K. L. LAETTNER

The Girl Who Captured Memories

First edition

This book was professionally typeset on Reedsy.
Find out more at reedsy.com

To my grandfather, Charles Hermann. I remember our last heart-to-heart, sitting on the porch bench, and how I felt the emotion of calm roll through me like a soft whisper. As something told my heart what would come, I smiled, knowing goodbye was only a word. You're looking down, watching, encouraging, and though the chats are spiritually, I embrace them. I hold close each memory, and I know you were there, if only as a hazy spirit mirage. You taught me to believe, and I do.

"A world in which there are monsters, and ghosts, and things that want to steal your heart is a world in which there are angels, and dreams and a world in which there is hope."

NEIL GAIMAN

Contents

Preface

When I finished The Girl Who Captured The Stars, I felt a strange hollowness, almost as if there was unfinished business regarding the story. My mind went gallivanting on its typical manic tangents, asking me, "well, come on now, author, what happens next? There must be more?"

Sometimes I answer my own questions, and other times, my dreams answer for me. This tale is of the latter variety. After tossing and turning, with three or four current works in progress, and under duress, I set my boundaries and said 'enough, already. If it will shut you up, I'll do this first.'

But The Girl had gone away, didn't she? So, where would this newest tale take me next? My amazing dreams filled in the spaces and The Girl Who Captured Memories was born.

With many things happening in my life and my age increasing by leaps and bounds, complete with a jolting, yet never-ending stream of AARP envelopes in the mailbox, I set off on a tirade of self improvements. I then tacked on some mental adjustment training, which I'm happy to say, I succeeded with. I've incorporated things I've learned on my personal journey within the pages, and in having written it, it has strengthened me tenfold. You're never too old to change your mindset, and I've found that by taking a stance on what's important to my soul will help in the long run to keep this author sane. The term and meaning of having boundaries has become my new favorite phrase, and they keep things in check. It's okay to say NO.

Please note: This book is fiction, and not autobiographical. I adore my mother… So relax, Mom.

About this story: Julien is a young man, like many young men I grew up with, and family dysfunction runs rampant for everyone I've ever met. No one is ever perfect because it doesn't exist. Perfection is, from what I've learned, a never ending battle for something that's like an illusion. We all have ghosts of a different life we chase when we crave a niche of peace to dwell in. Life often gets us down when we hit dead ends in the elusive search. It's a kind of keeping up with the Jones's scenario. If we have this or we look like that, we'll find happiness. Somewhere in between lies the sweet spot. How to feel blessed and appreciate what we have when much of the world feels dark and ugly? I have no answers, only a story to escape into for a while to take your mind off it. It's not much, but it's what I have. It's what I can give from the heart.

On ghosts: Someone once asked me if I believed in ghosts. The answer is yes, kind of, having seen two in my lifetime. I had no fear at the experience. Somehow, I tucked those special memories away for the day when I could write about 'that other world,' the one where spirits linger and long to be heard. For that, I am blessed. If you don't believe, that's fine, too. We all have our beliefs, and the best part of life is that we can allow others to be themselves, to hold their beliefs, and that we can respect them for it. It's what makes the world go round and a better place.

Welcome, dear readers, to The Girl Who Captured Memories. A poignant, and magical story about things that may or may not be real for a man on a quest in search of the truth. I hope you enjoy this adventure, and that when you turn the last page, it leaves you with a little hope in your heart, that sometimes things work out differently than you hoped, but ofttimes for the better. Life is a journey. It's best to enjoy each moment of the ride.

Acknowledgement

I foremost want to give a tremendous shout out to my husband, Jeffery. He keeps my world spinning in an upright manner, with his superb cooking, sage advice, hugs, and by being the best husband in the world a woman can have. I couldn't do this without him and am blessed to have him as the other half of me, my better half, and the one that makes me whole. (Which is the best, not better half, right?) I love you to the ends of the earth, my love. Never forget that.

Thank you to my Aunt Peg Hermann. I don't know if she knows it, but she lives in a haunted house… Or at least it was when I was young. It is the home of my grandparents, and as a child, I sat in awe as my grandmother told me about the strange blue lights that would bounce around the bedroom. As I had weekend sleepovers, and that old grandfather clock would chime every hour, I'd peer out from the blankets, waiting… And hoping that the ghost would stop and say hello. I believed. I still do. But my Aunt Peg is one of those folks who's ten kinds of amazing and has a never-ending stream of encouragement for each of my tales. Flowers, hugs, and just being the woman she is, I forgive her for the gift of socks at Christmas. (says with a chuckle) Everyone needs socks, unless you live in Florida, then it's footies for the sneakers. Thank you for being in my corner every time.

Thanks to a college professor who told me I had talent. He knew I was bristling with irritation at being there taking classes that bored me senseless. I had a creative streak, and he told me to follow that path. Be happy with what you do, always. Life's too short to waste time not doing what you have a passion for. Sorry it took me so long to remember those long ago words, and your name. I think it was Rob.

To the Island Gift Nook on West Venice Ave. You took a chance on an unknown indie author by carrying my books, and two and a half years later, you now carry five of them happily. You folks are always so friendly as I drop in to do inventory counts and always ask me what's coming next. I am blessed to have you pushing along-side me to sell some wonderful tales.

To my family, your endless support encourages me to be the best me, to stand up for what I need to be a whole soul, and to the laughter that you fill me with each time we get together. When my cup is running dry, you're there to fill me right back up again. You make my heart lighter, and that's an amazing gift to give. Thank you, and if I don't say it enough, thank you again.

To my amazing readers who keep grabbing my books, reviewing them, and giving me encouragement when I think no one wants to read them. You folks lift me with each page read, purchase, or feedback that helps make me a better writer. Thank you.

To the ghosts who fill my mind with lavish stories, inspirational quotes, and the nudge to just get on with it… They do the talking and my fingers just type the words. Keep it up, I'm listening.

To Simone, Damien, and Julien: Thanks for letting me use your names for the tales, and I'm glad that the characters are so far removed from who you are. Maybe some day I'll give them a last name, but no fear, it won't be yours… Giggles…

Thank you to my medical team, first Donna, then Sara… I've learned that I'm strong, that I can rise above, and I've proved to myself I'm capable of change. Now I've got the boundaries in place and am just saying NO. That's made all the difference, and the stress level has blown to the zero range most days, along with becoming a healthier author. I might live forever at this rate. I know, watch the carbs…

To Donna Pfohl, the bestest lady friend that a girl could have. Thanks for being such an inspiration and for the amazing talks when I needed them. You keep me smiling and I am blessed to have you in my life. Cheers to doggies and sunflowers.

To my dogs, Apple and Chi, that gives me purpose. As a door opener, food delivery service, snack delivery service, and you pay me with the smiles you bring as you greet me at the door after a long day's work. Those girls are always happy to see me. I wish you could live forever and, though the days grow shorter, know that I love you with all of my heart and soul. Thanks for being the speed bumps in the writing room, and for the puppy dreams that jar me out of my writing thoughts. Please, when you're a ghostly spirit someday, haunt me, even if only in my dreams. I welcome the intrusion with open arms and mind.

Thank you Chris at KUDI-Designs for bringing my story to visual life with this amazing cover. Perfection!

There are so many I need to thank, and I don't mean to leave anyone out. Thank you, everyone, for being along with me on this journey. I'm embracing the bliss of following my dream, and am so happy you're there with me.

Life is a strange journey, taking us on roads we never imagined existed. New doors open, old ones close, but it is we who choose which way to go. This life has blessed me, and I thank the good Lord above, who never ceases to amaze me with the unfolding of this journey. The fine folks you bring into my life, for reasons and purposes, fill the voids when needed, and I am amazed at what I've learned about myself and the spirit. You make me whole and for that; I am blessed.

One

On the Unbelievable... And Becoming Whole

T his was my dad's home until he disappeared over a year ago. It was a place I spent little time in as a kid, but a house I adored, none-the-less. The recollections of my visits here escaped me through the years, replaced by contempt and a philosophy of not giving, as he would say, a hill of beans. But attitudes evolve, people change, and this is a story of something bigger than all of us.

If you would've asked me a year ago if I believed in the 'other' realm where mystical spirits roamed, I would have replied that you're ten shades of crazy. Yeah, I'm sorry, but that's how I felt.

My mother would say I'm Julien, one of those want-to-be goth artist types, as her eyes roll and her mouth purses tight in a sneer. True, I love hanging out in graveyards and sport the blackest of clothes. I scour thrift stores for cheap finds and vintage punk t-shirts, because as a college student and at the charity of my mom's pocketbook, I've no choice. To see me out and about, you'd say vampire blood rushed like a river through my veins. No, I'm not one of those mysterious souls of the night. And this isn't a story about vampires. I'm not wishing to be one, so if that's what you're seeking, close this tale and search for something else. You'll meet no blood-suckers here. What you will find is a soul-sucking one and some good folks who previously resided on this tattered earth.

My story defies everything I'd ever held true, and shifted me from who I'd been, which most say was tough and inaccessible, into a more attentive-type of soul. In my case, my body was a sanctuary of seething resentment, even though I ably managed it through various channels. Some could've wrecked me. I'm any guy you'd pass on the street and I generally function like those who survive in the shadows. Introverted is an expression that comes to mind, and I prefer my company best. I don't know, I'm only me and I'll make no excuses.

The tale you'll find here is mind-blowing, and not what I would have imagined as I came to linger in my father's dwelling. His home was as I was, worn, crumbling, and drained of life. The wooden architecture style was what they call old-school Florida. Set out in the boonies and shuttered tight against the weather, they'd nestled it close to a river called Peace. Crafted before the explosion of the million homes that cropped up like St. Augustine grass after a spate of rain, it was a relic of the past. Raised into existence when the forests were bountiful with wild animals and thicker than molasses, it fit into the landscape naturally.

My father's haven, due to my recent troubles, is where I disappeared to. My aim was to piece my life together and figure out where to go to next. You don't have to accept what I'll tell, but if you do, thank you. Your acceptance means I'm not crazy. I now understand that magical, mysterious things happen when least expected.

I don't know what else I can tell you, but I'll try my best to describe situations that some days I find hard to comprehend. This is the story of my father, a man I barely remember, me, and a house by a river called Peace.

Two

The Devil's Lair

My mother believed this house killed my father. Though I realized a physical structure could do no such thing, I'd often wondered the same thing myself. Something here changed him, though.

I stared from my stance in the shade of the porch to beyond the yard and across the old dirt-crusted road. The heavy machinery had taken root, sun bleached like dying bones in an almost vacant field. Rust-speckled, the once yellow Caterpillar bulldozer took on the essence of an antique relic on a poor farmers' land.

Once upon a time, isolation and quiet reigned in this neck of the woods. But, as urban sprawl happens, Dad's little slice of heaven would find itself overrun with fancy rich-folk's houses. They would complete their communities with a security gate meant to keep people who looked like me out. For now, they'd called a moratorium to halt the progress because of the plethora of Gopher tortoise nests the diggers attempted to bury as if they'd never existed. At least, that's what the lady in town at the diner told me. Burrowing owls took up residence in the overgrown meadow at the far edge of the acreage, or had when I was younger. I wondered if they'd moved on.

The old oak tree near the driveway had grown bigger. Though some of its lower limbs, I noticed, seemed culled back like amputated body parts.

Severed, flat spaces became worn and faded with the weather. Things never stop growing here, and as needed, get kept in check like unruly kids bent on having fun, regardless of the circumstances. This land is wild, but inch by inch, the wildness is being tamed out of it. A soul loses hope when that happens, and the crushing pain washed through me as I know it must have for him. The air still smelled thick and rich of earth and decayed wetness, just as I'd remembered, and a calm moved through me with each breath I took.

Remnants of a thick braided rope I climbed as a boy, now frayed, remained and I watched as it swung languidly in the breeze. I loved that old tree. Some of my few memories were of climbing high and pretending I could see forever from my hidden position. My father waited below, ready to catch me if I fell. Long tendrils of Spanish moss grew thicker through the years, giving it a sinister look. But I wasn't ten anymore. We reserve fear of things that go bump in the night for children. Grown, I now laughed, seeing the wild, dangling stuff for what it was. I shook my head at the thoughts I'd once held as I took a minute to absorb everything I saw.

With a heavy sigh, I leaned against the rail and felt the sagging, unstable wood at my hip. The porch post was rotting, and I couldn't remember if he'd ever done an upgrade or if this was the original. My fingers pressed into the soft wood, which crumbled. I flicked off the remnants that stuck beneath my black polished fingernails. The chipped, pale blue robin's egg hued particulate fell on my dusty Doc Martin boot, and I kicked it away. I slid my hand below the rail in search of the spare key he'd housed there, and a moment later, found it. As I twirled it in my fingers, I imagined my father's hand wrapped around it. To see him again in the forgotten memory shocked me. His fingers twisting it into the lock I was about to use, a sad smile rose on my face.

They had boarded the windows up at some point, and it seemed like no one had been there since. I wondered who'd taken care of sealing it against the storms, but of course it wasn't my mom. Perhaps a hurricane had been coming and Dad took the same precautions many who lived along the river did. He respected the moods of nature, but had always been sensible, or at

4

least that's how I remember him. My thoughts get cloudy, and I realize I should remember the good and let the rest go, but I haven't mastered that yet. Some days booze helped, but other times, not so much.

My mother refused to step foot in this place, and I shouldn't have been there either. But if I went home, she'd complain non stop about the cost of school. With what she'd paid to get me in to where I thought I wanted to be, it was a battle I had no heart to engage in.

But, my father had loved this archaic place, and as a child I shared his passion. My mother, Simone, and sister, Keira, tolerated it, but they'd stare at each other with an occasional eye roll and I knew something was amiss. They were thick as thieves and I guess after a while; it became me and Dad against the two of them.

Vacations here dwindled to next to nothing, and once my mother became obstinate about it, our visits stopped. She tried to drag my father away to come home to us, but it was like pulling wisdom teeth. Once that man dug in, he was hard pressed to let go. Dad rarely ventured to our home back up north.

If my mom knew I was here, she'd blow a gasket. Part of me wanted to call, just to hear it, but I wasn't ready to deal with what she might do afterwards. She and I don't get along, which is the same for me and my sister, Keira. I keep my distance, which is why I chose a school far from both of them. Florida was where my dad grew up, and something pulled at me, egging me on to show face in his last place of peace.

Heck, maybe it was time for me to figure out what happened to my life? I don't know. It's not that it was bad, but it could have been better. For myself, school wasn't something I wanted to deal with, and in hindsight, it never had been. I was only there because my mother wanted me to carry on the family business.

My passion was art. Bold, dynamic painting suited my soul, but through the many lectures, I came to believe it would be a fruitless endeavor. If I wanted to make a living, I needed to expand my horizons to architecture and design, like my folks had. So, relenting through clenched teeth, I chose a college out of state. Out of state, out of mind, right? But my dreams couldn't

5

get crushed that easily, and grew larger the more I tried to fit in to their world. Perhaps her dreams for me wasn't my gig.

My room-mate and I used to sit up late at night and hash out the idea of traveling to Europe and seeing the world in an RV. Two days ago, we had what you would call a falling out. His fist connected with my face after a party, and I knew it was time to switch gears. I needed to figure out what I wanted to do, because dorms and school weren't it anymore.

So, aimlessly driving down the I-75, I began thinking of my father and this place. Maybe it's because I needed answers. Unfortunately, I didn't know who'd give them to me. Heaven knows I won't glean any wisdom from my mother on the subject. She has nothing nice to say about my dad since the divorce or even before that, for the most part.

When Simone walked away, it was for keeps, and my mother isn't one to look back, not even after he disappeared last year. They never found him, and maybe that's what hurts the most. Is he alive or dead? I like to think he passed away somewhere doing what he loved, but without a body, no one knows.

His bank account was intact, and his wallet, mom said, sat on the bedside table. Time covered the pickup truck in the driveway with a thick layer of dust, and knowing how much he loved that thing, if he was taking off, that would be his preferred ride. Death doesn't bug me, but lately, lost chances do. My mother's voice rose to my thoughts, and I flinched.

"Too much to look forward to. Why would anyone want to live a life like that is beyond me?" The venom in her voice would cut like a knife. Though I loved him, I went along with her endless tirades or else get labeled as a supporter of "that piece of crap." I heard her talking to Grandma. Little bits of this and that, then a "Serves him right. He can keep her in his warped little world of make-believe, but I'm not sitting still to watch." Those harsh words joined others I'd grown up hearing from her lips. He never took the time to reach out to us. I figured a hot chick was keeping him company in his little sultry get-away home. What else could drag him away from us kids?

The place had changed little. I hadn't been in here since I was ten years old and hadn't talked to him since a quick drive-by visit when I was twelve.

Seven years is a long time, but who's counting?

No one had ever built anything on the land that ran past this place, but it was only a matter of time and money. Time was something I had in abundance. I figured I'd get a job, hang tight to keep out of sight from mom, and figure out what the heck I was doing here.

My hair stuck to my cheek. I pushed it away and tucked it behind my ear, then pulled the Cinnamon Schnapps from my pant pocket. A second later, I grinned as I gulped down a hefty swig. I took a quick glance around, as if there was anyone to see me, and feeling unsure, slid the liquor bottle out of sight. My lips burned as I swallowed it, but I loved the warmth as it flowed from my throat to my stomach.

My courage now shored up, I turned the key in the fancy lock my father had put in and pushed on the thick wood door. I found it swelled up from lack of use and gave it a mighty shove. The portal creaked open. Long-lost familiar aromas of my childhood assaulted my nose. Not even the cinnamon on my tongue could cover that scent. Old things and secrets waiting to be discovered and it made me shiver. The smell reminded me of the first time we'd come as little kids, and it shot a chill through my bones, just as it had when I was five. I hoped I'd made the right choice in coming here.

Pressing my hands against my leg, I took a breath, then closed my eyes. Hesitating, I wiped the remnants of the liquor off of my mouth, a twinge of fear rising within me that he wouldn't approve of what I'd done. My feet felt cemented in place, but I lifted one, and then the other. I stepped over the tattered welcome mat and entered the devil's lair.

"I'm home, Dad. It's me, Julien."

Three

Joy and Rain

I t was dark and musty as a cave. This place, when I was young, held light and laughter. But now, it felt like a home of despair. Someone stacked papers on the side table, but overall, it seemed more barren than I remembered. The scent was strong, and I glanced up at the old eucalyptus that hung over the door. Long speckled with mold, the twigs hung like tired dying remains. A candle sat in the middle of the table, and I pulled out my lighter and fired it up to give myself some light to see by. The soft scent of flowers hit my nose, and I realized that this was another odor that lingered here. I figured my mother must have bought it, because I don't remember my father ever being into the candle thing. It looked newer, though, so perhaps it was from his lady-friend.

"God, it's too dark. Ugh, gotta pull the wood off and get some air in here before I die," I muttered as I escaped back out to the porch. At least there was a little breeze out there. My heart was beating like a drum, and I took the steps two at a time and opened the trunk. I had crammed my toolbox behind my bags of clothes, and found the small crowbar nestled at the bottom of my junk. Eyeing the height of the shuttered windows, I knew I could do it without the use of a ladder, but I didn't want to break them in case a storm came and I needed to get them back up. I would tackle the front of the house first, I thought, as I wedged the bar beneath the corner. Philip's head screws held the thing in place, and I grinned.

"Easy peasy, lemon squeezy…" The words filled my head and I let out a small laugh. It was one of my dad's favorite sayings. I had forgotten it until now, and I glanced around as if expecting to see him standing there with that goofy grin across his face. The wind stayed calm, and with a sigh, I returned to my mission. I ran back out to the car and grabbed a screwdriver and loosened the front fixtures, slid the wood off, then propped them in a standing stack against the peeling wood siding. One after another, I worked my way around the house as the sun beat down on my back. My hair dripped with sweat, and I prayed the water inside was functioning. I'd need a shower when finished.

I made it around to the side of the house. When I was younger, this had been my bedroom. It was the same size as Keira's, and my parents had built a larger room off the back of the house for their own sleeping quarters. Not that they spent much time there, perhaps only a few years before their lives fell apart. I wondered if he'd changed up any of the rooms since then? The curtains were closed, but were now faded. The blue looked worn and dull from what I remembered, and I was eager to finish and get cleaned up. I ran my sweat soaked hands down my pant leg and pried my shirt up to wipe my face. With my skin tone, I worried I'd burn, but this side had some shade. It took me years of sun avoidance to master my pale, vampire-toned alabaster skin. Leaning against the window, I closed my eyes and felt the wind shift. A cool breeze was now coming from the back of the house where the river was and I took a deep breath.

"Is there a division for joy?" The voice jolted me out of my stance, and I jumped. A young girl stood a few feet away, her finger pointing at me.

"What?" I said, my tone edged with irritation. I didn't understand what she was asking me and I wiped at my eyes, wondering if she was a mirage.

"I said, is there a division for joy? Is it like a club or something?" She rocked from foot to foot and as I stared at her long auburn hair. She seemed familiar. Her finger pointed at my shirt and she took a step forward. I looked down, now understanding what she'd asked. Though soaked, the faded Joy

9

Division album cover stood out on my chest. I shook my head at her.

"It's a really cool band. Haven't you ever heard of them? 'Love Will Tear Us Apart' was one of their most popular songs. They're right up there with Bauhaus and The Cult. Excellent stuff. You're missing out." She seemed perplexed, then shook her head.

"He isn't home anymore. Why are you taking the boards off?" I blinked at her in shock.

"He may not be home, but I'm here. He's my dad, and he knew I was coming. No fear, kid, he's cool with it." I wasn't sure who she was or where she came from, but her laughter lit the air like a refreshing breeze.

"Okay, if you say so. Then you're Julien, right?" I breathed a sigh of relief, knowing she wouldn't be calling the cops. She must know my dad, or she'd be running to tattle within seconds. "Don't worry, I will tell no one you're here. It would defeat your purpose, right? Mums the word, I've got your back." She stopped for a moment and her mouth turned down in a frown. "Love doesn't tear apart, it heals, so that's a stupid name for a song." She turned her attention to the bedroom window and shook her head. "It's a shame he let it go, but I suppose he couldn't help it. That's okay, you're here now and I'm sure you'll get it shipshape in no time flat. It was always a rather nice place."

I nodded at her and looked back towards the river as the wind kicked up a notch. The skies were growing darker, and I wanted to finish before the rain set in. It was ominous out there and I felt a chill move over me. Ghosts walking over me is how my dad always termed it. It was odd, the phrases that were coming back to me. I cleared my mind of the thought and glanced at the girl.

"Hey, I'm just gonna keep on motoring, okay? Got a lot to do, and it looks like it's gonna piss on us any moment." She looked at the clouds and a smile broke across her face.

"Rain is a beautiful thing. It washes clean like nothing else can. Let it be a part of you, and you'll get over not liking it. It's a fact of life here, and you'll grow to love it. Trust me. Many things get clearer after a good cleanse." She began walking in the opposite direction as I turned to tackle the next window. I glanced back to ask her name, but she had already left.

I moved towards the front of the house, figuring I'd see her go into the house next door, but she had disappeared. Shrugging, I trudged around the corner to start on the back of the house. I stuck the screwdriver into the screw head and stopped. Dang, something was pulling at my mind, and her face kept moving through my head in a hazy cloud. The look in her eyes struck a chord with me, but I couldn't put my finger on it exactly. A second later, I heard the rumble of thunder in the distance. The rest of the windows could wait. I just hope the power was easy enough to turn on and that dad had installed modern conveniences like air-conditioning at some point.

Four

Blue Moon and Memories

W ith the wooden shutters removed, the house had become lighter, but with the approaching storm, a strange greenish hue hung over everything. I made a beeline to the breaker box as I stripped my shirt from my body and I threw it in the kitchen sink. It was dripping wet with sweat, and I wasn't sure where else to put it. First things first, I told myself, air conditioning. I flicked all the breakers on and I could hear the refrigerator spring to life. Tomorrow I'd head back into town and pick up some supplies, but I'd wait to make sure the fridge was working before I stockpiled it with beer.

I pulled the door open and the interior light came on and I smiled. I could feel a little coolness stirring within and I shut it tight. Beside the fridge, two twelve packs of beer sat, and I crossed my fingers that there'd be some full bottles inside the dusty cardboard boxes. A smile lit my face as I opened the first case to find only one bottle gone. The brand was out of my pay grade as a college student, but seeing the Blue Moon Belgian white emblem made me giddy.

"Pretty fancy stuff, Dad. Don't mind if I do," I said as I grabbed the box. Blowing the dust off, I snorted as the sneezing began. "Man, I've got my work cut out for me cleaning up this joint, but thanks." I grabbed my shirt from the sink, rubbed my nose, then wiped off the grime from the box. Sliding it into the fridge, I knew it would be hours before it got cold, so I threw two of them into the freezer.

"What was I doing? Ah, yes, air. Let's get some air flowing in this crypt." I headed back out to the living room and glanced at the ceiling, but saw no vents. A thermostat was MIA, too, and I shook my head. Behind the living room chair, I discovered a window air-conditioning unit, and I giggled.

"Thank the Lord. Something is better than nothing," I said as I hefted the thing around in front of me. "Please work, please, please work." I slid it out and carefully pushed the coating of dust off the top, then plugged it in. Turning the knob, the musty-smelling blast of air hit my face.

"Ah, that's what I'm talking about. Yes, Virginia, there is a Santa Claus." I leaned back and shook my head in shock. That had been another of his favorite sayings. The man had been full of them. I hefted myself up and opened the window, then put the unit inside and re-closed the window in the seam. There were gaps, but I figured I'd jam some towels in them until I could find something better. I turned the chair around and let the thing blow itself in my face. With time to kill before the beer would be cold, I pulled out my schnapps and eyed the contents. I still had half left. Unsure who I could sucker into buying me booze in this hick town, I took a sip, and then another.

"Fire is good, feel the burn, baby. Feel the burn. Ah, now that's what I'm talking about." The cold air felt like heaven, and though I was feeling filthy and damp, I just sat there and let the thing work its magic. The chair reclined, and I closed my eyes as I heard the first pellets of rain strike the tin roof. A rumble of thunder hit somewhere close by, and I set the bottle aside as my body decompressed into a lump.

"Where else on earth would you rather be, then right here with me?" My father's voice filtered through my head and I nodded off to sleep as the rain fell above me.

* * *

13

"You know I love you, sport? I always have, and this won't change that. Trust me. You trust your dad, right?" As I glanced over, I watched as the tears wavered in his eyes, but he blinked them away as fast as they came. I smiled as he hugged me tight to his chest. I could feel the beating of his heart against my chest, and it was a sound of thundering drums, played to the tune of heartbreak. He released me a minute later.

"I know, Dad, but why can't you come home? Why do you and mom have to keep fighting? It's not fair. Peter's parents got divorced, and he got a new dad, but he's not nice. He hits Peter when his ma's not looking. What if Mom gets a new dad for us and he's mean?" My father glanced up at the moon and shook his head.

"Your mom's gonna do what she's gonna do. I love her, but it isn't working anymore. Things have changed, and it's time to get away from each other for a bit. No one said anything about divorce."

I didn't tell him I had heard my mother talking about the 'D' word to grandma, and to tell him would betray her. I nodded and tucked myself closer to his side. Things were always nice when we came here on vacation, but as he'd said, things had changed. The air crackled with electricity when they were in a room together, and I could sense my mother on edge. She hated it here. She told grandma that ghosts lingered and interfered with her peaceful mojo. I never saw a ghost, but grandma believed her.

"You should sell the house and come home, then we can be a family again." I felt his hand squeeze me tighter as he let out a breath.

"Look up, Julien. Do you see that? It's a sky with unlimited stars as far as the eye can see. That's the Milky Way." I thought he meant the candy, and I watched him, waiting for him to unearth a sweet from his pocket. He merely continued to gaze upwards. "And that moon, ah, I'll always remember this moment. Sometimes I feel like I can reach out and touch it. When I'm up there at the other house, this doesn't happen. I find it magical here. Except for you guys up there, I feel empty when I'm there. You won't understand, but when you grow up, maybe you will. Never stop looking for the magic, because when it's gone, it's hard to find it again." I sat still in his embrace and stared at the backyard. Everything was quiet, except the soft sounds of the river in the distance. I could only go there with Dad, because Mom freaked out otherwise. She was afraid we'd drown or something. But back here in the yard, it was alive, as if the night were moving through on its way somewhere. Flickers lit the distance, and I heard him chuckle.

"Fireflies… Do you see them? They are the keepers of the magic. I used to catch them, but then learned to let them do their thing. Things do best when they're set free to their own devices. That includes people, too. You can't keep something captive and expect it to thrive. Fireflies will die if kept in jars, just as people's souls will wither and disappear, too. Remember that, sport, okay?" I nodded, and he kissed me on the top of my head, then released me.

"I think it's past your time for bed. Your ma will get pissed if she knew we stayed out this late. Tomorrow will come soon enough and we'll deal with what it will bring." He stood up and took my hand, then pulled me to my feet.

"Promise me you'll remember, Julien." I felt something rip inside me, and I wanted to gather every image of each moment and tuck it deep within me.

"Yeah, I promise, Dad, I'll keep it right in here." I tapped my chest and saw him smile, then he wiped at his eyes again. Following him, he held open the door, then closed it. He walked me to my room, then watched as I tucked myself in bed. The creak of the couch on the other side of the wall filled the space of silence. As I lay there, I thought about the fireflies, then tucked the memory away and fell into a deep sleep. He wasn't around when I woke up, and we carried our things to the car. My mother moved like a soldier, direct and on point, and neither Keira nor I said anything to set her off. She shoved us into the car, and I clicked my seat belt as she backed the car around and drove off. I leaned back in my seat to see if he was there watching, but as I turned back around, her eyes met mine in the rear view mirror.

"Give it up, Julien. This is for the best. We can do this on our own and we will, so stop looking for him. Besides, true to form, he's not looking for you." I nestled down and pulled my baseball cap over my eyes. I wouldn't let her see me cry.

My body jolted awake as a loud crack of lightning hit close by. Rushing to the window, I could see the smoke rise from across the street. Unsure if it hit the Caterpillar, I smiled. Even mother nature doesn't want them to develop the land, I thought to myself. I gave a quick nod and eased my way back into the seat. My thoughts moved to the dream, or should I say, my memories. Something about this house was stirring my long-buried brain crevices, and I wasn't sure if I should be happy about that or sad. Releasing a sigh, I wondered if the beers were cold enough yet. The rain was falling like a spasmodic drummer and I flinched as another bolt of lightning lit the sky. I feared storms like these when I was a kid, but now I embraced the aliveness and wonder of something that could kill without being seen. Death filled my thoughts when storms hit or when I wandered amongst the dead in a cemetery. I loved hanging out with departed strangers. They couldn't talk back, and I liked to wonder who they were and create stories about their lives. Maybe they'd been happy or sad to be gone, but I always gave them some kind of tragic bent on why they were six feet under. There's a cemetery behind the house here. My dad tended to it when we vacationed here, but I'm sure no one's touched it since he left. Tomorrow I'd check it out.

Yawning, I made my way to the kitchen, but stopped at the table and picked up the candle I had lit. The three wicks were white and fresh, as if they'd never been used. I wondered if I'd blown it out before removing the shutters or looking for the air conditioner. I get forgetful when I'm catching a buzz, but that's all right by me, because sometimes it's better to lose the thoughts than dwell on them. Those things eat you alive. I set the candle down and headed for the land of brewskis. The fridge was now cooler, and I grabbed one from the freezer and replaced it with another from the case in the fridge. My fingers twisted off the top, and I swallowed it down, then repeated the process.

"Ah… Now that's the cat's ass. Tasty little brews," I said, licking my lips. My words, now loosened by the alcohol, echoed in the empty kitchen. I moved to the cupboards and began poking around. Canned soup seemed the mainstay and some quick cook rice, but other than that, one dented can of peaches and a box of dog biscuits remained. I lifted the red box of Milk Bones that sported a grinning canine and peered inside. One lonely biscuit sat at the bottom and I shook my head.

"Maybe your neighbor had a pooch, huh? You always did like dogs." With no one to answer me, I slid the box back into the cupboard, but changing my mind, set it on the counter top. The thing was probably stale, but I would not take a bite to find out. I took another swig of beer and leaned against the counter. This place hadn't changed since I was ten, and if my dad had a lady friend, he didn't let her fix it up. It still looked the same as how my mom decorated it when he inherited it.

I finished the beer and moved to grab the next in line. Another bolt of lightning flashed through the sky, and though I hadn't gotten the shutters back here undone, it lit the front room like a midnight rave party. It was then I heard the knock on the door. My first thought was it was the cops, and my heart raced.

"Crap, what am I gonna tell 'em?" I ditched the beer bottle beneath my shirt in the sink and walked nonchalantly to the door, my fingers twitching as the sweat beaded up on my forehead. "God, what if Mom knows I'm here and sent them to ship my butt home?" My thoughts ran rampant as my hand shook. I stood up straight as I turned the knob and took a deep breath, steeling myself as my mind tried to concoct a believable lie.

Five

Coming Through in Waves

꧁ꕥ꧂

She stood on the porch, her clothes dry as a bone. It was the girl from earlier and she waited for me to say hello, but I just stood there staring at her. Our standoff lasted a minute, and I stepped outside. To ask her inside felt weird, because she looked like she was fourteen and I didn't need to be accused of doing anything. I eyed her and waited, but she grinned and shook her head, then wagged her finger at me. She broke the ice first.

"You shouldn't be drinking, you know. You're not old enough, number one, and number two, your dad wouldn't approve." I leaned against the door and I'm sure my look told her I didn't give a crap. Figuring she had more lecturing to do, I waited in silence, now slightly amused at how irritating she could be. A trick mastered in college. I'd learned that if you stay quiet, it makes folks uncomfortable, and they started yammering at you because they realize you're in control. They want to get you to talk, but you don't, which unnerves them even more. I enjoyed being in control, and the girl was falling right into the mode like everyone else. She opened her mouth, then shut it. With a wide grin, she crossed her hands across her chest, but said nothing. This change in tactics intrigued me, and I cleared my throat as I stepped in front of her to lean on the rail. She watched me with a smirk,

18

but stayed silent, and I chuckled while I shook my head. A second later, my body slammed backwards as that piece of crap porch rail gave way. I landed on my back with a resounding splash into the deep puddle on the ground.

"Ugh…!" The taste of muddy water hit my mouth and made me want to gag. Her laughter filled the air, but she stayed where she was. Moving to my knees, I trudged my way back up to the porch, my eyes shooting daggers at the rotted old piece of wood that lay in the filthy brown water.

"What's so freaking funny? You shouldn't laugh. It could have killed me. If I fell on the post and it rammed through my chest like one of those horror movies, I'd be stone-cold dead and that would be on you." She shook her head as she doubled over. And I wanted to laugh, too, but I'd be damned if I gave in.

"Julien, that wouldn't have happened, so don't worry. Besides, they'd call the rescue squad to fix you up lickety-split." She stopped laughing, yet her mouth was terse. "I don't know why you're such a grump. You used to be so much more fun." I stopped and stared at her as the skanky water ran from my hair down my face. Trying to squeeze some out, I realize I'd lost my hair tie, which angered me more. I'd only brought one.

"I've never met you before today, so I don't know what you mean by 'I used to be more fun,'" I said in a high-pitched, whiny girl voice. "How would you know?" She shrugged and slid past me, then walked into the house like she owned it. "Hey! You can't just walk in…" I followed her as she stood in the dining area and looked around. She touched the candle on the table and giggled as she took a sniff.

"Your dad loves jasmine. He used to take clippings and get them to root, then he planted them behind the house near your parent's room. They're not blooming yet, though. But come Spring you'll see what I mean. They look like a thousand little stars when they open. Nature's like that, and all the time the wheels are turning…" She gave a brief grin as she eyed me and then slid into the wooden chair behind her as she hummed. A second later, she stopped, as if coming out of a trance, and her eyes looked tired and sad. "Picture me and then you start watching…" I slid into the seat beside her, now a little impressed.

"So, you hit up Google and did your homework, huh? But that's New Order, a spin-off from Joy Division, but I'll give you high marks for trying." She nodded at me and patted her knee absentmindedly, her mouth pursed as if she was concentrating on some deep thought.

"I need to get some jars. Your father was keeping them for me until I needed them, but I have had no need, but now I do." Her head nodded as if she was keeping beat to a song in her head, then she turned serious. "That song's about suicide, right?" I eyed her and shook my head, then stood up and made a beeline for the fridge. If I was going to deal with her, I was going to drink to do it. She had unnerved me, and I didn't want to talk to her, but felt like I had to. I grabbed a beer from the freezer and walked back into the room. But she was now standing in the doorway to Keira's bedroom. I shot forward and went to close the door and usher her out.

"That's my sister's room. She's up in New York at SU." She gave me a quizzical look. "That's in Syracuse. We live in New York, but I go to school down here. That's why I'm here taking a break. I thought I'd check out the old stomping grounds." She nodded as I spoke. My brain kicked into gear and I grinned as she eyed me suspiciously. "Hey, you never told me your name, you know." I said, as I attempted to gear her out of the bedroom. She took a step forward, then stared at the walls. They once held Disney princess posters when we were kids, but Dad must have removed them. Brandon Lee in his Crow garb stared down from his lofty position at the head of the bed. An old faded Marilyn Monroe, James Dean, and some other old movie star dude hung side by each on the other wall. I stared around the room in shock. It was like my sister had never been here. The decorations resembled something out of the seventies, complete with a groovy bedspread. A bookshelf that used to house Barbie dolls now held jars, and the girl made a move towards them.

"What the heck did he do? This is Keira's room," The shock hit me like ice water through my veins. She giggled and reached for a purple jar. Its lid sat in front of it, but they capped all the rest of the jars.

"Yes, it was, and it still is. Don't get your panties in a bunch. Chill, Phil." I looked at her as she blew in the jar, knowing that if it was like the beer boxes, a bunch of dust particles would rain down in the air. "I only need a few, and don't worry, I'll bring them back because, in reality, they're for you. Your dad would be cool with it, I promise." She tucked two jars in her pocket while still grasping the purple one, then she strode by me like a breeze. I detected a faint whiff of jasmine as she passed, and I closed the door before following her into the dining room.

"What are you going to do with the jars? Who are you, really?" She closed her eyes and shook her head, then moved towards the door.

"All in good time, grasshopper. All in good time," she as she gave a little bow. I exhaled loudly and plopped down in the chair. "Don't worry, I'll be back, but I have to say something, and you'll think I'm a complete fruit loop, but bear with me and try not to get angry." Well, this was going to be good. I waited for her to continue.

"You came here for answers, right? And I may be able to help? But that's gonna depend on whether you're ready to hear them. You can't get drunk and understand. Being pie-eyed defeats the purpose. Try to get a handle on that, and then I'll tell you more." I rolled my eyes and ran my hand through my hair. "It's important, or I wouldn't ask."

Nodding like an apologetic child, I watched as she opened the door and left. Her tone was dead serious, and it sounded like something my dad would say, and that floored me. I set the beer bottle down and eyed it, then twisted the cap off for spite and swallowed down half of it. Leaning back, I wondered what the heck had just happened here?

Why did my dad change Keira's room and why the retro look? I chugged down the rest of the bottle, then went to grab another. Her words spun in my head and I stopped. "You can't get drunk and understand." I nodded and closed my eyes. There was a barometric shift to the room, and a cool breeze blew past me. I opened my eyes to find the door had opened. She must not have closed it, I thought, as I stumbled towards it.

"Were you born in a barn? Close the door for Pete's sake." My mother's voice rocketed through me and I flinched. I closed the door and peered over my shoulder, as if expecting to see my mother standing there, giving me her stink eye. Another bolt of lightning rattled the house, and the lights flickered,

21

then went dark.

"Ah, for crying out loud, that means no air, and no cold beer. Son of a…" I shut up and stalked over to the table to light the candle. "Nothing to do now but wait." I moved back out onto the porch, my mood shifting to agitation.

The rain had tapered off, and I yawned. Dealing with that girl had exhausted me, or maybe it was the beers. I pondered sleeping out here for the night. It was cooler than in the house. I slipped back inside to blow out the candle and looked down at the table. The purple jar sat beside the lighter that I'd set down, and I lifted it and held it up to the light. Eyeing the flickering spots that filled the interior, I ran my finger down the side of the bottle. I figured it had ridges or something to fragment the light, but it was smooth. The scent of jasmine drifted past me again and the front door closed with a quiet click. I let out the breath I held and settled down in the chair to ponder the latest freak-fest quirks of my father's home.

Six

Was it the Hand of Fate

A slamming door woke me, and I stared around, confused at where I was. The seven empty beer bottles on the table, a harsh reminder of the night before, registered in my brain and I yawned. I grabbed a bottle that held a few swallows, and with a shudder, forced the warm wetness down my gullet. The power flicked on at some point, and the window unit threw enough cool air to keep me comfortable for the night. Later, I'd put it in my old bedroom, but figured I'd only be in there to sleep. That was, if I fit in the bed anymore. I hadn't tried, and was almost afraid to. Not wanting to take over Dad's room, I hadn't looked in to see what that looked like now. This place was like a time-warp from my childhood, and being back here without him felt strange. I could almost sense him here, but chalked that up to too many brewskis the night before. I wrapped my fingers around the bottlenecks and moved to toss them back into the box. At some point, I had slid the other twelve-pack into the fridge, so I pulled out the partial to fill it with empties. In New York, you had to return them, but not in Florida. I dumped them into the garbage can, which I noticed needed a bag as the bottles hit bottom in a glass smashing symphony.

"Yep, gonna have to grab supplies," I thought as I made a mental note. "Man, I could go for a stack of pancakes right about now," was my stomach's reply,

23

as it growled in agreement. I patted it and shook my head. "Nope, shower first, then food, buddy." I tried the sink, but the water was still off. I'd have to retrieve my clothes from the car. But, I felt bad for crashing out in the chair with my filthy pants on. With no one to yell at me, the feeling left as quick as it came.

"Jules, you can do whatever the heck you want." I said to the walls. "You want to sleep like a pig, do it. You want to drink beer, you can do that, too. No one's gonna say a word and if they do…" I realized I was muttering to myself and began to chuckle. My father was often found talking to himself, too, I remembered suddenly.

Another car door slamming interrupting my chat with myself and I headed outside to find the valve to turn on the water. A moving van was backing up to the front porch of the house next door. My dad lived there as a boy with his aunt and uncle, but they'd croaked and then he inherited this shack from some lady who also died. He didn't talk about living there, except that he spent a lot of time down at the river and helping his relatives. I don't know what happened to his parents, and it wasn't something you asked when you were a little kid.

But this house, it held him like a vice and you could tell when he talked about it, it was as if it was alive. Maybe that's why my mom hated it so much. She never understood the attraction, but then again, her idea of camping is a Holiday Inn, so there's that.

My father liked and appreciated simple, and my mother strove to become someone people wouldn't forget and own the best of everything. She forged a name for herself in her designer/architect world, but even with all of her traveling and stuff, she never seemed like she was happy. That woman always had to do more, be more. I never have understood it myself, nor did I want to. Being better than the Jones's was her gig, not mine.

The yellow Penske truck was good sized, and I watched as a middle-aged dude and a young boy poked around in the cab, then went inside. A woman was pulling boxes out of the back and barking orders like a drill-sergeant. "Be a love and take this one in the kitchen, and don't drop it. It's fragile. And when you're done, there's five more. Don't drop it. That's your grandma's china in there and it would devastate me if anything happened to it." The girl looked to be around seventeen and was cute beyond words. Her long hair was dark and pulled back in a high, perky ponytail, and I laughed as she rolled her eyes behind her mother's back.

"If you don't want your china broken, why don't you lug it in yourself, you lazy cow?" My brain added mockingly, and if that were my mom, I would have said it out loud. This girl looked like she was used to it.

I hung to the shadows and watched mama witch on a roll. The girl kept returning, stoically grabbing each box her mother lobbed her way, but at some point, she looked over and eyed me. A slight grin crossed her face, and I felt a tingle of excitement. I still hadn't put on a shirt, but I didn't move as her eyes took me in. Her mother must have said something to her, because she turned around as the witch tried to shove another box her way. Unprepared for the hand-off, cutie fumbled it, and the box hit the ground like a bomb going off. The girl looked down in shock and her hands rose to her mouth as she took a quick look at her mom.

"You're lucky that was only towels, Em. If that were the china I would have up and died." Her words cut short, and she eyed her daughter. "What are you staring at?" The girl must have glanced over, but I backed out of view. So, her name was Em. I wondered if it was Emma. My room-mate's girlfriend was an Emma, and it wasn't a favorite name in my brain anymore. That one was a witch with a capital B.

I waited until they'd gone in, then slipped around the other side of the house to find the water valve. It was in the back corner, and though stiff, I got the thing into the On position. "Score one for Jules, now, some fresh clothes and a shower." The husband was lugging in some chairs as I turned the corner, and he eyed me from head to toe, shook his head, and strode into the house. I glanced down at my black pants. Streaked in muddy grime, I saw my chest still mucked up, too. My long hair hung in wild tendrils in my face. I headed to the front of the house and found my hair-tie submerged in the puddle. After I squeezed it out, I gave it a sniff, wiped it on my pant leg, then tied my hair into a knot on top of my head. My hair was dirty anyway, so what's the difference? The girl came back out and slipped into the rear of the van, then came out carrying another kitchen chair.

"I hope they're paying you well to do all that bull work? Tell 'em you demand a raise," I yelled out to her, just to be a smart-ass. Her head shot upwards, and I heard a small giggle. She shook her head and walked across the porch, dragging the chair as her father came back out. He glanced at me, said something to her, and shot me a look. Typical reaction, but I was used to it. Men don't like their daughters associating with me, but I take it as a challenge. This girl, Em, was sweet looking, and though I wasn't sure how long I'd be here, I hoped to find a time when I could get to know her.

The shower was nice, and I was glad my dad had shampoo and soap handy. His razor was missing, and I wondered if he'd grown a beard. No shaving cream, either. The towels that hung on the rod smelled musty, but I found some in the cabinet behind the door that weren't as bad. No sense in taking a shower just to stink like an old run-down house. I'd forgotten to bring in my clothes from the car and tamped down the idea to put my grungy pants back on. Wrapping the towel around my waist, I figured if nothing else, I'd piss Em's dad off even worse by strutting around the front yard in a towel. No one was outside, though, and I was a little disappointed. I grabbed my duffel bag and headed inside.

* * *

The town had grown. Not that I remembered much about it, but not finding a Walmart, I pulled into Publix. I had my mental list going, and I grabbed a cart. Of course it had a wobble wheel, and it squealed like a pig each time I turned a corner. People turned to stare at me, like they always do, and I moved from aisle to aisle, grabbing a few things as quick as I could. Publix wasn't bad, but I preferred Walmart. When you're in college, you learn that beer money is more important than anything else. I had passed a Dollar Tree and figured I'd grab a razor and shaving cream there to save some bucks. Then, I'd use the plastic bags they put my groceries in for garbage. Happy with myself for being smart, I'd skip buying fancy ones, and I crossed that off my list. Not wanting to dip into my bank account more than I had to, I laughed, knowing my mother wouldn't freak out with the small amount I spent. I doubted she'd even notice, but with my luck, she would.

I eyed the beer, but no one in the aisle seemed friendly enough to approach to entice them to buy it for me. My fake ID was pretty crappy, and I knew those sharp-eyed sally's at the register would be too worried about losing their jobs to accept it. At school, they turned a blind eye to my ID at the liquor store. You forked out more for the beer, but at least you could get it. I paid for my stuff and headed back out to the car, then trudged down the plaza to the Dollar Tree. The line was atrocious, and I changed my mind and left. I hit the McDonalds further down the road, using my last five bucks on pancakes and a coffee. I sat in my car and devoured it, then pondered my next move. Heading out of town towards home, I hit an ATM and grabbed some money. Maybe I'd take pretty little Em for a coffee at some point. The thought made me smile.

Seven

Down the Hole we Fall

T he Penske truck now took up space across the street in the dirt, and a shiny BMW resided in the driveway. No one was out and about, and I carried my goods inside. The sun beat down on me with its intense heat, and I thought about mowing the lawn. After having taken a shower, decided I'd wait another day. I wondered if the girl from yesterday would show up again. She didn't live next door, and I wondered where she lived as there were no other houses on the street. Filling my water jug, I decided to head down to the river. Without my mother here to tell me not to, I gleaned satisfaction because life seemed much easier without her sharp tongue criticizing everything I did wrong. The world was my oyster, and I chuckled as the tune, "Welcome To The Pleasure Dome," began blasting in my head. The song fit my current mood and I bopped my head along to my internal sound machine. Beside the door hung a coat hook, and my father's old hat sat on a peg. Dad always wore hats outside, and I remembered I called this one his safari hat. I slapped the worn thing on my head and chuckled.

"Aye, mate, we're heading into the bush today in search of the wild and secretive beast, the Em." I shook my head and shut the door behind me as I chuckled. Alongside the path, Dad had put up stakes and in spots I noticed string attached between the poles. Maybe he did this when the house next door went up for sale to mark off the boundary lines? I vaguely recalled the way to get to the river, though things had gotten completely overgrown. As I stopped, I wondered if I could still have access to our bench. Would that old thing even be around anymore? My feet trudged through the hip high grass and I sensed his voice in my head. "Always watch where you're going. There're snakes here and some aren't kind. They'll bite, not that they intend to hurt. That's just their way. Gotta be aware, always." My eyes moved down to the path in front of me and I now recalled the thin stick that stood beside the hat. "Fool, you should have brought the stick, just in case."

Too late now. I slowed my pace and followed the thin metal rods impaled in the ground. They were painted black, though it had worn off, but black was better than green. I'd never notice them if they'd painted them to match the over-grown weeds. A few minutes later, I detected the sound of water in the distance, and with the rains, figured the swollen river was running fast. I reached the bend in the back corner of the yard and glanced over to where the cemetery had been. Time had covered it in vines and I found it no longer recognizable.

"Add it to your list of honey-do's, Jules," I said with a chuckle as I moved around a clump of bushes and continued on the non-existent path. The water roared in the distance and I found it hard to believe how wild it had become. The bench was there, but in disrepair. Several of the wooden pieces had rotted away or been beaten up by flooding or storms. It made me sad, because I had a few memories of sitting out here with him. "I should fix this first. Dad would want his star-gazing bench to be like it was." The thought made me smile. Vines grew all the way to the bank, but there was one area that was churned up and muddy. I took one step forward and stopped as her words reached my ears.

"You might want to be careful. Roger doesn't like it when you sneak up on him, you know." I turned at the sound of the voice and saw the girl standing there. Surprised, I felt a little let down. I had hoped it was Em from next door. The jar girl stood there staring at me and I shook my head.

"I don't see any Roger here, Rabbit, or otherwise. Who is he, a homeless person?" I heard a snort, then a large splash. Jumping, I spun around and stared in shock as this log-like thing moved out a few feet from the shore, its cold eyes gazing at me before it slipped below the water and disappeared.

"That, as you can see, is Roger. He lives down here and likes to lie on the side of the bank. He'll move along, but be sure you make a racket as you approach. Like I said, he doesn't like to be snuck up on. It might be a Ramona, but I've never lifted the tail to find out," she said as she chuckled lightly. My father had told me there were gators in the river, but as a kid, I'd seen none except at the state parks or at Alligator Land.

"Can you tell if it's a boy or girl that way?" I asked, as she took a few steps forward.

"How would I know? I don't get close enough to find out, or at least I haven't in a while. I respect their space, as should you. What are you doing down here?" I took the hat off as a bead of sweat ran down my forehead. In the shade, with the breeze, it seemed cooler with my head uncovered. Her eyebrows drew together as she frowned.

"You've got girlie hair. Men shouldn't have girlie hair, but then again, men shouldn't have their nails painted or wear eye-liner, either. Do you do it for fun? You must, because Halloween is months away. I loved Halloween." No one normally had the guts to ask me that to my face, and it was a refreshing change of pace.

"Listen, chickie, I don't know who told you that, but then again, you know nothing about cool clothes or music from what I can tell. I do what I want, wear what suits me, and this is styling and hip. Go home and pull up the punk scene on your computer and then you might understand. Yeah, Google Sid Vicious, Iggy Pop, or Robert Smith." She smirked at me, shook her head, and looked at her fingernails.

"I suppose you're right, but I'm more into classical fare. Your dad taught me about music, and he listened to a lot of classical music. You know, concerto's and orchestral kinds of stuff. I guess in some ways you're nothing like him. But he would have still loved you for who you are. That's how he was." I glared at her.

"You know nothing about me, girlie, and I wouldn't want to be like him, anyway. He was a useless father who didn't give a crap about us. Maybe he used you as a replacement kid because we weren't living with him, but he wasn't around for us. My old man couldn't bother to deal with his own family. Oh, and classical music blows, and it's boring. God! Mozart and Beethoven, I mean, what a joke. They're like Shakespeare. Old dead dudes who should stay in the century they were buried in and forgotten. That's not music, it's crappy church noise." The girl looked at me with a sad expression, and for a second I felt bad for saying it out loud. I turned away and shoved my hands in my pockets, watching for Roger to resurface and come splaying out of the water to get me for being such a jerk. When I turned, she had disappeared again, and I began heading back to find her, figuring I'd apologize, but I didn't see her anywhere.

The neighbors were nowhere in sight, and I felt around in my pocket for the rest of the schnapps, but realized I'd left it back on the table. As I meandered my way along the path, I pondered if I should just leave the bench to rot away. The idea of hanging out with Roger didn't appeal to me, and I eyed each step I took on my way back, wary of slithering creatures. Coming around the corner of the house, I saw the front door wide open. The soft sound of music found my ears, and I rushed up the porch to see who'd broken in. Music came from the living room. The wooden box in the room's corner was open, and the vinyl record was turning slowly, emitting a soft piano solo. They propped the album cover at the base of the stereo, and I lifted it up. Moonlight Sonata #14 by Beethoven was filling the room with this soothing, yet haunting melody. I glanced around, figuring it was the girl who'd done this.

"I'm sorry I said what I did." I listened as human silence echoed, yet the piano reverberated like a love song through the room. "Hey, yeah, this isn't bad. You're right and I was wrong. I'm always open to new things, and… Are you here?" There was no reply.

I set the record cover aside and sat down in the chair. Now weary, I closed my eyes and listened to the melancholy music as I imagined my dad sitting here, doing the same thing. The scent of cinnamon lingered, its aroma heavy in the air, and I opened my eyes and bolted upright. Moving to the table, there sat my half bottle of schnapps, sideways, cap off, with the precious remaining drops dribbling down the table leg onto the floor. I looked around and wondered if she'd done this, then figured maybe I forgot to cap it when I set it there and had bumped it. I lifted the bottle and inhaled the scent as the music stopped. A feeling of loneliness swept over me and I ran to the kitchen and threw the empty bottle in the garbage.

"There, are you happy? Fine, you win for now, but this isn't over, not by a long shot." I yelled out to the emptiness of this perplexing home, and not expecting an answer, wasn't disappointed.

Eight

Escape From your Cage

T he Penske van fired up an hour later as I washed the kitchen counters and I moved to the porch, hoping for a glimpse of Em. The man and boy sat in the truck and the Mrs. was in the BMW alone, waiting while Mr. turned the beast around. Minutes and five awkward turns later, the group headed down the road and out of sight. I wanted to grab a beer and sit on the porch, hoping the elusive Em would grow bored enough to venture out, and after fifteen minutes, I became impatient. A killer plan hit me a minute later. Yeah, I'd fire up the noisy mower and arouse her interest in the hot dude next door toiling away on his lawn. I changed into my dirty pants and my Joy Division shirt, then headed out to the tool shed where my dad had kept it. My spirits plummeted when I saw only a push mower. "Really, Dad? You couldn't fork out a few measly bucks for a real mower? What a joke."

The relic, long stuck in thick mud, looked like the last action it saw was when Vikings roamed the planet. I was already sweating like a pig, and ten minutes later, dislodged it from its resting place. I stared hopelessly at the yard, wondering what the heck I'd been thinking. She would hear nothing except me grunting expletives as I pushed this thing through the weeds. I jumped into action, ready as I could be.

33

"What the... Aw, come on, you can do it..." I wanted to swear, but something told me Em might expect class from a guy. I slogged that archaic piece of garbage mower back and forth, stopping what seemed like every ten seconds to yank the tangled weeds from the multitude of blades. Sweat poured down my red face as I huffed and puffed, and I nearly jumped out of my skin when I heard her voice. It was as I imagined it, sweet, and almost shy.

"I'm sure my dad would loan you our ride on. He's already complaining about your unkempt yard, so maybe he'd be willing to let you use it, if only to get in under control. Did your regular one die?" I shook my head as I burst out laughing, and wanting to sound cool, I said nothing. Words were ripping through my mind and none were winning the fight. She smiled and glanced at the road, as if expecting her folks to show up.

"I'm Emily Simonson. We just moved here from Wisconsin." She said nothing more, and I wiped my cheek off on my shoulder. My hands were filthy from pulling clumps from the machine, and she was too perfect to soil her hands by shaking them. I moved from foot to foot and eyed her. Tongue-tied, I coughed and my hand reached for my schnapps pocket. I stopped halfway there and gripped the mower handle instead.

"I'm Jules, or Julien, but my friends call me Jules or J-man. It's nice to meet you Emily from Wisconsin." She grinned and looked up as the sun drifted behind a bank of clouds. I relaxed and leaned against the mower, which took that moment to roll backwards. As I stumbled, I caught myself before falling over and could feel my cheeks turn to red.

"My father already warned me to steer clear of you, but you seem a nice enough sort. Besides, he's always wrong. He shouldn't judge someone based on appearance. Thank God I don't take after him, huh?" I liked her. She was smart and friendly, and I wondered how long we'd have until they returned. I eyed the rest of the lawn and sighed.

"If you think he'd lend it to me, I'd appreciate that, but I don't know if it would even make it through this jungle. I just got here. This is... Was, my father's place. Someone must have kept it up, but not recently." She nodded as I rambled, a smile stretching itself across her face. "I'm gonna be here and

34

wanted to keep my neighbors happy. That's what I'm attempting but failing to do." She nodded as her mouth turned wider in a knowing grin.

"Well, I'll leave you to it, then. Just don't kill your shirt, that's a classic. Oh, I'll send my dad over when he gets back. His name is Franklin, but if he likes you, he'll let you call him Frank. He's not a bad dude, just likes things a certain way. It's my mom who's a nag, but you've already seen her in action. Wanda likes everything perfect. Very OCD... but you knew that, too, right?" I wanted to agree, but I heard a car coming.

"You better go now. I think they're coming, Emily from Wisconsin." She gave me a wink and a small wave and headed back to her house, and I turned and continued my next trek through the lawn. The BMW pulled in a minute later and I felt like someone was watching me. Turning, I saw Franklin standing beside the car, eyeing me as I slogged my way through the next row. He gave a nod, then walked into the house.

"Well, sorry, Frankie old boy, but I'm not asking..." So, realizing this would take days to work through, I stopped fifteen minutes later and wondered if I should ask. As I stood beneath the blazing sun, I was out of breath and exhausted. My hand swiped the sweat from my forehead, but it was pointless. I felt like I was standing in a sauna. Leaning over to stretch my back out, I rested my head on the handle and cursed my father for leaving me with this mess to clean up. A sound pulled me out of my thoughts and I looked up to see neighbor Frank heading my way on a snazzy ride-on mower. He held a weed whacker in his free hand and gave me a wave with it.

"Looks like you got your work cut out for you, young man. Em said you've been toiling away and I must say, it's good to know someone's taking an interest in this place." I wanted to cry, but I just stood watching and waiting to see what he'd do next. "When I was looking to buy, the Realtor said the owner had gone missing, but his family was living somewhere up north. Let me help you out. Brett took care of your yard, I guess, once the owner disappeared, but he moved months ago. I can see they brought no one to do it since." I offered a sincere smile and wanted to fall at his feet in undying thanks.

"Um, I'd appreciate that... It's my dad's house. I'm Julien. Yeah, it needs a severe trimming, but…" I didn't know what else to say. He looked at me and nodded, then handed me the weed whacker.

"Here, you knock some of it down and I'll follow along. My ticker ain't great, and I can only hang onto that for a few minutes. Oh, and nice to meet you, neighbor. I'm Franklin, but just call me Frank, okay?" I nodded and felt a slow, happy feeling drift through me. Thankful he was giving me a chance, I fired the machinery up and began trimming as he kept a steady pace behind me. After two hours and some gas refills later, we'd cleared most of the backyard. Frank's face was red, and he'd grabbed a hat and a big jug of water when we knocked off. I grabbed two glasses, and we stood in the house's shade in between fill-ups. He chugged down two glassfuls and eyed me.

"Well, we did pretty good for today. You got me out of unpacking boxes and listening to the harpy all day. Hard work is good for a man. You'll have callouses on your soft hands in no time. Stick with me, and together we'll get it done." I'm not sure if he felt bad because my dad had disappeared, or if he was just a genuinely nice guy, but I enjoyed his company, even though we'd hardly said a handful of words to each other. Frank emptied the last of the water jug into my glass and eyed the sky.

"Gonna rain tonight, I suppose. I'll put the mower away, and you just hang on to the whacker for now. Keep at it, and I'll help you again if it doesn't rain tomorrow. Sound like a plan, Stan?" The glass was halfway to my mouth when I stopped, as yet another dad-ism quote found me. I felt a cool breeze blow over me and I smiled at Frank.

"Sounds perfect to me, and Frank?" He turned back around after he climbed on the mower and nodded. "Thank you. I owe you for this." He didn't say a word, just gave me a smile and drove that John Deere across the yard with a wave. I put the weed whacker in the shed, stripped off my soaking shirt, and smiled, feeling a sense of belonging for the first time since I'd arrived.

Nine

Just an Earth-Bound Misfit

⁕

I spied the spilled liquor puddle as I walked in, and headed to the kitchen to find a bucket and soap. It missed the area rug, so it would be a simple job. Beneath the sink I found what I needed, and as I stood, music played again. It was different this time, a slow song, but lighter than the first fare. I set the bucket aside and moved to the living room. The girl sat there in my chair near the air conditioner and her eyes were closed as she listened. I watched her for a minute. She was absorbing the noise like a sponge takes in water. She opened her eyes a second later and grinned.

"I've missed hearing this. It was one of my favorites, but since your dad left, I couldn't come and listen. Things always sound better on vinyl, he said, and he was right." Her hand moved rhythmically in the air and I left her to it. Not wanting to track the schnapps across the floor, I returned to the kitchen and filled the bucket, and added a splash of Pine-Sol to the mixture. The lemon scent was overpowering, and I wasn't sure how it'd fare with cinnamon thrown in. In the living room, music was still playing, and I went about cleaning my sticky mess. The floor wasn't dirty, which surprised me, so there was no need to scour the entire thing. After dumping out the water, I slipped back into the living room. The girl, now absent, but sitting on the chair was one of those bottles she'd taken on her first visit here. I lifted it up and eyed it. They were funky little bottles and had something sparkling in them.

"Are you still here? You left your bottle behind." Of course, I heard nothing and started the record over. Sweat soaked from mowing, sitting in front of the air, cooled my core, and I set the bottle aside, figuring she'd return in short order. The record cover hung half-way out of the pile, and I leaned forward and slid it out. Rhapsody on a Theme of Paganini, op. 43: Variations 16-18 by Martino Tirimo. It looked familiar to me, and after a few seconds, I realized my mother used to play this in her room when she was working. Unsure whether to turn it off at the memory or do as the girl had done earlier and absorb it, my body made the choice for me. I leaned back, and turning so the air blasted over my face, I wondered where she'd gone. The thought slid from my mind as I yawned, then drifted into a deep sleep.

* * *

"There's a subtle beauty in the right music, Jules. When it fills you up like your first sighting of the ocean blue as it washes over you, you can sense the change in your bones. I guess it would be like floating on clouds, too, but I love the water, so we'll go with that analogy. You'll grow up and find what fills your vessel. Let no one tell you what they like is better than what you like. Everyone has their own tastes. It can be good or bad, but it's for them to choose." I sat beside him on the bench by the river, listening to the small transistor radio that was spinning golden oldies. Another in a line of lazy days. We were heading to the ocean tomorrow on a family excursion. Excitement filled me, but he seemed calm, laid back and taking it all in.

"Can we come back on Christmas break? Mom said we wouldn't, but I thought you can talk her into it. I like it here, and I miss you." He patted my hair and gave me a wistful smile, the one that told my heart the answer would be no.

"We'll see when the time gets closer. I enjoy having you here, too. There's something about being on the river with you that calms my soul. Perhaps you sense it, too, but the smell in the air, the rains that wash the world clean.

I don't know, but this is home to me." He hadn't answered yes or no, so that gave me hope. If I asked Mom, her answer would be a resounding no, and I didn't want to hear that. Dad pointed up at the oak a few feet away and nudged me.

"In that clump where those two limbs form a V lived an owl. As a kid, it thrilled me to watch it raise its family. Well, I was fifteen, but I guess still a kid. That bird was beautiful. I wait for the day it returns. Things come and go, and you're left wondering if you'll glimpse it again. But I guess you hold the memory close, pray for the best, and someday, get surprised." I could see the tattered remnants of the nest and shook my head. Did he think of us in the same way when we left? Wondering if he'd be with us again? He stood a minute later and stretched out his back, then looked at me.

"Time has a way of easing things, Jules. What seems to hurt us now strengthens us in the long run. You're still young, but you'll find out when you grow to be an old man like me." He said it with a smile. My father was young, but things he said made him seem a wise old wizard. My dad was magical to me, and I grinned at him.

"I know, Dad, you're so old, you're moldy like cheese." He chuckled, and it made me happy to know I could make him laugh. I don't remember him laughing enough, and maybe I thought that he'd remember me better for that when we returned home.

"I'm as old as time and young as a second, young man. But yeah, I'm probably as moldy as cave-aged cheddar cheese, or even that dreaded bleu cheese." I cringed, because I hated the smell of bleu cheese dressing. His hand tousled my hair, and I smirked, picturing him as a walking brick of cheese. My mother's distant voice intruded on the moment and a frown crossed his face. It disappeared as fast as it came. "Your ma is ready to go to town, Jules. I guess we better head out before she gets angry." I nodded, though not caring if she was mad or not. She always ruined the best moments, and I didn't want to walk through boring stores and buy endless stupid stuff. Not being with him often, I wanted to be next to him any chance I could get. Mom stood on the front porch, her foot tapping impatiently, and my sister, Keira, her mini-clone, was doing the same. I rolled my eyes at them and slipped past them into the house.

"Make sure you brush your teeth and comb your hair. I'm not taking you downtown looking like a vagabond. Geez, did you have to keep him down there for so long, Damien? You knew we were going shopping. I've got to get a new swimsuit for tomorrow, and some suntan lotion. You'd think you'd have something as basic as suntan lotion here. Skin cancer happens to those who hang out too long in the sun. Look at you, D, your skin is going to peel off if you get any browner." I listened as she griped at him, then heard the door shut and his footsteps as he came to the bathroom.

"I'm going to stay here, sport. Play nice and I'll catch you all when you get back." He turned and strode away, his shoulders stooped, almost as if in defeat. Every time we came, it happened, and I watched him shrink beneath her harsh tone. It made me hate her more, and I wondered if she'd ever let me come alone, just so we'd have man time together. I doubted it. Her voice rose to a feverish pitch, and I eyed myself in the mirror.

"Come on Julien, get your rear in gear, times a wasting…" I sighed and watched as my shoulders sunk, too. I pulled them back and shook my head.

"You will not kill my spirit, too, Mom. I won't let you do it!"

Saying it aloud made me feel strong, but as I turned the corner and saw her face, I let go of my bravado and hung my head.

"I'm coming. Sorry, Mom, I didn't mean to make you wait." She gave a nod of her head, pivoted around, and stalked out the door. I peeked into the living room on my way outside and saw my father. He was sitting in a chair, his fingers moving easily, and soft music was playing. It made me happy that he found some solace in his music, and until I'd returned, I had forgotten that aspect of him. "I love you, Dad…"

He turned and gave me a smile, nodded at me, then closed his eyes and lay his head back on the headrest. I walked out to the car, wishing I, too, could sit beside him and just be.

A rumble of thunder and the needle reaching the end of the record woke me. I contemplated re-starting it and peered around to see if the girl had returned. The bottle sat beside me where I left it, but its lid was now off. The sparkling essence long gone. I lifted the bottle to my eye and peered inside. It lay empty, with only a faint essence of jasmine emanating from within. With a heavy sigh, I set it aside, turned off the record and slid it back into its sheath, then went to grab myself a beer.

Ten

Tongue Tied and Twisted

I t took me two days to finish the yard, or at least the weed whacking of it. The rain left everything messy, and Frank stopped by on the second day. He eyed the skies and shook his head.

"Gotta take the nag to town, so I can't help. If you want to borrow the mower, I leave the key to the shed beneath the stupid gnome in the garden beside it. I hate those things. They give me the creeps." His finger pointed out the peculiar rainbow painted creature, and I understood what he was saying. I nodded in agreement, not seeing the attraction myself. "Wanda did a stint with ceramics class, and the darn things took over the house. They were everywhere. When we moved, I made her unload a bunch of them at our garage sale, but that one's Em's favorite, so it had to come. Whatever makes my little girl happy, right?" I now knew to not say anything derogatory about the gnome in Em's company. I could learn to love them. Frank turned around, and I watched him head towards the car where Wanda stood eyeing us both. She shook her head, and jumped in to drive, as Frank shrugged and jumped into the passenger seat. I hadn't met her yet, but she already reminded me of my mother. She held the tone that you almost expected to see flames and smoke blow out of her mouth. Dad always called them dragon ladies, and I learned to spot the type a mile away and to steer clear.

My room-mate's girlfriend was just such an example.

The whacker fired up easily. I began edging around the house, cleaning up the growth and driving out any vermin that might have taken residence. I saw a black snake slither beneath the house, and remembered that those were the good ones, or at least I hoped so. At one point a hundred years ago, mother had put in flowers, but he had replaced them with small, compact shrubs. I'd have to ask Frank if he had trimmers, because I didn't see a set in the shed. I'd made it three-quarters of the way around the house when her voice broke through my reverie.

"Ready to take a break yet? The folks headed to an appointment and won't be back for a bit. Oh, and I made some lemonade if you want some?" After I jumped at the sound, I turned and smiled. Em stood there looking as fresh as a field of daisies. I say that because it literally covered her dress with daisies. I set the tool aside and nodded.

"Best thing I've heard all day, Em, from Wisconsin. Haven't had homemade lemonade since I was a kid." She turned and began walking towards her house and I followed along like a love-sick puppy. Her dress swayed in the breeze, and she turned and caught me staring. I brought my eyes up quick, but she knew, and gave a soft giggle. Drenched with sweat, I eyed my clothes as I walked up the steps. Their furniture had immaculate white and turquoise striped cushions. Hesitating, she turned to me and smiled.

"Don't worry, we'll sit on the steps. God forbid we dirty Wanda's new upholstery job." I breathed a sigh of relief and nodded. There was a tray with a pitcher of yellow liquid, two glasses, and a bowl of cut lemons. She poured out a glass and plunked a sliver of lemon into it and handed it to me, then grabbed one for herself. I took my cue from her and we sat apart on the steps in the shade.

"You've got your work cut out for you with that yard. I don't envy you that task at all." I chugged the lemonade, and it surprised me when I went to take a sip and found the glass empty. The ice cubes flew up and smacked me in the mouth, and Em began giggling. I loved the sound of that giggle, and I shook my head. She oozed happiness, which was something I found lacking in my life lately.

"Um… Yeah, it's a lot of work. Your lemonade was terrific." She reached for my glass, refilled it, and sat down again.

"Thanks, I use edible essential oil in it. I love oils and making distinct scents from them. The stuff's expensive as all get out, but Dad always buys me a new collection for my birthday and Christmas. This was a Christmas one, but in Wisconsin, no one drinks lemonade in the wintertime. I'll burn through it here in no time. Perhaps I should hint to him about a larger bottle." I sipped my drink more slowly this time and watched her as she eyed the machinery across the street with a frown.

"My dad hopes they don't build there. It's a shame. Ten years from now, he said that there will be a subdivision and houses that all look the same. I wonder what it looked like before they stripped the land?" I blew out a breath and shook my head.

"Cookie cutter houses, my dad calls them. It used to be a lush jungle, filled with trees and wild things. Burrowing owls lived way down there at the field on the end," I said as I pointed down the road, "and Gopher tortoises lived in the thickly wooded parts. You would hear them coming through the dead leaves, and you'd stop, wondering if it was some venomous snake or a bobcat, only to see this goofy turtle motoring along on his way to somewhere. It was nice. I hope they don't build it up, too." She took a sip of her drink and set her glass aside.

"How long have you been here?" I didn't know whether to tell her the truth, but it's not like she'd tell my mom, or anything, so I relaxed.

"I just got here. I go to college an hour away, and took a brief break. This house was my dad's. He left us a year or more ago, but something compelled me to come. I guess I just needed to decompress and figure some things out. I don't live here, and our house is up in Western New York, but I like here, better." She listened, and I eyed the bracelet on her wrist. It was silver and had two charms on it, and her fingers kept playing with them. She must have noticed me eyeing it and, stopping, she grabbed her glass again and took a sip.

"What did your dad pass from? Was it expected, or… God, I shouldn't be so nosy. I'm sorry." Not sure how to answer, I pushed my hair back and shrugged.

"Don't be sorry. And I don't know. He just disappeared. Boom, gone, and no one knows where, but he left everything behind as if he were coming right back. Mom thinks he... That he killed himself and that we won't ever find him. I don't think that happened, though. He thrived on life, and he was a peaceful guy who loved staring at the stars and moon, and probably hugged a few trees, too. Suicide wouldn't be his bag. At least I hope it wasn't. There was no note or anything, and I'd think he'd at least have said goodbye or something." My mind hoped he would have, but having not spoken to him in years, I was unsure about that. I changed the subject.

"So, Em, from Wisconsin, what made your folks move here? I've never been to Wisconsin, but it's up near Canada, right? Must be colder than a witches ti... I mean, freezing in the winter?" She nodded and grimaced. So I knew my guess was correct. "Summer is pretty hot down here, but my dad said it never snows this far south." Em relaxed and sipped her drink, then stretched her long legs out in front of her. I eyed her basic white Chuck Connors and smiled. Her feet were tiny, and I knew the girls were all doing the dress thing with sneakers these days, so she fit the image of a typical high school teenager, something I didn't resemble in the least.

"We needed a change of scenery. It's a really long story and someday I'll tell you, but let's just say we're processing as best we can. Dad wanted to move to the warmth and far away from... Well, we needed a new start." Her words had me intrigued, and I hoped for the day she felt comfortable telling me. She sighed and finished her drink, then eyed my glass.

"Do you want another? I have some left." I shook my head and stood.

"Nah, I'm good. Got to be getting back to work before the rain sets in. Not that it wasn't good, but save some for your folks. I'm sure they'll appreciate it, too." She stood and gathered the glasses and gave me a smile.

"I'm glad you took a break. Dad said you're a 'hard-working young man,' so that's a wonderful compliment. He doesn't dish them out very often, but I think you remind him of someone he used to know and feels the need to take you under his wing. I'm not sure if that's a good thing or not, but you'll figure it out. At least if he likes you, he'll let us hang out. Wanda is a different story, and she hates everyone mostly. She wasn't always that way... But things change. People change, and maybe someday she'll soften up. I hope so, because she used to be cool." Em pressed her hands against her daisy dress, smoothing it out, and then she resumed playing with the charms on her bracelet. I wondered what had happened in their life that made them who they were. Not knowing them before, I had nothing to compare it to, but Em had a sad softness about her. She wasn't fragile, but she looked like she could break easily if pushed. I smiled at her and nodded.

"I know what you mean. When my folks were together and we were little, life was so much easier. I don't know my dad too well, because I haven't seen him in over seven years, but he and I were once tight. My mom has changed into someone I don't want to know, but I don't know if he ever changed. That's why I came. Maybe it's closing the chapter of my life that I wonder about, or maybe it's just to apologize in a way for not trying harder to be there for him." I shrugged and turned to get back to my work. Her voice called from behind and I listened to the words of wisdom she imparted.

"I don't think it's true that you have to love someone just because they're family. One of the biggest lies ever told is, 'Blood makes you family.' No, blood makes you related; loyalty, love, and trust makes you family." Her soft laugh followed. "I wish I could say that was my creation, but alas, I'm a fraud... I found that as a meme online, but I think it's true. Follow what you feel in your heart, Julien. It will take you farther than anything else ever will." I turned and gave her a solemn nod, then walked away, the words striking home in my heart.

Eleven

A Man Lies and Dreams

I kept at the yard for another hour until I heard the rumble of thunder. Frank and Wanda returned and it must have been a heated event. I pretended not to watch as Wanda grabbed some bags out of the trunk, slammed it hard, and stalked past Frank. Frank hung his head and followed her into the house. I could hear the beep of the car lock a second later and wondered why they'd be so worried. I'm not sure what the crime rate was where they lived, but there was no one near us to break in here in this Podunk town. My hair tie kept slipping, and I ran my hand down my face, wiping the beads of sweat off.

"Friggin' hair, it's too hot to deal with this." My stomach growled, and I realized I hadn't eaten in hours. After throwing the whacker in the shed, I headed in to grab a bite and a quick shower. The house was cool, and I was thankful for the air-conditioner that seemed to function nicely. Thunder boomed closer and the rain would follow shortly. If my mother was here, she'd be griping to not shower in the storm. "Lightning will get you anywhere, even through a window. The water, oh, water is the best way for it to travel. Back in the day when we had land lines, you always hung up when there was thunder and lightning." Her voice felt like it was right here, live, and I shivered. I wonder if it was an old wives' tale, or something drilled into her

47

from her mother? Determined to snub the warnings, I jumped in the spray with a laugh and sang a lively tune from The Cure. Minutes later, 'Singing In The Rain,' popped into my mind and I stopped as the soap ran down my body and swirled at the drain like a circular funnel cloud. I hadn't heard that old song in years, but remember my father singing it at the top of his lungs every time he took a shower. This place did that, bringing to my attention all the little details I'd forgotten about.

"If you're almost done in there, song bird, we need to talk..." I jumped and looked around. The door was open, because being here alone, why the heck would I close it? I pulled aside the curtain a bit and peered out. The girl stood in the door and smiled.

"I enjoy singing in the rain, too, but I'll leave you to your privacy. Sorry, I let myself in. Hope you don't mind." What could I say? She turned and walked away, closing the door behind her, and I finished up, choosing to take my time. I refused to be dictated to by anyone, and that was that. Wrapping a towel around my waist, I squeezed the water out of my hair and searched for my tie. Not finding it, I combed it back and grabbed my clean clothes. As I reached for the doorknob, I stopped. I hadn't been singing, 'Singing In The Rain.' I'd only thought about it. My skin broke out in goosebumps and I wiped the mirror with the towel and stared at myself. The black color in my hair was fading, and my roots were turning back to dirty blond. I must have lost weight because my cheekbones were more pronounced, almost skeletal in a way. Staring at the mirror, I was face to face with how I remembered my father looked, and it floored me. The towel dropped from my hand and I left it where it lay, slipped into a fresh T and cargo pants, then went to find my visitor.

She sat in the living room, the turntable once again playing a soothing, beautiful piece. The string instruments brought the room alive, and even with the storm beyond the panes, it gave a sense of comfort. Her eyes were closed, and I slipped in and took a seat across from her, watching as she smiled.

"It is amazing, don't you think, how something so simple as music can have such a soothing effect on the body? I miss this, and I hope you don't mind that I came in. I didn't intend to trespass." Her eyes opened and a melancholy look crossed her face. She was the one who stole her way in, so I waited to hear what else she had to say. Lifting her hand, her fingers moved on air to the vibrant music.

"This is 'Gabriel's Oboe.' by Ennio Morricone, in case you wondered. He did a lot of music for films, but I think this is his best. He's Italian, and has this incredible ear for what will tug the heartstrings, don't you think?" I wondered what being Italian had anything to do with it, but I nodded and contemplated grabbing a beer.

"Sometimes you need to cut away the weight you're carrying. Life is a hard enough journey, shouldn't we embrace it and move freely, without constraint?" She looked at me as if she were looking through me and it made me uncomfortable.

"I'm grabbing a beer. Want one?" Offering a beer to an underage kid suddenly didn't faze me, and she shook her head.

"I would have thought you'd let that go by now. After all, you won't understand if your head is in a cloud. Maybe I was wrong. I thought you wanted answers." She stood as if to leave, and I sat down and held up my hand.

"Fine, you win, I won't drink, but you still haven't told me your name, and you keep turning up out of the blue. I need some answers first." She grinned and shook her head as she looked up at the ceiling.

"As you wish, young Julien. I'm Sara Elridge, and I used to live next door. I had a sense you were coming and so I came. When your dad lived here, I used to help him out, but then my folks moved, but now you're here." I knew I didn't need her help with anything, and I wondered if her parents knew she was still creeping around her old stomping grounds.

"Well, Sara, I don't need any help, except with some yard work, and I'm probably not going to be hanging around permanently. While I'm here, if you ask nicely, you can listen to Dad's albums. I'm not sure if Mom's gonna sell the place or what her plans are." Sara nodded, and I relaxed. "How old are you? Because I don't want any trouble. I'm nineteen and you're probably bait. The last thing I need is to get busted for corrupting a minor or something."

Sara burst out in giggles and shook her head.

"Sixteen years, ten months, and three days, but perpetually young at heart, so how's that? I have no plans of doing anything except helping you on your mission." That one threw me.

"What mission? I'm not on a mission. I needed a break, and that's why I'm here. Your dad used to do the lawn, but since y'all moved, I've now got that covered. What happens after I'm gone, well, that remains to be seen." I shook my head. Mission?

"I've brought you another jar, because I think you could probably handle it at this point. You haven't turned tail and run, not that I expected that. Damien always said you were brave, and I believe that to be true."

"I doubt he talked about me much. It's certainly easy to desert your kids and walk away, so what he knows about being brave... Well, who the heck knows." I folded my arms across my chest and closed my eyes as the jealousy crept over me like a wool blanket. It felt suffocating and left me empty. "I don't need your jars, they're yours, so why don't you take them and go." A yawn escaped my lips and my thoughts turned back to the beers in the fridge. "Yeah, I'm pretty tired and ready for bed. You should go." Sara gave a sly grin and waggled her finger at me.

"No can do, buckaroo... You want, no, you need a beer, am I right? Of course I'm right. That's why he trusted me to fill in the spaces again. You need to see the truth before it's too late. Your dad wanted this, and you need THIS, not a beer." I eyed her through the hair that fell forward on my face and shook my head. I'd had enough.

"I'm not your buckaroo..." The words came back to haunt me as she held out the bottle with a knowing look etched across her face. I could see the twinkling lights within the pale pink jar and I watched with trepidation as her fingers carefully unscrewed the top. A slight waft of smoke and sparkles erupted from within, and I sat back, mesmerized, as the oboes on the album played their haunting melody.

"You've got to cut the weight loose, Jules, or you will never be free. Lies cloud one's judgment, and only truth will rise to the surface, if you allow it. You've got to allow it, Jules, let him in again so you can release him with a clear heart." My mind drifted into a zone unlike anything I'd ever experienced before and I wondered if she had some kind of drug in there that intoxicated by fumes. I leaned back in the chair and felt my eyes close. His words filtered through my head and I drifted into the memory.

Twelve

And He Talks to the River

❦

I watched us. My Father and I hung by the bench at the river where Roger now lives, talking man to child. This should have scared me, but it comforted me, if that's possible.

"Your sister shares a name with a young girl I once knew." He slid his fingers through his wavy hair and eyed me from the bench as I skipped stones into the river, just like he'd taught me. "I met her when I was fifteen, and though I was never one to believe in that hoodoo, ghosts from another world garbage, she made me believe in magic. She's gone now, so you'll never meet her. At least I doubt you will, but it changed my life after I met Keira. I still feel her presence when I listen to the wind blow, and when the jasmine blooms, it's almost like she's still here." I peered around in the darkness, looking for a strange girl to walk out of the bushes, but saw nothing.

"Let's just say that I helped to set her free, and I guess she did the same for me." I listened as any stoic ten-year-old boy could as I sat down beside him. He wrapped his arm around me and I smiled. But I wasn't grasping anything except for the way his face came so alive when he told his story. Not wanting to speak and break the spell, I tucked myself deeper under his arm and listened for a girl's voice on the wind. Hearing only cicada's and the movement of the water, I stifled the yawn. I wasn't ready for bed yet and wanted to listen more.

"She was the girl who captured the stars, and I could tell you everything, but I think telling the story would diminish it, or diminish who she was. Besides, you'll think your old man's gone to the kazoo factory. But she existed, and she knew things." He leaned back and settled himself on the bench. "If you ever meet someone and they seem far-fetched, or they tug at something inside you, where you don't want to be out of their sight, trust that it's real, and follow where it goes. That, my son, is how you find the magic." I nodded as I listened and watched the ripples settle on the water.

"I could have turned out differently had I stayed at home with my mom, but when I moved here, it allowed me to be a new person. The girl with the stars awakened an affinity with the universe in me after she left. It left me shiny and clean. I became whole again. There was no taint to my broken spirit any longer. Simplicity and truth is a cherished gift. Remember that, okay?" I watched my young self nod and something tickled my memory, and I knew that this had happened. I just hadn't remembered it.

"Where is the girl now?" My father looked up at the sky and a wistful smile crossed the plane of his face. He gazed at me and pointed up.

"She's everywhere, Jules. She's with the stars, and we will all be there someday, too. Some just get there sooner than they should. You'll grow old, and maybe you'll understand and maybe you won't. There's always a shift happening, like a portal. It sweeps you away when you least expect it, and if you're lucky, you come out the other side better. Maybe you'll meet a girl and she'll give you a poke right there in your heart," he said as he tapped my chest, "and you'll be like a newborn, seeing another soul for the first time and you'll know it's the one. If the stars align, you'll get to move through the journey together. But, like taking a trip, sometimes you take a wrong turn, and, well, that happens too. Just enjoy the scenery and know that there's something better ahead, maybe even right around the corner." I watched my young self yawn, and he caught the sight and smirked, then he kissed the top of my head and pulled me tighter.

"I could sit here forever with you and just tell you so many things. But, I think it's best if I stop now and shuffle you off to bed." His smile was sad and

I shook my head.

"I want to stay here with you. Who cares if mom gets mad? I don't! Let me stay here with you for a while longer, and you can tell me more about the girl, okay? Mom can suck eggs, right, Dad?" He wiped a tear from his eye and shook his head.

"Someday I'll tell you everything, but for now, it's time for sleep. You'll have sweet dreams and maybe you'll see the girl in them. I still do, though she's gone away. But, you never know. Maybe if you ask, she'll come. We don't want your ma angry, so let's go, sport." I nodded and yawned again, and he pulled me to my feet. We walked together down the path in silence, and I turned back once to stare at the stars. One shot across the dark blue atmosphere and I nodded, knowing that maybe that was her sign, that she was listening out there somewhere.

* * *

The funeral dirge on my phone startled me, and I looked around. The girl had disappeared, and the empty jar remained in the seat where she'd been. I noticed the record now stopped, too, and my eyes looked for the source of the ringtone. My phone was out on the table and I grabbed it, steeling myself for the wrath of Simone. Something tingled in my senses, and I had a feeling in the pit of my stomach that she knew where I was, and that she wasn't happy about it. My brain debated hard about letting it go to voicemail, but it clicked on before I could answer. I set the phone down and let her spew into my inbox, and my eyes lit on the refrigerator.

"It's five o'clock somewhere, right, sport?" His words filtered through my head. My Dad hadn't been one to drink to excess, but when on vacation, he and mom would sit out in the oak's shade and enjoy minty cocktails. He gave me a sip once, but it was nasty, and I'd never asked for amother. Now my body was screaming for a beer and I walked to the refrigerator and leaned against it as my hands shook. As I pushed my hair back, I sighed heavily.

"Are you still here, Sara, because I need to ask you some questions?" I listened, hoping to hear her voice, but found only the hum of the motor behind me. What the heck had just happened? Why, suddenly, were these forgotten memories plaguing me? I glanced over at the closed door off the kitchen. It had been his and my mother's room. I'd yet to open it, and it's not because I was afraid. I think it felt like an intrusion. At some point I would, but not today.

"Dad, if you can hear me, give me a sign…" My voice wavered as I said it. I was nervous, expecting a loud booming voice to come thundering down from the heavens, and I felt like crying. Maybe I was losing my mind, I thought, and I jumped as my phone rang again. The funeral ringtone screeched at me like an owl in the night. I grabbed a beer, pocketed my phone, and headed to the porch to deal with whatever she wanted.

"Geez, mom, give it a break, already. I was in the shower. Do you know how long it takes to grab one when you're sharing it with the entire floor?" I felt no remorse for lying to her. I just wanted her to chill out.

"Julien, I've been trying to get a hold of you. It's not like you to not answer the phone, but that's fine. I'm heading to Europe on a trip tomorrow and didn't want you to worry if you couldn't reach me. Sometimes Wi-Fi is wacky over there, and…" her words trailed off as I rolled my eyes. I could give a crap if she went to Europe or hell. I never call her, nor did I intend to.

"Why would I call you? I'm fine, have fun, and don't take any wooden nickels…" I tried to stop the words and could hear the sharp intake of her breath. My father's favorite phrase of all time. I knew it would rile her.

"Ugh… Really, Julien, why did you say that? You know I hate that phrase. Your father spewed it endlessly, and I hated it then and hate it now." I grinned widely, wishing she could see it. "I hope school's going well and you're studying more than partying. You know how much that school is costing me." I offered up another eye-roll at the endless money/school tirade. With her, it never ended.

"I'm going to Europe on part business, too. Gotta keep making the bucks to keep you kids in your fancy schools, right? Don't worry, when you graduate, you can work for me and get the money paid back in no time flat." My mother never changed, and I clenched my fists, happy she wasn't standing right in front of me. Frank took that moment to pull into the driveway, shut the car off, and yelled over.

"I'll come give you a hand tomorrow, Julien. My back's feeling better after the chiropractor adjusted it and I'm almost as good as new." I could hear my mother's eagle ears tuning in on the Frank frequency and I flinched.

"Who was that? Are you outside? I thought you said you just got out of the shower?" My mind raced, and I chuckled, as I lied through my teeth.

"Ma, I'm in my room and looking out the window. It's this guy, Frank, and we're working on a project together. He's been out for a few days with a messed up back from basketball, but he just got back. Geez, why are you harassing me?" She sighed heavily, as if I was tormenting her in some odd way.

"Fine, but I'll be there for two weeks, maybe three, tops, and Carlos is going with me. I just hope Greece is nice this time of year, though I doubt it." I could see her and Carlos shacking up in some little Air B&B somewhere on the Mediterranean and they'd be doing more than work. Carlos was just another pony in her stable of men, or should I say, almost men. Not that I cared, but Carlos was four years older than me and was one of those guys that the girls creamed over. Dark hair, olive skin, sparkling white choppers that filled his face like a neon sign, and he looked at me like he was my superior. Alpha male want-to-be, I thought with disgust. Whatever, I just wanted to hang up and drink.

"Have a delightful trip, Ma, and... Have a nice trip," I went to hang up the phone and her pathetic voice reached my ears, and I paused.

"Aren't you going to say you love me, Jules? I love you, you know. It wouldn't hurt to hear it from your lips once in a while. What if my plane crashes? You'd feel horrid for not saying I love you." I refused to take the bait, as her neediness hit me like nails on a chalkboard.

"Yeah, whatever, Mom, well, have fun." I hung up the phone and stared at the Caterpillar across the street. "Stuck in yesterday, always stuck... No escape, ever." I slid the phone into my pocket and cracked the beer.

Thirteen

Sorrow Lies Over the Land

I woke up with a splitting headache and the sound of a lawn mower droning in the distance and figured it was Frank. After I hit the head, I stumbled like a zombie into the kitchen and peered out the window. Frank was teaching the boy how to use the mower and I rolled my eyes. Typical parents, treat the kids like hired help, without the pay. I chastised myself a second later, because Frank had been cool with me. On second thought, maybe it was good to teach the kid some responsibility? Eyeing the empties, I swallowed down the remnants in the eight bottles, because I figured, why waste it? I knew my supply was getting dangerously low and wondered how cool Frank would be if I asked him to buy me more. I'd worry about that later, I thought as I headed to the porch.

Frank came striding over a minute later, glancing back periodically as the boy rode the mower around the curves like a pro. "Don't go too fast!" He yelled, and the kid nodded, watching to make sure his lines were right on. He'd obviously done this before, and I relaxed.

"I don't know about that boy. He loves to mow the lawn, and God knows he'll get his practice here. This lawn is twice the size of our other one back in Portage. He's gonna tackle yours when he's done with ours." My eyebrows must have risen, because he cut in, all nervous. "You don't have to pay him or anything. Like I said, he loves doing it. He races go-carts back home, and I hear they have some tracks around here. Part of the deal of moving to Florida is that he wouldn't have to give that up. Whatever, I guess, but as a kid, I rode a bike and played ball with my friends, but my boys... Well, the need for speed must come from Wanda. Gotta go, gotta go, you know?" I smiled and sat down in the old rocker on the porch. It creaked but held, and Frank shimmied himself into the Kennedy chair, then relaxed.

"What's your sons' names and where's the other one?" Frank fidgeted a minute and glanced behind his shoulder, then sighed.

"That one's Jasper, and he turned eleven last weekend. My other son was... " he stopped talking, and I realized maybe this was the reason they moved, the story Em wouldn't talk about yet. I waited and glanced across the street to take the pressure off, and Frank cleared his throat. "Well, we had another son who... Passed away in an automobile accident two years ago." I knew better than to delve into his business, and debated changing the course of the conversation, but took my cue from him.

"Franklin was coming home from a party, you know, the typical story, kids partying, too much to drink, and no sense. Eight kids pile into a car, no seat belts... Your typical evening news fodder, but when it's your kid, well... That changes things, I guess. He was fifteen, and into the racing thing, too. He wasn't driving, but you can't change it. Things I'm trying to get a handle on, but it gets hard. I had such hopes for him, too." He brushed the wetness from his eyes and ran his hand down his pant leg. "I shouldn't be bothering you with this. You're a stranger, and no one likes a downer, right? If Wanda were here, she'd be shushing me with daggers from her eyes. I'm sorry, I should go."

I sighed and shook my head as I held up my hand. "Frank, you can talk to me whenever you'd like. My Dad and I used to have a lot of heart-to-hearts when I was a kid. I'd say I wish he were still here, but... That's another story for another day. Everyone deals with loss differently, and if it makes you feel good to vent, then I'll be here to listen. I'm not a stranger. I'm Julien, or Jules, if you prefer." Frank looked over at Jasper as he moved effortlessly and perfectly across the green grass, and a small smile lit the corners of his mouth.

"It takes everything in me not to grab that kid and hold on tight. It seems with every year that passes, he grows bigger and farther away from me. Losing Frankie Jr. killed me, and I try not to dwell on it, but when you lose someone, you lose a piece of yourself. Wanda throws herself into hobbies, Jasper has his racing, and Em, she disappears into her world of books to escape. I hoped moving here would give us all a change of scenery, and maybe something new to look forward to, at least I hope so." I nodded as his eyes turned to the cleared land across from us.

"I hope they allow it to grow back to its former glory. Em said that you told her it was woodsy and jungle-like over there. I liked the joint we bought because the river runs behind it, so no one will build over that. Land is a precious commodity, as is life. We shouldn't ever take it for granted." He leaned his head back and closed his eyes. I knew I wouldn't be asking him to buy me beer. Shifting in his seat, he stood. "So, you're okay with Jas mowing your yard? If so, I'll let him know." I nodded and gave him a smile.

"Sure, if he wants to mow, I need to tackle the back… Cemetery. It's old, but my dad always loved sitting back there. Who knows, maybe he was talking to ghosts or something," I said with a light laugh. Frank nodded and eyed me.

"Ain't nothing wrong with talking to the dead, Jules. I still talk to Frankie Jr, but oh how I wish he could talk back. Man, I'd give my eye-teeth for one more talk with him. I'll let you get to it. We'll chat soon, okay?" I stood, and he held out his hand, and I took it in mine. He'd gotten teary eyed again, and I was afraid to say anything. It surprised me when he pulled me forward and gave me a brief pat on the back, like I was a small child he was afraid to touch.

"Thanks for listening, Jules. I appreciate it." He turned and walked towards his house, his hand wiping at his face as he made his way up to his porch and through the door. I could almost see Em tucking herself away in a fairy tale girlie room, immersing herself in books, forgetting about the broken hearts that moved like phantoms around their home, silent in their tragedy, longing to be heard. It hurt my heart, and it made me want to sit with her and break through to let some light in. Something told me she was okay, though, and that maybe I was the one who needed her to let my heart see past the darkness I dwelled in.

Jasper waved at me as he swung around the front porch, and he put it in neutral and eyed me. "Dad said I could mow your yard if it's okay... You don't mind, right?" I shook my head and gave him my best grin.

"Heck, buddy, I hate mowing lawns, and all I have is one of those antique push suckers. Mow away, as often as you want. If you get bogged down in the thick stuff, I'll be in the back and I'll help you out." Jasper nodded, pulled his baseball hat down and put it in gear, then went zipping on his way. The scent of the freshly cut grass smelled good, and I hoped he'd watch for any snakes. I contemplated flagging him down and mentioning it, but no sooner did the thought rise, Jasper came to a screeching halt, and I watched as his eyes traveled along the ground. The black racer came zipping my way, and he gave a quick glance to me. I offered a thumbs up, and he grinned, then set it into motion again. With a reprieve from mowing, I headed out to the shed to grab the weed whacker. A pair of gloves hung on the shed wall, and I scooped them up and eyed their worn appearance. They must have been my dad's, and it felt weird putting them on, like a child stepping into their parents' shoes. They fit perfectly, and were smooth from use. I pictured him toiling away amongst the stones, culling the weeds and making it respectable again.

"Don't worry, Dad, I'll get it as right as rain. It will be just how you like it, if not better." I thought of hitting a garden center and picking up flowers to plant back there, to lighten it up a bit, but figured it could wait for another day. First things first, I had to make it good again. I had a decent sized pile of refuse an hour later, and the stones were once again visible. Jasper rumbled by occasionally and eyed the cemetery like it was the last place he wanted to go near and I'd give him a wave, then return to my mission. I never noticed him finishing, and lost in my thoughts, her voice sent me rocketing forward as I leaned over to grab a wayward stem that kept just out of reach.

"Dad wanted me to invite you to dinner tonight, that is, if you ever eat. You're as thin as a rail. I hear being in college makes you gain at least fifteen, so if that's true, you must have been a stick before you got there." Her laugh filled the air, and I wiped my sleeve across my face, pushing the sweat away. She was wearing a pale pink sundress and the same sneakers. I felt my heart thudding in my chest as I eyed her and I stood.

"Um… Sure, I guess. What time?" She peered down at the stones that stood behind my feet and worked her way around me to see better.

"I guess five o'clock, but who's buried here? Are these your relatives or something?" Her hand reached out, and she kneeled down and ran her fingers across Keira's stone. It had a small angel on it and the year of birth and death. "She was so young. Gosh, I'm sorry, Jules." I shrugged and watched the way the sun glinted off her hair. I wanted to reach out and touch it, and she blushed when she turned around and looked at me. She stood and stepped away, creating a distance between us.

"Yeah, I think she lived here before my dad inherited the house. I don't know who the others were, but I think her ma, maybe her dad? I was told there are family pets in here, but beyond that, I'm not sure, so don't be sorry." Em smiled lightly and eyed the lawn.

"Jasper's gonna love having two lawns to mow. If you end up heading back to school, you won't have to worry about who's going to take care of this. That should ease your mind a bit." It did, but I was in no hurry to leave. My mother's voice took that second to rip through my head and spill from my lips.

"Should I bring anything for dinner? I hate to show up empty-handed." Geez, no sooner did the words roll off my tongue, I regretted them. I sounded like a brown-nosing doofus. "Um, Ma always said it's impolite to show up without a gift for the hosts. I don't cook, but I could run into town and pick up a dessert or something…" Em chuckled as she shook her head.

"No, bring nothing except yourself. Wanda prides herself on her spreads and God forbid you show up with something that doesn't fit the theme. She'll be ten kinds of freaked out. Just you, Jules, and that will be enough." I wondered if I should tell her about my talk with Frank, but let it be. Maybe he'd tell her, or maybe he wouldn't, but in the meantime, if she felt the need to talk, I'd be better prepared. She looked into my eyes for a second, hesitating, as if she had something else to say, then she gave a wave and headed toward home, yelling out, "See you then, Jules, and I'm looking forward to it."

Em didn't look at me when she said it, and I wondered if she was blushing as much as I was. I grabbed my gear and headed in, done for the time being with the cemetery. "Flowers would be a pleasant touch, though," a voice sounded off in my head as I strode across the freshly shaved lawn. My next mission was to head into town and see what was available. Flowers would be a perfect offering, and I hoped they would bring a smile to Em's beautiful face.

Fourteen

Thunder Drowns Out what the Lightning Sees

❦

I paced the kitchen, my hands quivering like a tree in a hurricane, and I eyed my parents' bedroom door. I had a few beers left, and knew they'd calm my jitters, but I couldn't go over there smelling like alcohol. With what happened to Franklin Jr., it wouldn't feel right. Giving a quick glance at the bouquet of wildflowers I'd bought at Publix, I hoped they would suffice. I double-checked the water in the vase they came in again and resumed pacing. I hesitated in front of the door again. My hand trembled as I steeled myself and I gripped the doorknob, then released it a second later.

"Come on Jules, there's nothing in there that you haven't seen before. Get a hold of yourself. It's just a room for Pete's sake." I argued with myself, then angry at being such a baby, I turned the knob and walked in. With no sane reason for why I shouldn't be in there, I closed my eyes and inhaled deeply, then stared around the darkened room. The Queen-size bed still sat in the middle of the far wall, and a bedside table with a lamp sat beside it. Photos on the wall behind the bed capturing our vacations hung like a real-life museum, my life that I'd forgotten about. An image of my mother and father from their wedding, taken on a beach somewhere in South Carolina, hung front and center, and at least ten candid shots of mom, dad, and us kids hung around it. They were all close-ups of our faces, and I could tell we were happy. I don't remember when they took them, but he suspended them like a little time-capsule of our history. The room had a slight musty smell to it, and I opened the windows a crack to let some air in. Another air-conditioner sat on the floor on the other side of the bed, and I hefted it up, slid it into the window and plugged it in. The air blew warm at first, but then turned cool a minute later, and the floral scent of whatever thingie he had stuck in the vents filled the room.

"It's jasmine. He had those specially made because the blooms were only out for a month or two before they die. I told you, he loved that stuff. He always thought they looked like little stars. They are as beautiful to gaze at as the real deal. Day stars, he called them, though when it gets humid, they overpower the air with their scent." I turned sharply at the voice and Sara stood there leaning against the door frame. "The flowers are a perfect touch, and she'll love them, so stop worrying." I felt strange having her in here and ushered her out and closed the door behind me.

"Do you ever knock?" She gave me a sly grin and shrugged. "I've got to head to dinner, but hang out and listen to the records. I don't mind." What if Em sees her, though? What would I say? The thought moved through me, and I knew she'd be okay with it. Sara was just a girl who used to live in Em's new house, and maybe the girls could chat about that. Sara shook her head and smiled.

"So, I'm not here to talk to her. But, I'm here for you. I'll listen to the albums some other time, but tonight, when you get back, I've left a bottle for you. I grabbed a few more from the shelf, but it's sitting on the stereo. Now that you've entered the lair, bring it in here and open it. Relax, lay back, and let the magic do its thing." I shook my head, ignoring her, and headed back to the kitchen to grab the flowers. It was one minute to five, and I was going to be late. When I turned around, Sara had disappeared. The front door sat wide open. I rolled my eyes and headed out, closing it behind me. I didn't have time to dwell on what she'd said. Dinner was waiting, and I didn't want to upset Wanda by being late, or she'd never issue an invitation again.

64

* * *

Frank swung the door open with a wide smile and a Bass ale in his hand. He gestured me in, and I hid my look of shock as best as possible. "Welcome, Julien, and hey, what can I get you to drink?" My eyes moved to the beer in his hand and it took everything in me to keep from asking for one. Something told me to play it cool, and I peered around the room I stood in.

"Um… Do you have any lemonade, or… I don't know…" My voice wavered, and he eyed me, shrugged, and strode into the kitchen.

"Whatever suits your fancy, I just figured… Eh, never mind." His eyes looked into mine, as if he knew. "Wanda, we have any more lemonade left?" Wanda eyeballed me over her fancy glasses, as if surprised Frank wouldn't be lobbing a beer my way.

"Yeah, I think Em whipped up another batch earlier. Check the fridge, I'm busy here." Wanda was on super-speed, slicing and dicing, as her eyes darted nervously about. Frank wiggled his beer in the air.

"You sure now? It's not like you're driving anywhere, and I let Em have one now and then, though she's more partial to lemonade." I shrugged.

"Beer or lemonade is good, I'm easy." Frank nodded knowingly, a bright grin across his face.

"Us men should stick together. Have a beer, and we can go sit on the porch. Dinner's delayed a bit because the chicken wasn't cooperating with the Mrs." Wanda snorted and eyed him, then her eyes lit on the flowers in my hands.

"Just don't be getting drunk. I've worked hard for this and I want Julien to enjoy my culinary skills." Her eyes spoke volumes, and I watched as Frank's shoulders drooped. I took that moment to set the flowers down on the table, out of Wanda's way.

"Here, I guess it's a welcome to Florida and thank you for dinner bouquet." A wide smile crossed her face, and I knew I'd chosen something nice enough to appease her.

"Why thank you, Julien, it's Julien, right?" I nodded.

"Or, Jules, I answer to both, just don't call me late to dinner…" I stopped and shook my head. Here we go again with the blast from the past phrases.

65

Wanda must have heard it before, because she chuckled and waved her hand at me.

"You two boys go on now and get out of my hair. I've got some more stuff to do. Enjoy." Her tone had evened out, and I felt happy to have said something appropriate for a change. I grabbed the beer from Frank and followed him out. With no sign of Jasper or Em, I sat in the enormous chairs Wanda had had reupholstered. I sunk into the cushions and I waited for Frank to speak first.

"So, Jules, what is it you're going to school for? Theater?" I knew my clothes and hair seemed more in line with that, but I shook my head.

"I'm going for architectural design, but am taking a break right now. It's not really my thing, and the longer I'm there, the more I realize I'm wasting my time. But, it's what mom wants, and what mom wants, she gets." Frank nodded knowingly and grimaced.

"That's a darn shame, I'll say. A man should do what's in his heart. Heck, even a boy will get a certain feeling for things. Jasper and the racing is a perfect example. It's the one area I fight with Wanda on. That kid loves it, and when he's behind the wheel, you see the gleam in his eyes. You don't want to take that spark away. If we don't live our passion, well... We may as well be six feet under, don't you think?" I thought about my art studio at home. Walls of oil and acrylic paintings from years of dabbling hung, and though they weren't much to look at, they were a part of me. The idea of never painting again physically hurt, and I shook my head.

"Yeah, I know, but I can't make a living as an artist. If I want to get somewhere in life, I've got to tow the line and do something that brings in money." Frank swallowed down some beer and set it aside.

"Now, son, that's your parents talking right there. Think about it. Do you really believe that load of puckey that just fell out of your mouth? You may dress a little weird, and don't get me started on the black nail polish, but I see something in you that reminds me of me when I was your age. Fight against the man, or in your case, your mom. It's your life. Don't squander the time you're allotted on this earth, because I know it can all be over in the blink of an eye. If you knew you were going to die tomorrow, what would your regrets be?" I wasn't used to this line of questioning and I squirmed in my seat, which only set Frank to smiling more.

"You're afraid, Jules. Ain't nothing wrong with being afraid, but somewhere inside you is your truth. Trust the journey, and take whatever steps necessary to get where you'll be living a life you honestly and truly love. Everything else is secondary. People, places, this is your journey and no one else's. Don't forget that." He leaned back and ran his hand through his hair and pointed at the car.

"See that? I worked myself to the bone for that fancy car because Wanda had to have one, and for what? Four wheels and the status that comes with it? I'd be happier with an old beater that I could fix up and pass down to my son, or daughter, if she wanted it. I enjoy tinkering. Used to do a fair amount of it, as a matter of fact. But life gets in the way. Don't be like me, growing old and wondering what I could have done differently. Follow your dreams and don't let anyone tell you they're not worth a plug nickel." My mouth dropped open and Frank looked at me with an odd expression.

"My dad used to say stuff like that. I remember little about him, but since I've come here, these things are flashing back at me. It's like re-living your life, but it feels new, yet you know it's your history. When I showed up here, I wasn't sure why I came, but with each minute that passes by, I'm getting closer to him in a way. Does that sound strange? Sometimes I think I've lost my mind. I never went into my parents' bedroom until today, and again, I don't know why. He was such a jerk, according to my mom, and we never saw him. He left us behind for this house and never tried to connect after that. What kind of father would do that to his kids?" Frank's face took on a melancholy look, and he shook his head.

"You never know what drives a man, and you may never know, but maybe he was following his destiny, too. Perhaps he didn't intend on hurting you, and having not met him, I can't judge, but maybe give him a little leeway in your thoughts. Perhaps they forced him to do something and as his world opened here, it finally gave him peace. Well, a man who's haunted will settle once he finds his rightful place. It was his journey, you were just along for a little of it, and I bet you money, had he stuck around, as you grew into being a man, you would have sat with him like we're doing here and maybe you'd see he had to do this. Not that it doesn't hurt the heart to let go, but hanging on to anger and being miserable hurts a heck of a lot worse." Frank stopped talking, his eyes traveling to some place behind me. Em stood at the door, and I could tell she had heard at least part of the conversation. Her eyes moved to me and a small smile lit the corner of her mouth.

"Dinner's ready. Mom said to drag you both in before it gets cold." A blush rose to my face, and I looked at the beer in my hand, suddenly sorry that I'd accepted it. Frank jumped to his feet and motioned to the bottle.

"Can I grab you another one, sport? I've got a twelver in there. There's plenty." I shook my head and followed him in.

"I'm good, but thanks. I drink water with meals, but… Thanks…" Em smiled at that and I watched as her pink sun dressed swayed around her legs as she walked. Frank turned and saw where my eyes lay, gave me a small knock on my arm, and shook his head.

"Uh, huh… Yep, I see." I blushed and averted my eyes to the hallway in front of me.

Fifteen

When Light Gets into Your Heart

ollowing Frank, I eyed Wanda, who stood cross armed beside the table. The spread looked like a festive holiday meal, complete with a fancy tablecloth, and I wondered if there were more people expected. I noted five place settings, which answered my question, and Wanda pointed to a spot beside another setting. She and Frank took a seat at each end of the table like warlords presiding over their minions. I shelved the thought and grinned when Em sat beside me. Jasper came flying down the stairs a few seconds later and slid into his seat like he was stealing second base. Wanda reached over and tugged the hat off his head and dropped it to the floor with a dirty look. Her eagle eyes then perused everything before moving to the flowers I'd brought, which now took center stage on the table.

"Well, Julien, I'm glad you could make it over, and I hope you like it. It's a new recipe, and normally I'd only serve what I know is good, so this is a kind of experiment." I knew even if it tasted like dog food, I'd tell her it was delicious. Wanda watched as we each passed platters and filled our plates, and it surprised me when Em handed the chicken my way, taking none. Wanda must have noticed my gaze and cleared her throat.

"Our Emily is going through one of those stupid teenage phases right now and has decided she no longer wants to eat meat. Says it's murder, or some nonsense like that. I'm glad to see that you're not following that trend. Tell her it's okay to eat meat, because if the Lord didn't want us to eat meat, he wouldn't have created the animals and saved them all on that ark." I took a quick glance at Frank, who was eating. I'm not sure if he was ignoring her, but his mouth seemed relaxed and his head bobbed as he chewed. Perhaps it was always like this at their home. I would not tell Em any such thing, and she gave me a smile as I stayed silent and tried Wanda's cooking.

"Wanda, this is so amazing, and did you put cheese and ham in there?" Her eyes brightened up, and she made a face at Franklin.

"See, honey, Jules appreciates my cooking. Yes, it's called chicken cordon bleu, and that's a high-end Swiss I adore, oh, and it's smoked ham, too. Make sure you take more of it, because I made plenty." I swallowed another bite and started on the broccoli. Broccoli is my favorite vegetable and I knew you couldn't screw it up too badly, but Wanda's version needed some flavor seasoning or something to perk it up with. Em picked at her salad and veggies as the table grew quiet. Jasper was bopping his head like he was listening to music in it, and I smiled. I'd been the same way as a kid, impatient to finish and get back to playing. He made eye contact with me, then grinned with a mouth filled with chicken.

"So, Julien, I hear you're going to college. That's always good when children pursue higher education. What do you want to be when you become grown?" I refrained from choking on my broccoli and grabbed my water to wash the woody chunks down my throat. Frank nudged me, and I nodded.

"Um, I want to be an artist, when I… Grow up. But right now I'm studying architecture and design with the goal of working for my mother. But yeah, I paint in oils, acrylic, and do a little mixed media work. I enjoy doing that more than anything." Wanda eyed me, her lips pursed tight, and Em got an animated look on her face.

"Ooh, I do so love the arts. Do you have any pics on your phone of your paintings, because I'd love to see some?" I wanted to be funny and ask her to head over to my lair to see my etchings, but I didn't think Wanda would appreciate it. Frank might, but Wanda, nope. I felt around for my phone and stopped.

"I left my phone on the table at the house. Maybe sometime when you're not busy, I'll bring it out and show them to you. They're kind of dark, but it's kind of the mood I'm in when I create." Em looked enchanted by my offer, and I blushed, unsure whether she'd even like my stuff. I jumped when Jasper slammed backwards out of his chair. His plate was clean as a whistle and Wanda wagged her finger at him as he grabbed his cap from the floor.

"Take your plate in and wash it, and afterwards, you can go outside and play, but make sure you stay away from the river. Your Dad will take you down there later, maybe." Jasper swept up his dishes and ran to the kitchen like he was on fire. Wanda reminded me of my mother, with the words of admonishment on the river. This family was similar in ways to ours, but Em's parents were still together, so I guess they were different after all. I finished my meal and looked around. Everyone else had finished their meal, and I felt like I had been eating at a snail's pace.

"I'm sorry, Wanda, y'all got done eating, and it's like I just started. It's rarely I get a home-cooked meal, and this was out of this world spectacular. Heck, I don't even remember the last time our family sat down together to eat. Too long, I guess." Wanda grinned at me.

"Tell me about your family, Julien. Do you have any siblings?" I really didn't want to talk about them, and I think Frank must have realized this, because he cut in hastily.

"Next time Jules comes over, he can tell you all about it, dear. Now we're going to clear our plates, then go sit on the porch and have a beer." He turned to me and winked. "You want one, right?" as his head bobbed up and down. I guess it was the only way I'd get out of sitting for the Wanda chat and I grinned.

"Em, are you coming out too? I can grab my phone and show you my artwork." Em shook her head and sighed.

"Nah, you and dad go on, I'll help mom clean the kitchen up and get things squared away in there. I'll pop out later when I'm done." Frank hit the kitchen and returned carrying a shiny silver pail filled with ice and four bottles submerged in it. He grabbed my arm and hustled me out the door. I turned back to thank Wanda for her hospitality, but she'd already disappeared.

71

Frank giggled as he sat down.

"Good thing you took me up on the offer. You're gonna find with her that one question will lead into another, and yet another. Before you know it, she's criticized every choice you make, everything you've done, and will tell you how to do it her way. Which, according to Wanda, is the only right way to get things done." He handed me a bottle.

"If you don't want it, I don't mind. It was just an excuse to escape the Wanda wrath which would follow." My hand reached for the beer, and Frank eased back into the cushions and sighed.

"Kind of hot out here today, and would you look at those skies? My guess is we're gonna see some rain soon. I hope it staves off, because I'm not ready to be sequestered in there with her. Unfortunately, she's taken up knitting now. First the painted ceramics crap, now knitting doilies, scarves, and mittens. I'm like, 'honey, we live in Florida now. What are we gonna do with it all?' and of course she has an answer for everything. She plans on shipping some up north to friends, although her friends were pleased as punch when she told them we were moving. Supposedly they look forward to coming to visit, but I think it elated them to get her out of sight. Whatever, at least I've made a new friend. You don't need any mittens, do you?" I let out a giggle and shook my head.

"Um... No, but if she can wrangle a scarf in black, I'd use that when I head north again." The idea of going home felt foreign to me, and I took another swig and eyed my house. I could vaguely hear another piano song emanating from within, and I switched positions to focus on Frank again. If the girl was there, I could introduce them if she finished and came out.

"I really want to go over and see if I can get that Cat to run. Wouldn't that be fun, rumbling over all that open space, sitting on top of the world in that beast? I'd probably get arrested. Yeah, the headlines read 'Fifty-eight-year-old caught drinking and driving on stolen equipment,' news at eleven, right?" I sensed Frank had had a few before I'd arrived and could see a little of myself in him. I'd always wondered what brought people into your life and for what reasons. Sara, and Em, for example. The whys of life, my dad always called them. I chose to just let things ride themselves out and worry about it when

I had to. Frank giggled again, dunked his empty in the bucket, grinned, and grabbed a full one. "You ready for another round, sport?" It amused me, hearing myself referred to as sport again, as no one but my father had ever called me that. Maybe it was just a dad thing to say. I shook my head and finished the one in my hand.

"Nah, I'm good, but thanks. Jasper did a fab job in the yard. I think he did better than you or I would have. Lawn care isn't up my alley, but it had to be done. Oh, I met the girl who used to live here. She and Em would be fast friends, I'm thinking." Frank gave me a strange look, then took another sip. "Anyway, I'm glad you folks will cover the lawn when I leave. I'll make sure mom sends him some money for his trouble, even though you said we didn't have to, he should earn a fair wage for his work. When I was his age, I did odd jobs and bought art supplies with the cash. Jasper can save up to buy a race car or something he wants." Frank nodded and looked behind me as Em stepped out of the doorway.

"I'd love to see your art, if you still want to show it to me..." She seemed hesitant and I saw her eyes travel to Frank, who offered a shooing motion with his hands.

"Yeah, you two go look at art, and I'll get heading in. Yeah, it's dang hot out here. Think it's time to fire the air up a little higher. Oh, and bye, Jules, I'll see you kids later." I watched as he stashed another empty in the bucket, added mine, then slipped past us to head in. Giving a quick glance at the house, I could no longer hear the piano playing. I wasn't sure how to broach the subject of Em to Sara. They were close in age, but the way I felt about Sara paled compared to my feelings for Em. Sara was like an annoying kid sister, and I would know, having had one all my life. I didn't want Em to get jealous or anything. We walked through the lawn and the front door was open, but no music.

"You're awfully trusting, leaving your door open like that. I guess you don't have central air, or you'd be sealing it up tight to keep the cold in." I nodded and hoped I hadn't left the place a mess. Holding out my hand, Em walked past me and into my home.

73

Sixteen

I'll Put us Back Together

The candle was burning, its light jasmine scent and flickering flames filling the room with a soft glow and aroma. Em relaxed as she moved towards it and I watched the way her hair hung down in the candle light. She turned and smiled.

"It's rarely I see a guy burn candles, but I love this scent. It's jasmine, right? In my oil box, I have two bottles. I go through them so fast, but Dad always gets me more. He told me he was going to sign up for the monthly subscription just for that scent. I mix it or Cassia with other things and wear it when I'm not home. My mom can't stand strong fragrances, and I can't wait for the day when I move out and can fill my world with things that make me happy. Oh, and bookshelves, I want lots and lots of bookshelves." She blushed, and I waved her into the living room, where I clicked the air to a higher setting. I offered her the seat by the vents, but she opted for the couch. Her eyes roamed the room, and she seemed comfortable and that relaxed me. Frank knew where she was, and didn't seem concerned with her being here, so that left me less anxious.

"My Dad said he painted this room first after he inherited the place. He fixed it up here and there, and I figured he would have done a lot more, but I guess maybe he liked it the way it was. There used to be an enormous palm

74

tree in the corner, but I think it either died or he planted it outside. I noticed your mom's orchid by the entrance-way. My mom collects those things like the tooth fairy collects teeth. I'm surprised they do as well up north as I see down here. I even saw one attached to a tree in the backyard and it's got tons of flowers. Maybe ma put that there... I don't know. I haven't been back here since I was ten. That was the last time." Em didn't talk, but sat politely, listening to me ramble, which made me nervous.

"Here, let me get my phone and I'll show you some of my paintings." I sprung up from the chair and bolted into the kitchen, where my phone sat. The light for voicemail was flashing, and I flicked to my photos, ignoring whoever was trying to track me down. When I returned, Em was standing by the record player with an album in her hand.

"I love this song. Did you ever see that movie 'Somewhere In Time' with Christopher Reeve and Jane Seymour? I've seen it a hundred times, at least. It gives me the shivers every time I think of the scene where he found the penny. Geez, look at me, I'm getting all teary-eyed just talking about it. Guess I'm just a silly romantic." I watched the way her face lit up when she spoke about the movie, and I wracked my brain, trying to remember if I'd seen it or not. I shrugged and watched as she peered at the turntable. She turned it on and set the needle in place. The piano began again, and I felt like time stopped. Her smile was serene, and she swayed gently as the music played, her fingers moving to the tempo of the song. I slid into my seat and watched her as she moved effortlessly, as if in some kind of trance. The candle's aroma filled the air, and spellbound, I watched this beautiful girl dance to this soulful song. I stood and moved towards her as a small giggle erupted from her when I held up my hand.

"May I have this dance, my lady?" She gave a small curtsy, giggled again, and placed my hand around hers. I held her close, but not too close, and we moved around the small area as the music played. Her back was warm beneath my hand, her dress soft, and I closed my eyes for a moment and wondered if this was all a dream. Every time we moved near the air, the cool breeze separated us and we began laughing. At one point, her face was close enough to kiss, but I looked down and backed away. I released her a few

75

minutes later, feeling the blush rise to my cheeks.

"Um… I never dance like that, not with a girl, anyway…" Her eyes lit on me and she grinned. "I don't mean that I dance that way with dudes. I mean, I don't dance that way, ever. It was nice, though, don't get me wrong." My hand went to my face, and I shook my head as I pushed my hair out of my eyes. "I'd dance with you anytime you wanted, Em, you're… Something about you makes me feel comfortable, like I can be myself." Another tendril of hair slipped down, and I yanked it back again. "You don't cut hair by any chance, do you? This is driving me crazy." It broke the moment, and she moved closer and ran her hands through it, pulling it back, then slipping a little forward, as if she was pondering something. She let it go and stepped away from me.

"I dabble a little in that once in a while. Why? Do you want me to cut it off for you? I bet it took a long time to grow it this long. My fear is that I'd do a chop job, you'd regret it, then never speak to me again, and I'd hate for that to happen." I grinned at her and shook my head at her concern.

"No, I'd never stop speaking to you, even if you shaved me as bald as a newborn. Besides, it's hot here, and my roots, as you can see, are growing out again. This haystack grows pretty quick. Trust me, you could take a weed whacker to it and the next day it would all come back with a vengeance." I was eager to feel her hands running through my hair, and I gave my best puppy eyes. "Want to do it tomorrow?" She thought about it for a fraction of a second and nodded, a wide smile stretched across her face. A moment later, her eyebrows drew together.

"Can you wait until after lunch, though? I've got to go buy yarn and stuff with Wanda, but then I can come over. Do you want me to color it back to normal, too? I think I can manage that. Worse case is it falls out and leaves you bald, right?" She started laughing, and I joined her.

"Yeah, that would work. Oh, and here are my paintings. I'm no Picasso or Warhol, but hey, it's me." I pulled up the file and after a minute search, chose my favorite from the lot. The black, blues, and purples I melded together in a tornado-like swirl, and small gray specks moved from small to large, entwined within the layers. The base color I used was a royal blue, and I'd

76

added layer upon layer until I finished and was content. I remember the mood I was in when I painted it, as I remember my moods from every piece I'd done. She took the phone and gazed at it, her fingers pushing in and out to enlarge, then shrink it back to size. Then she scrolled to the next, continuing until she reached the beginning again. Her eyes met mine, and she shook her head as she handed the phone back to me.

"I don't know what to say, except I see amazing depth and feeling in your work. I'm no judge of art, but I see you more clearly, and perhaps know you better for having seen them. They're incredible." I wanted to rush to New York right then, grab one from my studio, and gift it to her. My cheeks turned red, and I honestly didn't know what to say to her gracious compliments.

"I'm gonna head home before Wanda sends out a search party for me, but if nothing else, think of this. You have so much talent in you, and I don't think you realize what you're capable of. I've been to galleries and museums, and your work blows the famous stuff right out of the water. There's this unique talent in you, Julien, and you're crazy wasting your time in school on something that doesn't suit. Thanks for the music and the dance. I'll see you tomorrow, okay?" I nodded like a mute, love-sick dog and walked her to the door. She turned around and a curious expression flitted across her face. Then she took a step forward, then another back, before grinning.

"You've got a spirit here, Jules. I just walked through their essence, and the coolness dissipated, but it was there." Her eyes traveled the room and lit on the candle, which took that moment to go out. With a nod, she leaned forward.

"This is a good place you've got. Cherish it, and it will guide you. See you around noon." She headed out, her body moving breezily. I watched as she walked across the lawn, her steps light and almost childlike, and I wondered what the heck had just happened. I closed the door after she made it safely home and leaned against it. The candle flicked on, then off again, and I remembered the jar. I trekked back to the living room and saw it on the table. Em must have moved it when she put the record on, I thought, as I lifted it. I didn't see the little sparkles in it, but after the dance with Em, figured the sparkles paled compared to that. I carried it through the kitchen and stood in front of the door, my eyes lighting first on the fridge, my mouth watering for a cold, wet one. Shaking the thought away, I turned the knob and stepped into my parent's room. Nothing had changed since I'd been there this morning, and I think I almost expected Sara to leave behind a note of what exactly I should do while in here.

"Lay back and relax, open the bottle, and allow…" Her words trickled through my mind like a lullaby and I nodded, then did as she asked. This bottle was yellow and reminded me of the color of the sunflowers that grew in the neighbor's yard when I was young. "Where are the flowers now? Then again, where is my father?" I asked as I lay down. Something was guiding me, and I felt relaxed, though this should have freaked me right out. The floral scent was strong on the air, and I inhaled it, then breathed out, almost like a meditation I'd seen done on a YouTube video once. Closing my eyes, I twisted the cap off, lay the bottle beside me, then stretched out as my mind went blank. His voice beckoned, and with a start, I followed willingly.

Seventeen

Love is Like a Flame

❧◈❧

"Simone, you're talking like a crazy woman, you know that, right?" He paced back and forth, his head shaking, watching mom as she stood with her arms wrapped tight around her chest.

"I saw you, Damien, and I saw her. Three times since I've been here, you've slipped away at night with her, and you may think I'm stupid, but I'm not. I can only guess what y'all are doing down at the river. Probably skinny dipping or doing it on that old crap bench." He looked at her and sighed heavily.

"Simone, there is nobody else. I get insomnia and can't sleep. Would you rather I flip-flop in bed all night and keep you awake? There is no other woman and there never will be. You are my wife, and I love you. I don't know what you're imagining, but it's not real. Maybe you are sleepwalking and dreaming this fantasy up?" My mother shook her head, the water reaching the lids to her eyes before spilling down her cheeks. She wiped them off on her arm and sniffled. I looked around, confused at what I was seeing. The past mirage I'd been witness to had been moments I'd remembered as happening, but this was new. I stood in my parent's bedroom. The clock said two a.m., and I was unsure what to believe.

"She followed you down there, and she knew I was watching because she turned around and stared at me, then she smiled. Damn, I wanted to follow you, just to prove something I'd never thought in a million years was happening right in front of my gullible face. You two must have had a grand laugh over it. The poor wife's asleep and will never know her husband's messing around beneath her nose. God, how could I have been so stupid? Enough! We're leaving, Damien, tomorrow. You can stay with your woman and have a wonderful life, but you and I are over." My father looked like a bus had hit him. The shock and devastation etched on his red face in tormented tears, and I wanted so badly to punch him for hurting mom. He lifted his hand and moved towards her, and she batted it away.

"Don't touch me, D, don't you EVER touch me again. I'm calling a lawyer, and when I'm done with you, you'll wish you never existed." He crumbled then, his body tucked tight as a wracking sob came over him. I wondered if this had even happened, and I closed my eyes as I became teary-eyed. When my folks fought, it was never in front of us. Taking in a deep breath, something changed. I still stood in this room, but my mother was absent.

My father, looking older and more worn, came through the door and opened the closet. His hands shifted around as he tugged at something. Leaning back on his haunches, he held a thick file in his hand and an envelope in the other. He gazed at the envelope with a tortured expression and tucked it into the binder before crawling back into the closet. He stood, and took a few steps backwards, then stopped with a moan. As he moved forward, his hand rose to his forehead as if pained. His face pinched tight, as if he were about to crumble to the floor. I moved forward to steady him. Swaying, he grabbed the bedpost to right himself, then took several steps and walked towards the kitchen. I watched as he closed the door behind him. I was curious about what he'd been doing in the closet, but felt as if they glued my feet in place. The music clicked on and I heard voices. One sounded like Sara. She mentioned how she used to help him, so her being there would make sense.

Why was I seeing these particular mirages? I'd not been in here for them. I realized I was witnessing things through his eyes, a voyeur to his and mom's marriage struggles. These were my father's memories, and I was borrowing them. I didn't recognize them because I wasn't here. Filling in the spaces... Her words filtered through my mind and I opened my eyes. Night had fallen, and I slid off the bed.

"This is crazy. Ugh, now I really need a drink." I switched on the light and almost came unglued as I jumped, startled. Sara sat in the chair, as if patiently waiting for me to surface. She watched as I opened the fridge and grabbing a beer with a trembling hand, I slammed it on the table. Her body never moved a muscle, and I shook my head at her as I rolled my eyes, irritated by her presence.

"Tell me, are you even real, Sara? You keep coming and dropping these little bottle bombs on my brain and heck, I'm surprised that you're here now. What do you want?" She watched me without expression and that made me even angrier.

"Tell me, why are you showing me all of this? Yeah, my dad was a dirt-bag who cheated on my mother, right under her nose. I mean, come on, who would do that? Then, those crocodile tears? He didn't give a crap, and he never has. He's a coward, cheating, bas..." Sara's hand rocketed forward, and I stopped as she shook her head and glared at me.

"We're not done yet, Jules. Go through the progression to see the truth. You're making assumptions, just like your mother did. There's more to the story, and in time you'll see it's true. But being angry with him will not help things. You need to take a chill pill and accept that other people live their lives. Stuff happens, but mostly, that it isn't all about you. Go get some paint, work out your irritation, and you'll feel better. It's going to get a lot darker before you see the light at the end of the tunnel. I'm sorry for that, but it's the way it works, and I may not be very good at this, but I'm trying." Her mouth turned up in a small smile and she reached across towards me, then pulled her hand back, as if thinking twice about tempting me with the mood I was in.

"You're just like him, you know. Stubborn, unbelieving, but you know what? He let go of assuming and allowed, and that made all the difference. He had a journey to travel and you couldn't come along. It happens every day, and it's difficult, but it had to be that way. Bear with me a while longer and it'll become clear, I promise." Now mentally drained, I wanted to be alone, and I lay my head on the table, hoping this entire episode would fall away like a bad dream.

"I'm going, now. Sleep well, Jules." I looked up, and she had left. A cool breeze blew past me as I watched the front door open, then close.

"I need more beer," I muttered as I opened the fridge. Of course, I found it empty and wanted to scream.

* * *

Grabbing my car keys, I slammed the door behind me and headed towards town, hoping to find someone willing to buy me a case or more. With a fifty in my wallet, I figured that'd buy me a decent supply. Not wanting to bother Frank, he may have had some spares, but I didn't want him to know. The car Wi-Fi picked up my playlist on the radio, and I cranked it, feeling the throb of the bass rattling the windows. I needed to get away from that house, from the ghosts it was stirring up, and I ran my hands through my hair. I imagined Em running her fingers through it as she snipped bits here and there with scissors, when a man walking alongside the road came into view. He looked decent, and he held out his hand as I approached. We hitchhike a lot in college, and it never freaked me out. So, easing the car off the side of the road, the guy jogged forward with a wide grin. I rolled down the window while lowering the volume. He seemed quite animated and cool in his Grateful Dead T-shirt.

"Dude, I'm late for a party. Man, you heading to town by any chance?" He sounded like he'd had a few already and I nodded.

"How old are you?" I asked, although he seemed old enough to buy me beer. He smiled and shook his head, a wide gap-toothed grin crossing his face.

"Duuuude, you wouldn't be asking unless you were looking for me to score you booze. Am I right? Huh, am I, bet I'm right?" I grinned and nodded.

"I'll make you a deal. You buy me some beer, and I'll drive you to where ever you want to go, in town, of course. I ain't driving to the ocean or anything." The guy opened the door and slid in, the aroma of pot following him. He giggled and reaching into his pocket, handed a joint my way. "Some?" I shook my head. If nothing else, I'd learned you can lace that stuff with some killer drugs, and I wanted nothing to do with that. He tucked it back into his pocket. "Drive easy, man. I'm carrying some stuff and don't need no hassle with the cops. Ain't got nothing better to do than diving into my business. Hey, I got to make a living, too, so drive easy." I turned the radio down and monitored him, but said nothing.

"Hey, I'm Seb, and thanks, man. We can hit the 7-11 for beer. I don't do the grocery stores, 'cause they like to call the cops on me, and I don't need that. What kind of beer you want? Fancy? Regular? Or that watered down low-carb girlie crap?" I laughed and shook my head. There was a light ahead and traffic was getting heavier closer to town. I stopped at the red light and waited, eyeing the car that pulled up beside me, and in my rear view mirror, I saw a car full of girls, singing from the looks of it.

"Hey check out the chicks behind us…" Seb swiveled around in his seat and he eyed them, then pulled up his shirt and shook his chest at them. The light was taking forever, but I refrained from seeing if they flashed him back. But as I turned, I saw what looked like an unmarked cop car pull up behind the car beside me.

"Chill, Seb, I think those are the boys. Be cool, 'cause I don't want to get pulled over either." Seb's eyes went wide and, of course, he whipped around to see if it was true.

"Duuuuude, you are so right. Yeah, be cool, and don't speed, they love speeders down this strip." The light turned green, and I edged forward as Seb's finger shot into the air in front of my face. "Duuuuude, the 7-11's right there, ya gotta turn." He had startled me and I yanked the wheel just a little and swerved into the next lane. A car laid on its horn as it passed and I felt my heart racing, realized I'd almost side-swiped it.

"Geez, that was close," I muttered as the cops pulled up and eyed me and Seb. As I turned the radio even lower, I tried to control my breathing as I struggled to recall how much I had drunk. Would it be out of my system by now? I couldn't remember. I slowly made the turn and exhaled as the cop car slid past us. Seb hit his hand on the dashboard and his maniacal laugh filled the car.

"Dude, good job. You kept it together. We'll wait for a bit to see if they turn around. In the meantime, I gotta wait to get your booze, cause if they're watching, I don't want to get busted on some pissant trumped-up charge." I understood completely, because I didn't want to get nailed on a DUI. We sat in the parking lot and Seb walked in and came out a moment later carrying a bag of Doritos, sporting a huge grin. We sat on the bench outside the store and waited to see if the cops were still hanging around. Seb was a knock-off of Sean Penn from Fast Times at Ridgemont High, and I had to stop myself from laughing like a stoner each time he opened his mouth.

"Man... I got the munchies... But I love these things, don't you? I could eat a million bags of them and still have the munchies." I nodded and grabbed a few while he chewed loudly and giggled.

"If you ate a million bags, you'd be dead, orange, and the munchies would be done 'cause you'd be dead, Seb." Seb laughed harder, and I glanced at my watch. "Do you think the coast is clear to get the beer?" Seb kept piling chips into his mouth and nodding like a cow chewing grass.

"Dude, what kind you want and how much? Hey, lemme finish the bag, then I can use their restroom and I'll get you what you want." I fished the fifty out of my pocket. Seb didn't bat an eye as I handed it over, which made me wonder how much he sold his stuff for on the street. He had a small bag slung over his shoulder, and though worn, it looked pretty thick. With a nod, he stood and waltzed into the store, blew a kiss at the girl behind the register, then headed for the bathroom. I hoped there wasn't a back entrance, because that was the last cash I had and I really needed beer. He came out of the restroom a few minutes later and must have washed the orange Dorito dust from his face. I realized I hadn't told him what kind of beer.

"Crap, please get something decent," my lips moved, but he couldn't hear me unless I screamed. If I went in, they'd ID me for being with him. I grinned when he hefted up a twelve of Bud as he stared at me through the window and I nodded emphatically while holding up three fingers. He must have understood, because he stacked up one on top of the other, then hauled them all to the register. In the meantime, I opened my trunk. He came out a minute later and walked behind my car, then nestled the cases inside.

"Dude, here's your change. I didn't spend any of it either." He handed me four ones and some change and I handed it back.

"Keep it. You did me a favor, and now I'll drop you off. Just tell me where." Seb began laughing again and shook his head.

"Eh, we've pretty much landed. The house where all the lights are, see? Wanna come to a rocking party?" I thought about it, but with the cops cruising, I didn't want to get busted while at a shindig where drugs were flowing like water. I shook my head. Seb held up his hand, and I gave him a high five. "Thaas cool, man. Have a good one, and if you ever need old Seb to fix you up with something a little stronger, give me a jingle. You'll find me there most nights." He stepped off the curb, gave a little wave, and I watched as he walked away. Seb seemed like a cool enough guy, and reminded me of my room-mate, but older and not so wiser. Jumping in my car, I hit the rewind button and piped my tunes through again as I took a deep breath. My mind slipped back to what had happened earlier in my parent's room. I contemplated heading to the party instead of returning to the house of madness, but changed my mind. I slipped the car into gear. The traffic had gotten heavier, and I still felt buzzed. I waited for an opportunity to pull out, but slammed on the brakes as three police cars with lights flashing went tearing in front of me. My hands shook, and I closed my eyes and leaned my head back on the headrest, terrified of what would come next.

Eighteen

Burns You When it's Hot

The neon blue and red lights flashed in the air like a disco floor on speed, and I gripped the wheel. Two of the boys in blue cars flew around the corner and one whipped through the 7-11 driveway beside me. It cut off the exit that ran to the side street. I watched as the spotlight shone on Seb, who immediately thrust his hands in the air as he slid the bag off his shoulder and on to the road. He glanced at me, an uneasy frown crossing his face, and he dropped to the ground as the cops exited and ran towards him.

Something told me he'd done this before, because he hadn't run and never gave them a chance to question his motives. I wondered if he had any weapons on him, and I watched as the scene played out in slow motion. A cop straddled his back, patted him down, and slapped a set of cuffs on him while two stood with guns drawn. A fourth lifted the bag and shone a light into it, then said something to the two off to the side before launching the bag to them. People streamed like cattle fleeing slaughter from the house. Their forms meandered into the shadows, hustling down the street at a feverish pace. I waited for the cops to come after me, but I wasn't on their radar yet. As I pulled out of the parking lot, I turned away from the melee and headed in the opposite direction. Up the road, I slipped down a side street, hoping to circle around and end up far past that street where the bust was going down.

The canopy of oaks I drove beneath lent an eerie feeling to this road. Their dark shadows elongated in my headlights, and I kept making turns before exiting back onto the main drag. I pulled off into an empty plaza ten minutes later and caught my breath. My heart was racing, and I shook my head as I realized how lucky I had been.

I flicked the playlist up as a few cars passed me, then pulled back out onto the road, eager to get home. Traffic lightened up the further from town I drove, and I slowed my pace, not wishing to pique the interest of any other police cars. Fifteen minutes later, I made the turn onto my street and picked up the pace. My body was antsy and my brain was craving a beer or ten. My song ended, but I wanted to hear it again. I glanced down to hit the play-back button, and looking up, a scream erupted from my mouth.

The car crashed into Sara as she stood in the middle of the road. She had a sad smile across her face and I stared into her eyes in shock as the car connected with her small body. My hands gripped the wheel as I slammed on the brakes and put the car in park before my mind went blank. I jumped out, and in the glow of the brake lights, searched the ground for her body. There was nothing there. My breath came in gasps as I rushed to the car to grab a flashlight, then I began searching the ditches. Walking back the way I'd come, figuring with her size, I wondered if she'd gone airborne and landed farther away than I thought. High and low I looked, but I found nothing except a small blue bottle laying in the dirt beside my car. I picked it up and put it in my pocket. She had been there.

I yelled for her, calling her name over and over, hoping to hear her cry out to me, but heard nothing but the steady drone of the cicadas. A second later, they became silent, and I sat in the driver's seat with the door open and sobbed. The next thought rattled me to the core. I hadn't searched beneath the car and suddenly; I wanted to throw up. My body trembled as I slipped from the seat, and my hands shook as I grabbed the flashlight and got on my knees. The ray of light moved slowly from the front to the back of the car. There was no sign of Sara. I shook my head and got back in, wondering if I should go grab Frank to help me search, then wondered if I'd imagined the entire episode. As I slowly drove the length of the street, I glanced at Em's house and saw there was only a small light on in the upstairs; The rest was dark. My headlights flashed across my porch as I pulled in and my heart almost stopped. Sara sat in the rocker, her eyes staring at me without reaction. I parked the car and shut it down, opening and closing my eyes, not believing she was sitting there. As I got out, she stood and walked into the house, which I know I locked before I left. My mind was whirling, and I debated whether to grab the beer from the trunk. I left it there and followed her, unsure what to expect next.

The Beethoven moonlight song was once again on the turntable and the candle was glowing eerily, filling the room with ripples of orange-white light. Sara stood in the living room, her arms wrapped around her waist. She turned when I walked in, and I waited for her to speak first.

"I must be terrible at this, because you're still not getting it. I'm sorry I had to do that, but I couldn't think of anything else. You're spiraling into a dark place, Julien, and I'm trying my best, but… I don't know." I walked past her, flicked the air to a higher setting, and sat down in front of it. My clothes stuck to me, drenched with nervous sweat, and my hands trembled. As I shook my head, I felt the tears fall down my cheeks.

"You're doing fine, but I don't know what you're trying to do exactly. Why play these games, Sara? Can't you just tell me what you want me to 'get' and then you can get on with your life and I can get on with mine?" I watched as she slowly shook her head back and forth.

"Ah, I wish it were that easy, but this gig comes with rules, and one of them is that I can't just blast you with the truth. You need to go through the process, and though it's hard, it's got to be done. I asked that you trust me, but I get the sense you think this is some kind of game. Your lack of respect is disheartening, and I'd hoped to see more of your father in you than this." I snorted at that and shot out of my chair.

"I know you've got to do something, but badgering me and walking into my life and meddling in my affairs isn't welcome. I'm not my father, and from what I'm seeing, I'm as far as a body can get from being anything remotely like him. Here, I'll give you a few examples. I wrote to that man every week for years and you know what I got in response? Zip! That's right. He couldn't even bother to write me back. Phone calls? Ha, what phone calls? Visits? What are those? He couldn't come see poor little Jules and Keira, and I owe him nothing now. I don't care if he's alive or dead! If that man walked through the door right now, I think I'd punch the bas…" Sara's hand shot in the air rocket-fast and I closed my mouth.

"I'm leaving, and maybe I have to escalate things a bit more to knock some sense into you. I knew your father. He was one of the most courageous people I know, and he tried. If you paid attention to the messages from the bottles, and opened your perpetually closed eyes, you'd know. Go back and do it again, but this time, keep your own thoughts out of it and PAY ATTENTION! I can't do much more than that. I'm out of here. Good luck!" Sara stormed out, the door slammed behind her, which blew out the candle.

"Good, get the hell out, freak! I'm done with you, too!" I jumped up, flew back to my parent's room, and my eyes lit on the closet. They cracked the doors open, and I flung them wide, slamming them into the wall. "Get the message, she says… You're not listening, Julien, she says… Jesus, you sound like my freaking mother." I felt the bottle in my pocket grow warm and I slid it out and stared at it. The sparkling lights were floating around within, casting a glow, as if someone trapped a thousand fireflies inside. I twisted the cap off, and the lights swirled in the air around my head, a warm, woodsy scent filling the room with their presence. Watching, they whirled around and then moved in a cloud towards the lower back of the closet. I looked down and saw my father's shoes, and kneeled as the lights slipped into cracks in the wall. My hands pushed the shoes out and sent them sliding to each side of me and it was then I saw the knob.

"He had put something in here… Something important enough to hide in a crawl space." I pulled at the knob and a piece of wood slid forward. It was thin plywood, two feet high and one foot wide, and it was dark inside. The glittering lights had gone out, and I stood, then hit the light switch. The overhead light turned on and then, with a quiet pop, went out a second later. I headed out to grab the candle and realized my hands were shaking as I carried it back to the room, the oil sloshing around at the bottom, making the wick spit and flicker. Slowing down, I held it tighter, then set it on the floor in front of the closet. There were three small shelves within, filled with notebooks, a file, and stacks of letters. My hand reached for the letters and I hesitated. My heart was racing, and I saw the thin red ribbon that held the batch of them together in a stack. Did he get my letters and ignore them? My head told me I hoped so, so that I could throw them at Sara and show her my proof of what a jerk he was. I wanted so badly to be right and be justified in my anger. As my eyes moved down to the top one, my heart jumped to my throat, and the sob tore from me as they fell from my hand.

Nineteen

Pray Tomorrow Gets me Higher

❧

I leaned back and shook my head, wondering if this was real, or a trick from Sara. I wouldn't put it past her to attempt to get me to forgive the man who left me behind without a backwards glance. My fingers moved towards the thick pack, and I got to my feet. I carried it and the candle back to the living room, where I'd have more light to read. I settled for the chair, but started the album over, hoping for some added calm as I watched every lie I'd held crumble to dust. My fingers shook as I tugged the ribbon that held the envelopes together in their stack. There had to have been a hundred of them. As I propped them in my lap, flipping one after the other, keeping them in order. The postmarks spanned the last six years of my life without him. I flinched at my own feelings towards him.

He addressed each envelope to my sister or myself. The last two were for me. The large red "return to sender" stamp glared at me, and I wondered how that had happened. We hadn't moved. What about the ones I'd sent to him? I took in a deep breath and contemplated reading them, but it terrified me thinking about what could be in them. I set them aside, grabbed the candle, and walked back to the closet to see what else it held on the shelves. A thick file, marked research, sat alone at the bottom, and the leather-bound books were journals. I flipped through a small, slender one. They had written in this before I'd been born. A picture slipped out of it and wafted like a dying leaf to the floor by my foot. I lifted it and eyed the woman in the picture. From the angle, I knew this must have been when dad lived next door. The faded image was of a girl standing on Em's front porch waving, and in the background, a young girl stood in the window of what was now Keira's room. I flipped it over and read the name. Tina and the year 1973, penned in a loopy, feminine scrawl. Was this my father's mother, I wondered, and set it aside, then pulled the stacks of journals out? The last book found was in braille, and I slid that one back. Carrying them to the table, I was unsure about which pile to tackle first. For the first time in forever, I wanted to hear in his own words what had happened. A yawn broke free of my mouth and I didn't think once about the beer in my trunk. The woodsy scent had filled the air, and I smiled, realizing it was some kind of pine. We'd spent weekends camping as children with both my parents when they were in love, before everything had gone to hell. I closed my eyes and inhaled, content that perhaps I'd have some answers. Tomorrow would be a new day, and this was too much to handle in my mental state. I blew out the candle and went to lie on the couch and allow the sound of the piano to lull me into a deathlike slumber.

* * *

Startled, I woke to the sound of knocking and I looked around, forgetting for a minute where I was. My mind felt somehow lighter, and as I moved forward to answer it, I grabbed my phone, noting it was five past twelve. I opened the door while stifling a yawn. Em stood before me sporting a bright grin on her face, her hands clutching a paper bag and a coffee, which she thrust at me.

"Hey Jules, I didn't see you around this morning and noticed you came in late last night. I was up reading, and… Good morning, sunshine." My eyes were unfocused, and I shook my head as my fists rubbed them.

"Um… I just woke up, if you can believe that. Come in, I forgot about the hair cut, sorry." She nodded, and I opened the door farther. She brushed past me and a light scent of coconut and something else wafted in the air behind her. It made me shiver, and a smile found its way to my face.

"That's okay, and I wasn't sure what you take in your coffee, if you even drink coffee, but I left it black. I had to run to town with mom and I grabbed the bleach and hair color I thought would be closest to your roots." I grinned and took a sip, reveling in the dark, heady taste. "It's a Columbia dark roast. Frank loves the stuff. I'm surprised he doesn't hook an IV up to himself every day with the amount he sucks down."

I drank it when I had exams, but this was doing the trick of waking up my brain. Em eyed the stacks of journals and letters on the table. She didn't ask, and I picked them up, then walked to my dad's bedroom where I set them down, then closed the door behind me. She set the bag aside and pulled out a box, which held a silky cape, and she draped it over the chair.

"We can do this another time if you're not up for it? I don't mind." She eyed me and I realized I was still in walking zombie mode. I grinned at her and shook my head.

"No, the sooner, the better, because it's driving me nuts. It'll feel better short again." She pulled out a picture she must have gotten from the computer and handed it to me.

"I found this last night," she eyed the picture, smiling. "This style would look great on you, but if you don't like it, I can wing it and do something different. Or how about a Mohawk, or something shaved?" I shook my head and made a scared face, which sent her into a fit of giggles.

"No… I like this, and if you can manage it, I'll wear it. Do you want me to take a shower, or I can just wash it in the sink? It'll only take me a few." She pulled out a chair at the table and shooed me away.

"Go take a shower. That should wake you up, because to get the black out, I'm going to strip it. Afterwards, I use another dye, so this might take a while. May as well be bright eyed and bushy tailed for my magnificent chop job, right?" I grinned, and she nodded. "Yep, I think this cut will bring your dimples out, don't you?" I took another glance at the image and rolled my eyes.

"Nobody's ever cared about my dimples before, so as long as I don't look like Frankenstein with a bowl cut, I'll be happy." I lifted my arms like the movie monster. With an "argh," I stumbled to the bathroom, stopping first to grab a clean set of clothes, glancing back as she called to me.

"Mind if I put on music? There's nothing like a little classical to soothe the beast." I nodded at her and she walked into the living room. In the bathroom, I smiled, trying to see the dimples she was talking about. As I pulled my hair back from my face, I realized with what she was intending, I'd look like my father when he was younger. The movie song she loved began filling the house with its symphonic sound, and I figured this must have been the flip side to the album. It was the same song, but different somehow. Putting it in gear, I grabbed a shower, glanced at my face, and opted to shave later. My morning growth gave me a tough appearance, and I walked out fifteen minutes later, then took my seat. Em wrapped the cape around me and I glanced at the table where a bunch of pink clips sat. She ran the comb through my hair, gathering the segmented areas and clipped them tight, then repeated the process. Her body flitted around me like a butterfly while she eyed the picture propped up against the candle.

"This is the easiest part, believe it or not. The dyeing is a little trickier, but I do Jasper's hair when he's racing. He thinks it makes him look more wild, and that the other racers will fear him and get out of his way. But, he's an amazing driver, so he doesn't have to worry about the others too much. That kid wins almost every race." I listened to her voice as she hefted the scissors, and I watched as large black strands of hair slid down the cape on their way to a pile on the floor.

"My mom always wanted us to look respectable, and it wasn't until my senior year that I rebelled and grew it longer. She hates it this long, and I love it when she gets pissed. That probably sounds bad, but... I think everyone enjoys irritating their parents. It's like a rite of passage, doing the opposite of what they want, just to get a rise out of them." Em nodded, and a giggle escaped as she lopped off a large wad of hair. "Oops..." I moved and swiveled around to see her face, figuring she'd made a mistake.

"I'm just kidding, Jules. It's coming along nicely. Just a little hairdressing humor, I guess." I relaxed and turned back around.

"What kinds of books do you read? Frank said you're a bookworm." She went silent for a minute.

"Well, you're going to laugh at me if I tell you, so perhaps I should stay mum."

"There are no bad books... Well, yeah, I guess there are. Do you want me to guess? Hmm... What books would the lovely Em read in the confines of her tower?" She gave me a little punch in the arm and a giggle erupted from her.

"I don't escape and I don't have a tower, but I love anything remotely fairy tale-like or young adult fantasy, mostly. Although I'm still digesting Harry Potter. You'll never see me reading that Fifty Shades garbage, so if that was going to be your guess, you'd be dead wrong." I'd heard about those, but that thought would have never crossed my mind. "Do you like to read? I saw your stack of books, although they looked old? Do you like old literature, like the classics, Shakespeare and those authors?" I shook my head in between snips, not wanting her to stab me in the head, and debated telling her what she'd seen.

"I found those last night in my dad's closet. I think they're his journals, and I was going to check them out, but my eyes wouldn't stay open. Perhaps later today I'll dive in. I'm sure they will not be best sellers, and our life was anything but a fairy-tale, so I'm sure you wouldn't enjoy the escapism in them." Em's hands stopped, and she came around in front of me.

"That's kind of cool... I guess?" She eyed me, waiting for my reaction, and I shrugged.

"I've blocked him out of my head for so long, figuring I knew everything I needed to know, so I guess it's kind of scary in a way. To read his words, well, you can't get much closer to a person than that. Since I got here, strange things have been happening. The girl who used to live in your house, I guess she used to help my dad out, with what, I don't know, but suddenly, these mental images are surfacing every time she shows up. Sometimes I don't know if I'm coming or going, and it's kind of freaking me out." I eyed the picture and stared into the guy's eyes. He seemed so confident, a wide, yet bashful smile across his face. As if he didn't have a care in the world, and maybe some beautiful woman captured the essence of a man who was whole. I felt so far removed from being like that guy and I longed for the day I would be. Em picked up the picture in her hands and brought it alongside my face. A soft smile found her and she handed it to me.

"I think I did pretty darn well. Go see…" I stood up and shook off any remaining hair, shocked at the pile on the floor, and my hand flew up to my head to see if there was anything left. "Don't worry, you're even cuter than he is. Now, go look and see if you want it any shorter and if not, we can proceed with turning it purple." My eyes grew wide, and she burst into a loud fit of laughter, her hand waving at me. "It was a joke, Jules, really, no purple, just a brownish-blonde, natural, just the way you wanted and God intended." I shook my head and walked to the bathroom. As I eyed myself in the mirror, I ran my fingers through it, giving it a little tousle. Then I grinned, trying to emulate the guy's face from the picture. Em came up beside me and we locked eyes in the mirror. Her hand reached around me and she fluffed it a little, and pushed it more off to one side. Once satisfied, she gave a nod. "Perfect." I turned to her, inhaling the soft scent of mint on her breath as her lips opened, and I moved forward, wanting to taste her lips on mine, wanting to feel my arms move around her, pulling her in close. She moved forward first, her lips feather soft as they grazed mine, and I took in a deep breath as I slipped my hands around her back and pulled her tighter to me. It lasted a minute, but it was a minute I'd cherish for the rest of my life. As I let her go, I turned back, seeing the blushes greet our faces in the reflection.

"Come on, let's get to the next step… You'll be amazing in your actual color, nothing against the black, but sometimes being yourself is best. We shall see the true Julien rise today, and I think you'll be happy." I wanted to tell her that standing in her essence was all the happiness I needed, but I followed her out and took my place in the chair again.

Twenty

Trying Hard to Fill the Emptiness

N either of us mentioned the kiss, and I found my thoughts drifting to the letters as she brushed the bleach over my hair. Two hours later, after rinsing the bleach and going through the next process of actual color, she set all of her equipment aside and stood before me, eyeing her work. She was quiet, not saying much, and I hoped it looked as good as she hoped. I wanted to be the dude in the picture, and I wanted her to want me just as much as I wanted her. Tossing the clips and stuff back into her bag, she pulled the cape off, gave it a shake, and grinned at me.

"I think, out of all the cuts and colors I've given, this is my best work yet. Can I take your picture to add to my files?" I nodded, and she slid out a phone and held it up as I attempted to recreate the smile of the guy in the picture.

"How about if we go outside and take one? The lights better, and you can get a background with the greenery. Anything's better than these boring walls." She nodded and moved towards the door. I motioned to her, and she followed me around the side of the house and to the back corner of the yard. There were some bushes with small yellow clumps of flowers on them. A wide smile hit her, and she nodded.

"That's perfect. The Ixora and your fresh color will be great. Now smile for me..." She held the camera up and I eyed her as a blush rose to my cheeks. Moving at different angles, she took several and then slid the camera into her pocket.

"Don't you want to make sure they came out all right?" Em shook her head and ran her fingers through my hair again, causing me to shiver.

"They're perfect, you're perfect, and when you leave, I'll have a visual to remember you by." I thought about her words and knew the last thing I'd do was leave if I knew she felt the same way. I'd never had a true crush before, but I believed this to be my hardest one ever. She turned to head back, and I watched as she walked. Her blue dress swayed in the breeze. She glanced back, and I longed for my phone, so I could capture the look she held as she offered me a sad smile. I followed behind her, wishing we had forever to learn more about each other. Em grabbed her stuff from the table and came back out.

"I'm gonna go now. But, I'm glad you love it, and I'm super happy I didn't mess it up terribly." My thoughts were racing, and I wanted her to stay.

"Do you want to go check out the river later? There's a huge alligator down there. That girl, Sara, told me about him and I startled it. He was big, though." Em thought about it for a second and gave a backward glance at her house.

"I'll ponder it, but I've got to help mom for a bit. We're still unpacking and I've got to get more of my boxes unloaded. She wants the cardboard compressed and out in the next trash pickup. That's Wanda... No clutter, no boxes in the way... No fun, basically. Can I let you know later?"

"Sure, just pop by. I'm not going anywhere. I'll probably read a bit and play what happened in daddy's life that turned him into such a jerk. So, lame reading, I guess. I'll catch you later, though." She gave a little wave and headed home while I cleaned up the hair pile and contemplated my next project. The books and letters were calling to me, but I shoved the thought aside, not yet ready to tackle that bundle of mysterious history, but I finally gave in, my curiosity getting the better of me.

I eyed the packet of envelopes and settled on his bed, using the remaining daylight to see by. Starting at the beginning by date, he addressed the first one to both Keira and myself. My hands trembled as I opened the envelope and pulled the paper out. He had never re-opened them, just stacked them up and wrapped them in the ribbon before hiding them away. The first was a typical miss you letter, how he hoped we were doing well and he figured at some point he'd head north if he didn't hear from us. By the third letter, which was addressed to me, his mood had transformed to more melancholy, and I felt the tears well in my eyes. I read each sentence slowly, as if I could savor his presence through his penmanship.

"Dear Jules,

They returned my last two letters, unopened, so I guess they upset your mother, and maybe I shouldn't blame her. There's so much more to the story than I think she's telling you, if she's telling you anything. I've tried to call, but again, there's no response. I miss you more than words can say, and if I could whisk you away to spend some time down here, there's nothing more I'd want. Sure, I don't relish being one of those dads that says, 'son, someday you'll understand,' because some days I don't understand it myself. Life keeps on keeping on and as can happen, when you least expect it, good and bad things can arise. I've tried my best to live my life as an honest and upstanding soul, and I've succeeded, except with my family. I love your mother, and still do, and that will never change, but she believes something happened that didn't and it wasn't until recently that I figured out what and why.

Years ago, I told you about the girl with the jars who collected what she called stars. She was real once, and then she passed away. Afterwards, she came to me for help. Her name was Keira, and trust me, your mother and I both chose your sister's name together, with no intended connection to my childhood Keira. It was just a coincidence. But this girl used to come to me. It wasn't physically her, and I don't know how to say it any other way than it was her spirit that was drifting amongst us. She needed to guide me because she couldn't rest until a long-forgotten mystery came to light. It took years, from the time I was fifteen until after you both were born. There was nothing between us, because you can't have that kind of relationship with a ghost. I know you're thinking I'm nuts, but trust me, nothing's farther from the truth. Your mother described a woman following along with me on my sleepless nights as I headed to the river when we used to come here for vacations.

99

It was there at the river where a lot of the interactions happened with "ghostly" Keira originally. For years I thought she had gone to a higher plane, that I'd never see her again, and I can't see her anymore now, but I think that it's her spirit that has returned and she followed me those nights, unbeknownst to me. Perhaps that's why I found peace when I was here, because she was holding something together in me. Crazy, right? But it's the only logical thing I can think of. I send this to you because you've always been my guy, the one who believed in me when things were falling to bits. Your mother will continue to keep us apart, and I'll do what I can to find you, but in the meantime, if this letter makes it to you, know that you're here in my heart, sport, and that I do and always will love you. Scout's honor. So, I'll keep writing, regardless. Man, I hope this doesn't sound whack-a-doodle. I just re-read it and it pretty much does. Whatever, it's the honest truth.

Love you, son,

Dad

I set the letter aside and took a deep breath, trying to picture some kind of phantom girl-ghost following my dad as my mother watched from their bedroom window. Not that I didn't believe in ghosts, but something in my head knew this had to be true, especially having Sara popping in and out at will. My hand reached for the next one and though trembling, I opened it.

Dear Jules,

The last letter came back same as those before it, but I don't care. Until I breathe my last breath, I will never stop trying. I received the divorce paperwork from your mother two weeks ago, and she demands full custody. Honestly, that one floored me, and I should fight it, but I don't want to make your life harder than it has to be.

I had a friend, Lenny, whose parents divorced. They shuttled that poor boy back and forth like a piece of luggage between states to their new homes. It was exhausting, each parent down talking about the other, etc... I'm sure you get the gist. Anyway, I don't want to be that father dragging you down here when you've got friends and school up there. Later, you'd resent me for the time you lost. Time is a precious commodity, and should be used to the fullest with things that bring you joy. I'd hope you'd have fun here, but it's the not knowing that makes me want to put up my hands and not argue. Maybe someday she'll have more sense. I can only hope. In the meantime, I brought a medium/psychic lady in and she senses the spirit of a woman lingering here. See, I'm not crazy after all. She asked if I wanted her to sage the place, but I see no point in that. If it was Keira, this is her home and I'll not be the one to banish her from it. I've taken apart your sister's room and put back up the old posters that were here when I got the place, just like it was before that Keira died. My ghost, Keira, will always be welcome, even if I'm not able to see her anymore.

Anyway, I've been getting wicked headaches lately, but am trying to get some renderings done between them to make money. Never mind, you don't need to hear me blubbering about such trivial things. Be well, my little man, and I pray every night that you still think of me, and that you remember the good times we had. I know I do, every time I think of you. Feels like I'm falling apart some days, but getting old is never fun. Take care, be good and do your schoolwork. Someday you'll be old enough and can take charge of your own life. Maybe you'll come visit and we can pick up right where we left off, just like the good old days. Okay, enough old speeches... Ha, your old man's kind of funny, huh? Oops, there I go again.

Don't take any wooden nickels in the meantime, and love you!!!
Dad

Each one I opened pulled another piece of hurt to the surface and I didn't realize tears rolled down my face until one landed on the page in my lap. I set the letter aside and glanced out the window. Rain had fallen and merely enhanced the way I felt. The pile was large, and I wondered if I'd find the same messages in each one. The ones solely addressed to Keira I left unopened. As I slid off the bed, I wondered if Sara would return to talk to me about what I read. What was her connection to my father and was that ghost still lingering around? Now aware of the reason for the change to Keira's room, I headed there to inspect it closer.

The door was ajar, and I flicked on the light. A bolt of lightning lit the sky beyond the tired window panes, startling me. I jumped at the resounding crash. A soft giggle came from behind me, and I turned to find Sara standing there. Her face held a comical expression.

"Ask and you shall receive, young Jules. Learn anything new?" I ignored her and walked into the room, my eyes peering at each poster on the wall, trying to discern if I could feel Keira's presence. Sara moved past me and sat on the bed. I eyed her speculatively and frowned.

"So, are you her? Are you Keira?" Sara shook her head as I crossed my arms and leaned against the dresser. "I don't get it. You come and go, so my brain tells me you're not real, especially after last night, but I don't know what you want with me. Am I allowed to ask you questions?" Sara closed her eyes and sighed.

"You can ask whatever you want, but that doesn't mean I can answer them. I think you already know most of the answers anyway, except for the ones about your dad, and that's what I'm here for. You need closure, but you also need truth. Keep digging, and you'll find it. That's all I can say on that matter, but it's for you to seek. If I just dropped the information at your feet, it wouldn't be the same. I'm sorry, it's just how it is." Music began playing in the living room and I turned towards the sound and smiled.

"Em must have come in. You should meet her. She lives in your old house now." When I turned back around, Sara disappeared. I took a fast breath and bolted to the living room, half expecting to see her now in there. "I'm not in the mood for parlor tricks, Sara. It's not funny." The room sat empty, and I walked over and lifted the album cover that was propped against the stereo. A piano was playing Debussy's 'Clare de Lune' and it filled the room with its melancholy mood. I slid into the seat and closed my eyes, wondering what my father thought on the lonely nights when he listened. Did he think of me, of what was so far from his touch, his heart? Any thoughts of Sara slipped out of my consciousness, and I broke down again and cried.

Twenty-One

The Sound of Things you Said Today

A knock on the door roused me. I must have drifted off. My brain felt spent, and I walked over and opened it to find Em standing in her raincoat, dripping wet. I'd forgotten that I'd asked her to come to see the river.

"It's probably not a good idea, but I didn't want to leave you hanging after you'd extended the invite to go see the alligator. I'll take a rain check, though, although preferably without the rain involved." A light smile rose on her face and my hand automatically moved to push the hair from my eyes. Laughing, I shook my head.

"I guess old habits die hard. Want to come in? I'd offer you a beer, but it's in my trunk and is as hot as the day." Em slipped past me and I closed the door. She slid her raincoat off and looked for a place to hang it. I grabbed it from her and glanced around. Finding no place, either, I took it to the bathroom and hung it on the shower head to dry. The music had kicked on again, but this time, it was more modern fare. Pink Floyd's 'Fearless' jammed to the hilt, and I walked in to find Em grinning from ear to ear.

"I haven't heard this song in forever. My brother Franklin broke my album because I played this song repeatedly. I still remember that day. Man, I wanted to kill him. Don't you think it's funny how songs take you back in time, almost throwing you into the moment all over again? This song will always be Frankie's and my song." Her eyes went from happy to kind of sad, and I wanted to hold her tight and make her smile, but I waited, letting her go through her reminiscing without interruption. She sat down as her fingers played air guitar along with the song. Her head, swaying back and forth, was the most beautiful thing I'd ever seen, and she sang silently along with the band. I slid onto the couch and watched, transfixed by the moment.

"Listen, in the background, you'll hear them sing 'You'll Never Walk Alone,' which is from the musical Carousel. My ma's big into musicals, if you can believe that. She took us to see it at the school when we were younger and the seniors put it on. When we got older, she begged Frankie to try out for the play, but that wasn't his gig, as he succinctly told her, much to her dismay. Then, she tried with me, but it petrified me to stand on a stage in front of people, let alone for a few hours, trying to remember my lines. Nope, wasn't having any of that, thank you very much." I nodded as I listened to her talk, jealous in a way of her and her brother's relationship. Keira and I were so far apart, we'd never be as tight as them.

"Do you think of him a lot? Your brother, I mean?" I face palmed and shook my head. "Jesus, I'm such a jerk. Of course you think of him. I'm sorry Em, I didn't mean to say that you didn't. Sometimes I don't know the right things to say, I guess." Em smiled at me and set the album cover aside.

"He and I were alike, yet different, but we had our good times and bad, just like any siblings do. Yes, I wish he were here, but then I wouldn't have met you, because we would still live in Portage. Life happens, and some things change you. I like to think I'm wiser and maybe a little kinder with losing him." She shrugged and her light smile crinkled up the corners of her eyes. "Eh, I don't know. You can't go back and change things. Take each day as it comes and make the best of it, I suppose. It's all we can do, right?" My mind drifted to the letters I had found, and I wondered what she'd make of them. We sat and listened to the album, and though I felt nervous and wanted a beer, Sara's words kept playing on repeat in my head ad nauseam. My hands shook a little, and I gripped my knees to keep them from doing their thing. Em didn't seem to notice, and for that I was happy.

"Why do you call your folks by their first names? I know I do it to rile mine up. Frank seems pretty cool, though. I have had little chance to talk to Wanda… Maybe that's a good thing?" I wasn't intending on prying into her life with her family, and I wasn't ready to expound on my own. Em leaned back, and a chuckle came from her mouth as she eyed me.

"Pretty much to rile them up, but Frank doesn't care. It's his name, after all. Why give us names if we can't use them, right? Mother, father, brother, sister, they're all just labels to peg us on the old family tree with. I'd introduce anyone to them by their name. You're not gonna call Wanda, mom, you know? She hates it, though, but Frank is cool. I think meeting you is giving him purpose. You're a little older than Frankie Jr. would have been, and you're nothing remotely like him, but Frank has taken to you, which doesn't happen very often. Feel honored, if nothing else. Have you given any thought to when you'd be heading back to school? I'm just asking because Frank asked me…" I felt like that was a tiny fib, and that she was the one who was interested in the answer.

"I haven't, no. Some things have cropped up. The letters and journals I told you about. I could take them back with me, but I need to be here. Reading them anywhere else wouldn't hold the same weight, so until I meander through them, I'm stuck here. But I don't mind. I'm just waiting for the day Simone finds out I've gone AWOL. Then all hell's gonna break loose. The only regret is that I didn't grab any of my art supplies. I'd love to get some painting done. I feel that with my mood shifts, these pieces would be something different from anything I'd ever done before. The idea excites me, but short of doodling in pen on paper, it wouldn't do me justice." Em stifled a little yawn, and I grinned.

"Sorry, if you want to head home, I understand. I'm cool with it." She nodded and shrugged.

"Nah, I don't go to bed until much later, but I'm comfortable hanging out here. Like I told you before, I sense some kind of spirit here. Now, something makes me long to bask in its essence. Have you felt it yet?" I shook my head, longing to hear more of her take on the situation with the spirits. "Sometimes when you move from room to room, it's like walking through a chilly mist. Man, it's wicked cool, if you ask me. I saw a ghost once when I was a kid. It was a classmate who died from the flu, and I swear to God, he walked the hallways as if he was late for class. Robbie Jenkins had been the brown-noser to end all brown-nosers in fifth grade and never missed a day of class until then. No one believed me, but I think Frank kind of did." She sighed and a sad smile found her.

"At our old house, after Frankie Jr. passed, I had days when I could sense him there. He was such a huge part of our lives that maybe the idea of him being physically gone was something that dad couldn't handle. None of us could, really. I never told him about feeling Frankie's spirit, but maybe he felt it, too. It crushed him, and that's part of the reason we moved. Frank couldn't be around there anymore. It was too close to a daily reminder of what we, and he, lost. The drinking escalated, and we thought with moving here, he'd taper it back a little, but he hasn't. Maybe with meeting you, y'all can go fishing or canoeing at some point. The truck is delivering that stuff at the end of the week, so act surprised if he shows up on your doorstep and whisks you away to the river for man-time." I got excited at the thought of that, then thought about old Roger the gator.

"Well, if we go, I hope he brings a weapon, because the idea of an alligator capsizing the boat would freak me out. At least if he shot the thing, we'd live to see another day." Em's eyes grew wide, and she burst into laughter as she shook her head emphatically.

"Frank is not a hunting enthusiast by any stretch of the imagination. Even picturing him holding a gun makes me laugh out loud. Nope, no guns or weapons with Frank. That's not his thing." The idea of gliding along on an alligator infested river suddenly lost its appeal, and I knew I'd take Frank down to meet Roger and he could make his mind up from there. Em squirmed and eyed me.

"You look like you want to ask me something… You can ask me anything, Em. I've got nothing to hide." Her head moved slightly, and she inhaled, then leaned back in the chair.

"What do you know about our new house's former occupants? And what did they tell you about your dad disappearing?" I pondered the question and shook my head.

"I don't know. My Dad lived in your house when he was a teen, and it belonged to his aunt and uncle. Dad loved them for taking him in when no one else probably would. I'm not sure why he had to go live with them, but they both died years ago. Marcy and Ralph were their names, and he told me his uncle could roll his eyeballs around in his head. He never could master it himself, and I've never seen it done, but I believe him. After that, I have no clue. As far as Dad disappearing, mom said little, only that she got a phone call. He had disappeared without a trace. She said they presumed he was dead, but I won't believe that. I can't believe that. Dad is not a topic high on my mother's give a crap about list." Em inhaled deeply again and exhaled, then closed her eyes.

"I'm not sure how to say this, so I'll just jump in. Brett Elridge lived in our house with his wife and two daughters. The girls slept upstairs, where mine and Jasper's rooms are. My room looks down on the side of your house, and I've seen shadows in the room's window I now know is off the dining room. It's a young girl, and she looks at me, then disappears. Other times, she's an adult, but she does the same thing, watches, then disappears. The Realtor told Frank when he came looking at the house that one of the Elridge girls drowned in the river. Now, I love a good ghost story, and with what I've been seeing and feeling when I'm here, I'm wondering if it's her." I sat blinking, caught in disbelief.

"It can't be. I haven't seen…" I stopped, wondering now if my thoughts on Sara were dead nuts correct. Em nodded.

"You've seen a girl named Sara, right? You said she lived in my house before we moved in. Well, I Googled the local papers from the last year and then past that. Sara Elridge drowned in the Peace River over a year ago. They found her body on the bank, untouched. The dog came to Brett's door, shivering and whimpering. It was your father's dog. When Brett came out, the dog led him to the riverbank where he found his daughter, Sara. They said except for being wet, she looked peaceful, as if she'd lain down to take a nap in the dirt. They never found your father, though, just his guide dog, Chino. The poor thing sat beside Sara, protecting her. Brett said the dog kept staring out at the water and crying. There was a school picture in the article of her. Do you want to see it? It wouldn't let me print out the article, though, so you'd have to come over and see it, or you can pull it up on your own if you want to." She grabbed her bag from beside the chair and slid the cut-out piece of paper from within, then hesitated before handing it to me. I felt the blood drain from my face and my hand shook as I took it from her.

Twenty-Two

There's Room for You Inside

E m stood and walked into the other room, giving me a minute to process the information. I held the picture in my hands and blinked twice. Sara Elridge was, in fact, the girl who'd been coming to me. I set the image aside and ran my hands through my hair as I shook my head. My thoughts ran to the alligator, Roger, and the day Sara'd come up on me while I stood on the riverbank. It might have been the same spot they found her body. A shiver ran through me and I felt sick to my stomach, wondering if her death was because of Roger. My father had been an excellent swimmer, and the idea of him drowning was unfathomable to me. Sara was there with my dad and his dog. I didn't even know he had one. If she drowned, where was my dad? Wouldn't they have searched the river if they knew he was missing? Did they leave him out there alone and needing help? I wanted to grab the letters and read through them, hoping they'd provide more answers to this latest bombshell. Em slipped back into the room, her raincoat on, and gave me a sad smile.

"I'm sorry to be the bearer of this, Jules. I hope you're not mad at me, but I thought it might clear some things up better for you. Sara is here, at least in spirit. That's my best guess, and maybe she's trying to tell you something. You may not believe in this kind of thing, but if I could say anything, it's trust in it. You came here for a reason, and if you allow it, maybe you'll get what you need most. Closure, or maybe a reassurance that maybe he's still lingering in the house, too, if he is in fact gone? I'm heading out, but I can swing by tomorrow?" I nodded at her as my eyes began watering. Not wanting her to see me cry, I blinked and stared at the ceiling. The door closed with a soft click. I longed to run and grab her and to ask her to sit with me while I lost my mind. I squelched the thought and leaned back.

"Sara, are you here? I know about you. Sara?" I heard nothing but the thundering beat of my heart. I sat for a few minutes and could feel the pull of the letters, begging me to read more. My brain now unhinged, I flipped the Pink Floyd album over, then wandered into my father's room to begin the process again. This time, I'd search deeper for clues about what may have happened and what role Sara played in it all. I hadn't changed the light bulb in the bedroom and it was too dark to read by, so I grabbed the bundle of letters and brought them into the dining room. I lit the candle, then after setting the stack down to get my courage up, I walked into Keira's room and turned on the light. As I sat on the bed, I eyed the two remaining jars on the small shelf. Blank circles formed in the dust where the others had been, and I wondered if Sara would surface with more, enticing me to remember again. My eyes stared at the posters, and I stroked the nubs on the worn, soft comforter. This wasn't Sara's room. It was the first Keira's, I thought, but at some point, my dad had given Sara the jars. That seemed odd to me, unless he knew she wanted them for something. This whole mess confused me and I stood, then left the room, shutting the light off, but leaving the door open. I sat in the chair where I had a view of her room, feeling that somehow, something was going to come from there. My brain was spinning, and I slumped down in the seat and grabbed the next letter. My fingers itched to grab the last one, but somehow I knew I had to read them in order for it all to make sense. As I sliced the envelope open, a cool breeze blew from the room and the candle flickered. Unsure if it was Keira or Sara, I guess it didn't really matter. As long as when I finished, I could sleep in peace.

Dearest Jules,

Hey Sport, it's me again. I've resigned myself to the fact that your mom will not let my words reach you, but I refuse to let that stop me from at least trying. If nothing else, when I do finally see you again, I'll hand over the whole kit-n-caboodle to you so that you know I tried. There's not much else I can do. As I write this, I realize what a coward I was. Driving to New York was a whim, and it was almost your birthday, but I hustled and made good time to wish my sport a happy twelfth. I parked down the road and watched as you played with your friends. It looked like a great game of touch football, and I didn't want to interrupt, so I watched. You're growing up to be such a fine young man, and I'm proud of you. As I waited for your friends to leave, I saw the pizza delivery guy show up, and you all piled into the house. Not wanting to ruin your get-together, I waited for hours until your friends left and you walked out to pick up the water bottles from the yard. You looked up and saw me, and seeing that smile spill across your face made the entire trip worthwhile. Man, you threw your shoulders back, walked down the street, unafraid, and seemed nervous, yet giddy. You made me proud to see you strong and sure. I'm glad I had the chance to wish you a happy birthday, and that I could see you again. I'm not sure if you told your mom that I came, but I cut it short so that she didn't make your life miserable by knowing I'd been there. God, I wish I could be there to watch you grow into yourself, to become a man and conquer the world like I know you will. There's more I could say, but I will not be that guy who speaks badly about the situation. I wish it could be different, but in the meantime, I'll keep writing, and the next time I make it up there, I'll hand deliver these to you both. Stay strong, stay well, and behave, though why I say that? I'm not sure, because I know you will. You're in my heart, sport, today and always. Love you, always and forever.

  Dad

There was a noticeable gap in dates from this one to the next, and I wondered if Mom may have kept some, read them, and from there, most likely burned them. I grabbed the next one that was dated three years after the last. The handwriting had changed.

My dearest Jules,

I guess you can see from the script that my penmanship's changed. Maybe that's for the better, although I never considered my style chicken scratch or worse. You may think differently, but that's fine. My neighbor, Brett, has a daughter named Sara, and she's helping me. I dictate and she writes it out, so if something's spelled wrong, know it's not me. Haha! Anyway, I'd been having these really horrible headaches, which I kind of ignored for a while, but I just chalked it up to stress and missing y'all. Well, the headaches turned to losing some of my peripheral sight, and of course, with what I do, I need my eyes to function properly. They keep running tests, and continue coming up with different theories, but I only want it fixed. Of course, driving is out of the question, because I'm also seeing stars. No, I can't blame it on the girl, because if she captured stars and poked them in my eyes, I'd kill her myself. Although she's dead, so I can't. Sorry, a little gallows humor, I'll stop. Now I have to explain to Sara about her, but that's okay.

My goal is to continue writing to you and to do that, I need Sara, so this way she won't think I've gone completely kazoo. Hey, do you remember when I took you to the kazoo factory? You were very young. I don't know, maybe seven or something. We had a lot of fun, and I bought you one to take home and practice. Do you still have it? I wonder if that place is still even there. This is so much easier having someone else to do the writing, but as you read, know that they're my words, okay? I go back to the Doctor in two weeks for more tests, so until then, I'll keep watching the stars, that seem to be internally watching me. Isn't that a creepy thought? Will talk soon. Sara is shaking her hand, so it must get tired, or she's just tired of hearing me talk. She's laughing... I made her write that. Anyway, I'll write more when I get more information on what's happening, but you won't be getting a drive-by visit from me until the situation gets resolved. Sorry, sport. Love you always, and will write again soon, hoping someday one of these gets through to you.

Dadio (Sara wrote that... See, she's funny, too) I'll let it fly. Bye!

Well, at least I now knew what part Sara was playing in helping my dad. There was another gap of about three months before the next letter. I grabbed the next in line and then the dreaded funeral dirge piped from my phone. Unsure if I wanted to talk to Mom, I looked at the letter and decided now was as good of time as any. What I had to say may ruin her trip, but I didn't care.

Twenty-Three

Should I Build the Wall

M y fingers reached for the phone. I took a deep breath and hit the button. "What's up?" I could hear some kind of weird music playing in the background and she began yelling at me across the miles.

"Where are you, Jules? The school called me, and it sounded kind of urgent, so of course that made me late to a meeting by taking it. Do you know how embarrassing it is to hear that your son is MIA for over a week and you do not know where he is? Where the hell are you?" I grinned, not feeling in the least bit bad about her drama queen moment.

"What's it matter, Ma? You're off gallivanting with your boy toy and having fun, so who cares what I'm doing? It's none of your business, anyway." I could hear the breath leave her and I held the phone away from my ear, knowing what would come next.

"Do not speak to me that way, Julien Michael! I am your mother and I have every right to know what you're doing. I'm paying an exorbitant amount of money for you to go to school, and the first chance you get, I leave for a much needed break and you up and disappear. What's wrong with you?" I could hear someone talking to her and she must have slipped her hand over the receiver. She popped back to full sound a second later.

"I thought you were there on a business trip? A much needed break? Your entire life is a much needed break. I left school, but you already know that or you wouldn't be calling to chew me out. No, I'm not at home, but maybe in a way I am. I'm at dads." You could hear a pin drop, and I could see her brain spinning on its axis as she floundered for a response.

"What... Why are you there? I had it all closed up, hoping, of course, the damn thing would burn down or get hit by lightning. I want you to go home immediately, and we will discuss this later. Now I have to curtail my excursions to deal with you. That does NOT make me happy, young man." I laughed into the receiver and hung up on her, knowing full well she'd call back in a heartbeat. I waited, and maybe she was yammering at Carlos or something, because it took her five minutes before the phone rang again.

"Okay, Jules. Take your time. Carlos said you're probably going through some teenage angst, girlfriend heartbreak stuff, and I should let you get it out of your system. I'm staying for the time being, but I hope whatever bug you have up your butt loosens itself because I'm at my wit's end with you. We will talk when I return in two weeks. Until then, I had better not find out you're partying and acting like a derelict. If you get arrested, you're on your own because I'm not bailing you out. Got it?" I could tell she was nearing the end of the tirade and I needed to get a dig in just because she deserved it.

"Oh, gee, thanks Mom, yeah, I think I'll stay here for however long I choose. We will talk when I feel like talking. Oh, and I found the most interesting things while poking around. You don't remember Dad sending, I don't know, like a hundred letters to me and Keira, do you? They came to our address, but there's this big red stamp on them that says return to sender. Do you possibly know who might have done that?" Silence met my ears, and I chuckled.

"Yeah, I figured you must know, because ten-year-old's don't run to the postbox daily because 'they're expecting something important.' You must really have hated him to do that to us. So, you have no right for any explanation out of me now about how I live my life. Obviously you needed to have control and dictate it for us, but I'm relieving you of your duties." I could hear her gasping for air, and it made me smile. "Yeah, being here makes me wonder what Dad ever saw in you. I see the picture from your wedding still hung behind the bed and it makes me want to burn it. But he's in it, and I'm wondering more and more about the lies you've concocted all these years. I'm done, bye!" I hung up the phone and leaned back, feeling the heavy weight lift from my soul. I watched the phone, waiting to see it light up with her face, or at least the one of the wicked witch I'd thrown on there to be funny, and the death knoll ringtone, but it remained silent. Now antsy, I shifted off the chair and walked to the porch to watch the rain fall. The thunder and lightning had moved off a bit, but the air still held a thick, crackling essence to it.

"Feels like me, charged and ready for battle." I sunk into the rocking chair and took a deep breath, then glanced over at Em's house. Frank was out on the front porch, a beer in his hand. His shoulders slumped, and he ran his hand across his face. The humidity was riding high, and I remembered how much he hated the extreme heat. "Poor guy must sweat his brains out just to avoid the Mrs." My mouth salivated as I watched him bring the beer to his lips, and he glanced over and saw me. After stopping mid-swig, a wide grin lit his face, and he stood, then grabbed his bucket of bottles. *"You're gonna get soaked, you fool. At least grab an umbrella."* Frank ran across the yard at a sprint, and I tensed up as I saw his foot slip. He caught himself, a childish grin slapped across his face, and he came tearing up on the porch like he was on fire.

"Eh, I'm glad you're out and about. Care for some company?" I nodded and gestured to the chair beside me, where he plopped himself down. Squeezing the wetness from his hair, he reached in the bucket and handed me a dripping, ice-cold beer.

"Thanks, Jules, if we run out, I've got more at home, unless you have some spares here?" I shook my head and chuckled.

"Matter of fact, I have three twelve-packs. Bad news is they're in my trunk, warm." Frank shrugged and tipped his bottle back. Finishing it a second later, he reached for another.

"Never get married, Jules. If I could give you any fatherly advice, that would be it. Ugh, I swear to God, when he invented women, I wonder what in the blazes that man was thinking." I chuckled, realizing that he and Wanda must have had a row over something. I settled back, took a sip, and set it down. My hand was shaking, and I pressed it tight to my thigh.

"Yep, never do it. Get this, now that woman wants to take up ballroom dancing. I'm like, fine, dear, go ahead. Whatever your heart's desires. That's the right thing to say, right? But noooo, she needs a partner, and guess who that partner is?" I hoped it wasn't me and had to keep from laughing as he made a horrified face. "Can you see me dancing? She's hooked on that stupid TV show, Dancing With The Stars, or whatever. More like dancing to get scars, I'd think. Wanda isn't the most graceful bird in the flock on a good day, and I'll be... No! I will not do it. She can find another partner because it ain't gonna be old Frankie, here. No, siree, nope." He settled down and I couldn't help but let the giggle escape. He eyed me and shook his head.

"Tell me you're with me on this, Jules. It's like I told you before, do what makes you happy, and I want to do what makes me happy. Ballroom dancing will NOT make me happy. It'll piss me off more than anything. But, she's already signed us up and next Saturday is our first lesson." He shook his head and an evil grin filled his face.

"Hey, I've got my canoe and fishing gear coming later in the week. How's about you and I get up at the crack of dawn on Saturday and spend the day out on the water, mano a mano. We'll accidentally lose track of time and oops, sorry dear, forgot about the lessons. Maybe next week... Ha, maybe never!" I could see him plotting, and he giggled, the sound now sinister. "Yeah, we're gonna go fishing. I'll bring some beers and even if we don't fish, we can ride the river, catch a buzz, and see where that takes us. We'll be like Tom Sawyer and Huck Finn. It'll be fun. You'll see." I thought about Roger and grabbed the beer, then swallowed the whole thing down and shook my head.

"Um, well, I told Em, but I don't think I mentioned it to you yet. There're alligators in the river. You realize that, right? Now I'm not a fraidy cat or anything, but they're huge, and can easily capsize a canoe. They'd eat us and no one would ever find us. We'd be gator happy meals, you and I, minus the fun prize inside. I'm not sure if that's a good thing. Would dancing be that terrible in comparison?" I could tell he was pondering it, and I hid the smile that was trying to find me.

"Well, I don't know about gators. I was hoping they'd be sleeping or something. Don't they sleep during the day and roam about at night to eat?" I shrugged, and that made him think harder, then I laid it on thick.

"I've heard of kayakers getting swept right off their craft and gobbled up. Oh, and there're venomous snakes, too. Water Moccasins, they call them and they swim on top of the water. If they get tired, they climb right onto your boat, almost like they're hitching a ride until you hit land and maybe, if you're lucky, they slither off and go about their business. But if you're freaking out, I guess they may get riled up and bite. Now that would be bad. Out there, no cell service. Heck, you wouldn't even know where you are. That poison hits lightning fast…" A bolt of lightning hit somewhere in the distance and I watched as Frank darn near jumped out of his skin. He began shaking his head.

"I guess I gotta think this plan over some more. Good thing you know about the river. I would have never guessed stuff like that happened. In Wisconsin, it's all fresh water. I wonder if they have any fresh-water lakes around here. Maybe we could go there instead?" He handed me the last beer, and I took it, happily.

"What if you tried a lesson once? If you end up hating it, or start stepping all over Wanda's feet, maybe she'll decide that you're just not cut out for dancing. Sometimes it's better to try, instead of arguing about it. No, it's not what you want to do, but maybe you'll have fun? You won't know if you don't give it a chance. Then, maybe if she persists, you can make a deal with her. You'll ballroom dance if she'll go canoeing with you. Then, if you see a gator, you can offer her up as a sacrifice. If Mr. Gator eats her, he won't be hungry anymore and you'll be Scot free." I was just kidding, of course, but Frank settled down and merely nodded. He stood a minute later.

"Thanks for the chat Jules, I appreciate it and I don't think I'd like to see her get eaten by a killer reptile. Maybe you're right, and I'll try it, but just once." He grinned as he saw me chuckling. "How did you grow up to be such a smart man? If Frankie Jr. were alive, he would have loved you. You two were nothing alike, but he was smart, too. I sure miss him." I nodded, and he turned and walked across the yard as the rain pelted down on him. He did not hunch his shoulders, but I hoped he gave what I'd said some thought. He seemed rather graceful, even with the beers flowing through his system, and Em, I knew, was very graceful. It must have been a trait she inherited from him. I headed in to continue my trek through the past, content and calmed by the beer surging through my veins.

Twenty-Four

I Tried so Hard to Stand

My eyes lit on the stack of letters, and I shifted gears and skipped to his journals. Without being addressed to me personally, maybe I could glean more insight from the man I barely knew. They made the first of pressed leather, and a sticker on the back said they crafted it in Italy. It was pretty fancy, and I liked the feel of the soft bindings in my hands. This was the oldest, besides the small book which was written, I assume, by his mother. I left that one behind, closed the bedroom door, and headed to the living room. The house seemed unnaturally quiet, and I glanced at the albums beneath the stereo. Music from every genre sat side by each, in alphabetical order, and I grabbed The Moody Blues with a grin. My folks played A Question of Balance often, and as the songs began, memories of our vacations in this house surfaced. Undeterred, I brushed the thoughts away, intent on reading my father's words. The first page held doodles of stars and symbols. I had no way of knowing the meaning of why they were there.

Time moves forward, with or without us, and I guess as I write this, I feel the weight of fewer days before me, and more trepidation about what is coming. At some point, I'll no longer see to write, so before that happens, it's my wish to pen as much as

I can. It's funny, but when you're a young boy, or even a not so young one, you think you have forever stretched out before you. Almost like one of those desert scenes, where dunes move with the wind and the sight you see goes on endlessly. I know now this is not true, but, in my mind's eye, I can still imagine it to be that way. I've come so far from where I began, and maybe that's as good a place to start as any.

My mother is someone I used to know. As a child, she was loving, adoring, and like any typical mother, but she did not end that way. I found a journal she'd written. This was when I was living with my Aunt Marcy and Uncle Ralph. She had a friend, Keira, the girl next door, and my mom witnessed something horrific happen to her friend. Her friend Keira was run down by a car in the street during a driving rainstorm. My mother locked that memory away for years, until she grew into adulthood and moved, got married, then watched as her own life imploded. I did not have a happy childhood once she divorced my father, and I'd like to say I knew him, but I didn't. I never wanted to be like my father, and I've done all I can, but it isn't enough. But back to my mom. They sent me away, which is a hard thing to deal with, but it saved me. Living with my relatives opened my eyes up to what a genuine family could be. My mom's boyfriend Gordon beat me senseless many times, under the guise of wanting me to be a man. Yet he taught me to stand up for myself, to fight back, but that too was too much for him to contend with. As I grew, I became stronger, and I don't know if he feared me, because the house of horrors I dwelled in became something from a nightmare.

Once in Florida, I learned to take my cues from my uncle, to work hard, keep my fists out of other's faces, and to be a kind man. I enjoyed living here. My mom, Gordon and the rest of the brood passed away in a fire after a heinous domestic episode. I should have felt sad, but I felt hope. It left me empty, yet free in a way. As I realized I'd never have to return to that, it lifted something in me, and I am thankful. That must sound bad, but you would have had to be in my shoes to understand. My dog, King, died in the fire, and that was the only soul I shed tears over.

I never want my kids to live in a paralyzing nightmare world as my childhood was, and I will never raise a hand to any of them. Kindness is my bag, always.

Brett is my neighbor, and he's been ferrying me to my Doctor appointments as needed, but I think it's at the point where they will dwindle now. I know what ails me, and can't fight it, but the ending of my story will be inevitable. I'd never owned another animal after my boyhood dog, but if things work out, I will gain a new companion. The waiting list for a seeing-eye dog is long, and they could match me with a dropout. He's trained, kind of, but for whatever reason, continued to fail some aspect of it. I don't care, I'll take him. My only regret is he will not be with me for very long. He is a Labrador Retriever mix, and I've met him once, but we hit it off immediately. He walks with a limp from a puppy injury that never healed right, and his name is Chino. The lady told me someone named him after the actor, Al Pacino, from The Scent of a Woman. I've never seen the movie, and may have to have Brett rent it for me. If nothing else, I can listen to it.

Chino comes home in a week, and I guess I'm as ready as I can be. We went to town to the Pet Supermarket and Brett and Sara helped me pick out the needed items. They don't have a dog either, so I guess we're all a little excited. Brett also helped by putting posts up to lead me to the river. We did that last week, and he ran a string through it. I never thought losing my sight would be so hard, and we sat down one night and I told him I'd miss listening to the river most of all. Many nights I go down there to sit, and this is one way I can still continue to do that. I've tried it out, and it's great. I try to keep my direction forward, because if I accidentally let go of the line, I lose track of where I am.

My headaches are still happening, but much worse. I sleep when I can, and Sara has been an enormous help in aiding me. By writing this, I hope someday my kids will read it and learn more about who I was, am, and will be. Hope is a beautiful word, and I use it daily when I wake. The doctors are not hopeful, but I refuse to let it all fall apart. There's so much more I wanted to do, stupid silly things that I can only now wish for.

1. *Skydive*
2. *Swim naked in the ocean with my wife, Simone.*
3. *Learn how to bake Baklava (I love that stuff)*
4. *Learn how to line dance (now I'd be crashing into people and disrupting the whole process, I'm sure)*
5. *Ride a horse at full gallop across a meadow. I'd ride a Palomino... They were*

always such a beautiful color

6. *See a rainbow in Ireland or some exotic locale*
7. *Watch the Jasmine bloom*
8. *Tour with a band and see the country from a tour bus (kind of like the Dead Heads, only a little more cleaner and without all the drugs... Although)*
9. *Watch my daughter walk down the aisle with her husband and have the traditional father dance with her*
10. *See my son Jules grow up and succeed at whatever his hearts desires, then see him marry and start a family*
11. *See my aunt and uncle one more time to thank them for saving me*

Well, as I think of more, I'll add them on, but you get the gist. My thoughts run the gamut from light to heavy, and I do my best to keep them more on the light side, so if I get melancholy or bore you with my ranting, skip to another page. My moods run like that, depending on the severity of the headache that's plaguing me. I'll try to keep it light. Nobody likes a Debby, or in my case, Damien downer. I can't think of anything else to write, but I made a goal to add some words of wisdom at the end of my ramblings, so... my wisdom nugget for today is this:

Let no one control you, or tell you who you can or cannot be. The world is an amazing place and doors will open and some will close. Choose the one that feels right to you. And if it was in error, slip back out that door and move on to the next one. Eventually, you'll find the one that's meant for you. Okay. That's it, so I'll write again at some point. Looking forward to Chino. I hope he likes Milk Bones, because we bought the jumbo sized box.

I set the ribbon attached to the book in that spot and a yawn slipped from my lips. The music was playing, and I realized I hadn't even heard it. For me, to read my father's words was like opening a time capsule, and I was glad that I had tackled the journal. I turned off the stereo and checked my phone. Mom hadn't called, so she must have taken Carlos, or whoever's advice, to back off and give me space. I thought about calling my sister Keira, but what would I say? Not ready to deal with her, I set the book on the table and eyed the closed door to my father's room. I turned the knob as I took a deep breath.

My steps carried me inward, and I lay down on his bed. My eyes, tired from reading his story, were heavy. Inhaling, the remnants of the scent of jasmine that blew softly from the air conditioner calmed my brain. The drone of the motor drowned out the falling rain beyond the windows, and I drifted off to sleep, content.

Twenty-Five

What will You Leave us this Time

⌘

Ten hours passed when I woke and I jumped from the bed, unsure of where I was. My eyes moved to the images on the wall behind the bed and I shifted around and stared at my parents' wedding picture. My mother was beaming, a fresh, radiant bride on her day, and my father carried a gentle smile. His eyes held a look of wonder as he gazed at her, and I shook my head. If what I'd read was true, two people fell apart because of something beyond their comprehension. I'd seen Sara, and though it seemed odd, it also felt natural. Perhaps I was more like my father than I thought.

"Why wouldn't she believe you, Dad? Was she really that insecure? You two were always as tight as a stack of pancakes stuck in syrup." It made me feel bad knowing had they come together and believed in something beyond belief, our lives would be so different.

"But you're not here, and I don't know if this is something I'm supposed to fix or learn from. If you're dead, why can't I see you like I can, Sara?" I jumped when the voice alerted me to her presence.

"Because he can't, and that's why I'm here. If he could, he would, but he can't. I wish it could be different and maybe someday it can be, but not now. How are you faring?" I slid off the bed and looked down at my wrinkled clothes. What could I say?

"I'm learning more, like you wanted, and I'm taking it as well as I can. Not having seen him in so long, learning more about his history is a shock, but it explains why he lived next door. Maybe at some point he'll delve more into thoughts about Keira, the ghost. I know how you were helping him. Thank you. I'm sure he said it many times, but I want you to know I appreciate it. If it weren't for you, I wouldn't be reading this stuff, I guess. What happened to Chino?" Sara smiled and shrugged.

"You'll find out in time, but keep going. You'll have most of what you need to know, and then, I'll fill in the last details." She disappeared into thin air and I chuckled.

"If you keep doing that, it's gonna drive me batty. At least say goodbye before you pop, or better yet, learn how to disappear in a puff of smoke. That would be something to see." I heard nothing in response and headed for the bathroom. If Em were standing here, would Sara pull the same tricks? Would Em even see her? Shaking my head as I eyed myself in the mirror, I'd ask her the next time she deemed it necessary to haunt me.

A knock on the door pulled me from my reverie and I opened the door to find no one there. A large box sat on the doorstep, and I walked past it and peered around, wondering who dropped it off. It wasn't an Amazon box, and there was no postmark showing anyone had delivered it. "Sara, if this is your idea of a joke, it's weird. You could have just told me." I heard a giggle, and I stepped off the porch as Em popped up from around the side of the house.

"It's supposed to be a surprise... So, SURPRISE!" I shook my head as a laugh escaped my lips.

"Well, considering it's not my birthday yet, I don't know what I've done to deserve a box? But it's a very nice box, so thank you." She came over and shoved my arm as she pointed at it.

"No, it's not your birthday, but I figured if you're going to be hanging around for a bit, I could commission you to paint me something. I can't afford to pay much, but if you take the materials as a trade, that would be wonderful. But it's up to you. I'm not sure how much you sell your pieces for, so maybe this wasn't such a good idea." Her eyes looked down at the

126

ground and I took the steps two at a time, trying to look eager and happy. I was ecstatic, but I didn't want to show her how much. No one had ever wanted my art, not that I showed it to anyone but Mom and Keira, and they both smiled and said it was nice, but to me, nice was just another word for okay or subpar.

"No, that works fine for me. I charge little," I said as I tore through the tape to see what lay inside. I felt like a kid at Christmas, and my thoughts began churning at what I'd create for this beautiful girl. Inside, I found a multitude of high quality oils. There were three stretched canvases and a sketchbook, a few charcoal pencils, a variety of brushes, and three plastic palettes. I could make do and I turned to stare at her, shocked by what she'd done. Her face held a blush, and she smiled at me like a bashful child.

"This is amazing, Em. I'll paint you something extraordinary, I promise. I'm not on a timetable for it, am I? I like to paint in layers and it takes days. If you're okay with that, I'm more than willing to paint you a few pieces. You didn't have to do this… But I'm glad you did. Thank you." She grinned, and I was glad that I said the right things. I stepped across the porch with my arms open, and she waited as I wrapped my arms around her. The hug felt like heaven, and I chuckled, then released her, but not before giving her a quick kiss. I'm pretty sure we both blushed, and I shook my head.

"It's funny, because that Cure song, Just Like Heaven, popped in my head as I held you. It seems kind of appropriate." I'm not sure if she even knew who the Cure was, but I didn't care. No one had ever given me such a gift before and I loved standing there with her, but I also wanted her to leave so I could capture this feeling on the canvas. A gift of gratitude, or maybe a gift of the heart? Either way, I was eager to paint. I heard her name called, and she turned to her house, a sad smile on her face.

"I've got to go help mom. We hit the farmer's market this morning, and she wants to try her hand at canning now that we live in the country. I don't think this is technically country," she said as her hand motioned across the street, "but I guess it's close enough. What'll be next? Let's go milk cows or goats and make cheese? At least it's edible and not useless ceramics. Enjoy your paints, Jules, and I look forward to seeing what you create for me. I'm sure whatever your mind imagines will be beautiful." I glanced back at the box as she headed home.

"It will be almost as beautiful as you, Em. I'm sure." I hefted the box up on my hip and carried it in, then sat it on the table. I glanced around, looking for the best place to set up my work spot. The river seemed the only logical place to fit my mood, and I gathered up a bag full of supplies, grabbed my father's hat and walking stick, then headed towards my favorite spot spent with dad. As I followed the posts and weathered string, I thought of my father's hand, sliding along the same path to his place of solitude, his trusted dog by his side. The thought stirred something in me that thrilled my soul. I realized I couldn't remember the last time I'd pulled the paints out and went to town on a blank canvas. Eager, yet allowing the feeling to move through me, I tried not to visualize the picture to come. It always worked better for me if I just allowed my hands to do the talking through oil, and this time would be no different. As I rounded the corner, I began talking out loud and swishing the stick through the bushes, hoping to get Roger to vacate the premises. Unsure if it was his normal routine to hang out there, I'd be brave and stake claim for the day. Had Dad spent a lot of time here, I'm sure Roger had learned to make himself scarce occasionally. The riverbank was void of life and I let out the breath I was holding. I'd forgotten that the bench was unusable, and I sighed. Maybe it hadn't been such a good idea after all. Disheartened, I lugged the bag back to the house and glanced over at the cemetery. The sunlight hadn't reached it yet, and I figured it was my next best option. After setting my gear down, I went to grab a porch chair and table to prop my paints on. The car was absent from Em's house, and I hoped to get a few layers down before anyone interrupted me.

Twenty-Six

Tell Me your Secrets

⟡⟡⟡

Two hours later, the sun was encroaching on my space, but I barely noticed, lost in my zone of art. A layer of Cerulean blue had blended with cobalt in a sky-tone of swirls. I leaned back and eyed the thick smears, then grabbed a butter knife and gently cut through it, giving texture. Painting always reminded me of life. You could mess up, yet go back later and try to fix your mistakes. I always drank when I painted, and it surprised me I didn't miss it while I worked. I added a touch of violet through the texture I made and eyed it again. It resembled a night sky, without the typical setting sun shades rippled through, but it was a melancholy image and I nodded in approval of my progress. A car door slamming brought me out of my thoughts, and I glanced over. Frank gave a slight wave and headed in with a case of beer and a bag hanging from his hand. I salivated at the familiar box and thought about the three twelve packs still festering in my trunk.

"You can do without, you have to…" A small voice intruded on my thoughts and I glanced around to see if someone was speaking to me, but I sat there alone. The more I thought about the beer, the more my hand began shaking. "You will do this. Em is depending on you. I'm depending on you." I think I closed my eyes because I saw my father in my mind, the way he looked when I was a boy. He smiled lightly and nodded before turning to a mist and disappearing. With a heavy sigh, I knew I was imagining what I wanted to see, not what was real. I never realized how much I missed him until that moment, and I nodded.

"I'll hold off for you, Dad. I'll try." The stupid Yoda quote flashed through me, 'do, not try,' and I chuckled. "Yeah, whatever, enough already!" I eyed the painting and began gathering my stuff up, being careful not to get any of the palette paint on the canvas. I juggled the gear and strode towards the house. As I turned the corner, I almost stepped on the stupid yard snake, and it startled me. Dropping the canvas, I watched as it toppled into the grass before coming to rest against the trellis where the jasmine grew. I set the palette down and gingerly pried the wet work from the greenery. The leaves had created swirled streaks in the paint and I shook my head. I set it aside and carried the rest of the stuff in, saving the canvas for last. "Maybe I can fix it," I thought as I went back out to retrieve it, and carrying it in, I set it down on the table and assessed the damage. The vines had left a curving softness embedded in the harsh lines I'd created, and I stood back to see it from afar. "It doesn't have to be perfect to be beautiful, you know." Her voice caused me to jump, and I spun around to see Sara standing there in the doorway, a look of awe etched across her face.

"You should be so proud of yourself. I think that's one of the most beautiful things I've ever seen, not that I've seen much. Vincent Van Gogh was one of my favorite artists of all time and this reminds me of his starry night piece." I shook my head and blushed.

"Yeah, if I could be as good as him, I'd be a millionaire. Alas, I'm just a starving artist." I began laughing, and she stepped forward, her hand reaching out towards the painting. I shook my head at her. "It's wet, don't touch it..." I thought about it for a moment. "Can you touch it? Is that something you're able to do?" She gave me a slight grin and took a seat at the table.

"I can do a few things, but I wouldn't touch your paint. That would be rude of me. What else are you going to add to it? Any stars?" I shrugged, unsure.

"I never know what's going to happen. Dab a little paint on the brush and just let my hand do its thing. I never consciously think about what I'm going to paint, it just happens. I'm not sure how other artists work, but it's what I do." She leaned back and pulled a jar from her pocket and slid it across the table to me.

"Don't open it now, but it may give you more guidance as you work on your masterpiece. I know she's going to love it, whatever you end up creating, but one thing I know, it will be beautiful." I eyed her speculatively and grinned.

"Do you know already what I'm going to do? Can you see the future and see what the finished product will look like?" Part of me hoped so, but the other part of me didn't want to be influenced by what she'd say. She rolled her eyes at me as a beaming smile broke across her face.

"All I can say is that even you will be impressed, and that for years to come, you'll see it and know in that moment when you splashed the last brush stroke, you will never do another quite like it or in the manner that you did it. It's all good, so don't freak out. Just keep going. You've got a long way to go." She slid off the chair and I held up my hand.

"Can you stay for a bit? I have some questions… If you don't mind answering them." She sat back down and watched me as she wrung her hands in her lap.

"I guess so, but I may not want to answer everything, but shoot. What do you want to know?" I took the seat across from her, giving her space, and I sighed.

"I don't know my dad as well as I'd liked, and he's not here to ask, but you were his scribe, so maybe you can tell me some basics. Like, what was his favorite color, or did he have a favorite shirt he wore… Stuff like that." I could see her visibly relax, and she planted her hands on her thighs and closed her eyes.

"Okay, his favorite color, from what I could tell, was a really pretty shade of blue, almost like royal, but it had purple tones to it. He got a shirt from a catalog that he bought, hoping that you'd see it someday and get a laugh out of it. It was almost like a Hawaiian shirt, but without all the goofy flowers all over it. It was more artsy than anything. He wore that thing until it was a useless mess, and I cut it up to make a bandana for Chino. That way, he still had a piece, even if he couldn't see it. You never got to see it, and I looked online for another for him, but he said he didn't want another. Is that it?" I shook my head, trying to visualize my dad, who lived in L. L. Bean up north, clad in an artsy shirt, but drew a complete blank.

"Um, what did he eat, and did you help him cook as he lost his sight?" A round of laughter broke from her.

"Well, that's a big no. Cooking was never one of my skills. That was more in my sister's wheelhouse. But mom would cook enough that she'd bring him some almost every day, and other than that, he did soup and stuff. Dad brought him a few of those Hungry Man dinner things, but he didn't have a microwave and didn't want one. He did it in the oven, because one time the house filled with smoke. Apparently he forgot he had it in there, and Chino wasn't much help except barking his head off about the smoke enough to alert us that something was up. My Dad came over and threw the burning mess out. Your Dad had been out on the porch daydreaming but he came to dinner that night. Chino was all stressed out over the incident, but he got an extra treat for not allowing the house to burn down. Dad said he never took the cover off the meal before throwing it in to cook. When Damien had a severe headache, he'd kind of blank out for a bit. After that, mom would pop in to check on him at lunchtime with a sandwich, just to ensure he was eating. Towards the end, his appetite left him…" Her eyes grew wet, and she shook her head. "I should get going now, but if you have questions, I'll answer them the next time. GOODBYE, Jules, there, is that better?" She disappeared before my eyes and I burst into laughter.

"Goodbye, Sara, and thanks. You've given me a gift. See you." I eyed the painting and saw it through her eyes. She was right. The accidental drop had given it a unique quality I would have never thought to produce. Perhaps it was meant to be, I thought, and went to wash my palette of paint and figure out what to do with the rest of the day.

Twenty-Seven

The Death of your Heart

I set my art equipment in Keira's room, just in case Em dropped by. Not ready to show her the piece until I finished, I knew it would come to no harm in there. The bottle that Sara had set on the table kept drawing my attention, but she'd given me no specific instruction for when I should open it. I could see the sparkles within it bouncing around, but knowing it would harbor some more deep messages, I wasn't sure if I was ready for it, so I pushed it out of my head. The cases in my trunk needed to be dealt with, and I figured I'd haul them over to Frank as a thank you gift for being nice to me. As I reached the door, my phone rang the dreaded funeral march song. My breath felt knocked from me and I shook my head. "Just my luck. Here I'm off to do a good deed and she calls…" I answered it and said nothing.

"Jules, are you there? Jules? It's me, Mom. Jules?" I was waiting for her to hang up, but something told me to just get it over with.

"Yeah, just washing up some paint off my hands. What's up? Is my detention time over already? If so, it wasn't long enough." I could hear her angry sigh on the other end and I smirked.

"Um, I just wanted to touch base and make sure you were doing okay. That house isn't right, Jules. Strange things happen there and I had a dream last night that you hated me and that something was turning you against me.

133

You know I love you, right? I'm sorry for what I've done with the letters, but I was only trying to protect you kids. Something happened to your father when he got that house, and he was not the same man I married when we split. I'd hate to see the same thing happen to you. Ugh, I should have burned that house to the ground years ago." I almost hung up on her for that, but waited her out.

"Jules, I'm sorry. I don't know what else to say. If you don't want to go to school, that's fine, but don't shut me out in the meantime. I'm your mother, for God's sake, and I've always had your best interest at heart. You may not believe it, and I don't know what you've been reading in his letters, but he made his choice to stay there in that… That house. I was only protecting you." I nodded as she babbled, unsure what to say. Something in me said to give her a chance, but the other part was too angry. Damn, I wanted a beer and my hands began trembling again.

"Look Ma, I can't talk right now. I've heard what you said, but I'm not leaving yet. Some things have come up…" My mind moved to Em and the painting and I felt my heart beat faster. "I'll head north when I'm ready to, but that day isn't today, sorry. Have fun on the rest of your trip and I'll catch you later." I hung up the phone, not wanting to hear her whining any longer, and I turned the phone off, in case she speed dialed me back. A second later, I heard a knock on the door, and expecting Em, I grinned as I swung it open. My mother stood there with her hand frozen in mid-air. I think it shocked her as much as it did me. Blinking, trying to make sense of why she was there, I stood like a rock as she waltzed past me, her trademark fragrance following her like a foreign cloud.

"Fine, we can talk in person then. Sorry for the surprise visit, but you kept hanging up on me, and that's unacceptable. I came to see what the heck has happened to you and to close this place up so it can rot. Oh, and I see you finally did something decent with your hair. I guess there's hope for you after all. But, you're still coming home." My mouth hung open, and I shook my head, still in shock at the audacity of her to come storming in like this. Her eyes took in the room and she wrinkled up her nose as if a skunk had just swept through, gracing the air with its putrid aroma. She shook her head and moved from room to room, but never went to her and Dad's bedroom, which made me happy.

"Ugh, it's just as beat up and ugly as I remember it being." Her eyes rested on me and a fake smile rose on her face. "He's gone, Jules, and I doubt he's coming back. Unfortunate, I know, but it is what it is. It's time you forget about this place and let it go. Once we declare him… Officially dead, I'm selling this place and getting it out of our lives once and for all. We had a will and if he's dead, it's mine to do with as I see fit. I'm impressed that they're finally doing something with the land. Those places across the street will go for big bucks. Maybe they'd be interested in grabbing up this piece. Perhaps they'd tear it down and make some kind of park so that the folks can access the river from across the street. Hmm…" I could see the wheels spinning in her head and it made me want to knock her senseless. Sara's voice in my head took that moment to pipe in, and I turned away from her.

"Violence will solve nothing. Give her time and it will all work out, just have faith." It bolstered my courage, and I whipped around to see her back as she strolled into the living room. The Moody Blues album still set propped against the stereo, and she reached for it, and a look of melancholy found her. She waved it in the air. "I remember this one. Your Dad bought it when we were on a trip out in Utah, that was long before you were born. Man, this is ancient. No one listens to this stuff anymore, but I give it credit. It was a great time back then, but that was before…" Her words cut off and I just let her roll. She eyed the turntable and then me. "Do you mind?" I shrugged, and she flicked it on and set the needle down on the record. The song 'Question' began, and it seemed to trigger something in her. Yes, I'm sure she had many questions, but would she stay calm enough to ask me? I hoped so, because I wanted this to go easy and for her to go back home and leave me alone. Her fingers tapped on the album cover to the beat of the song, and she smiled.

"I loved him, Jules, and I hope you don't think I didn't. The hardest thing was for me to realize that he didn't love me back. We had been closer than two people could be, but then he inherited this house, her house. He told me once about the girl and her mother who lived here, and I always got the

135

feeling there was something more that he wasn't telling me. I don't know what the big secret was, but it hurt being left out of it. For years, he gravitated to this place, and I'm sorry, but I never saw what the big attraction was. But I felt uncomfortable, like I didn't belong here, as if I were intruding. Does that make any sense?" I shrugged, not knowing what it was like because until we were older, we weren't really here much.

"When you kids were just babies, he wanted me to haul you and the gear and shack up here like some kind of refugee. I mean, come on… It didn't even have central air. I refused, but once you turned five, it was easier and I relented. But something here bothered me, and I could never put my finger on it until I started paying attention. He was always a light sleeper and would go out and read a book. I don't know how many times I had to go wake him to come to bed, but it was almost a daily occurrence. It never bothered me except for when we were here. He wouldn't go read, but he would walk to the river, he said, and it was then that I saw her. I don't know where she came from, but she would follow him as he took the path there. She wasn't hiding, because she wore a gown that you could see from a mile away. Oh, how I wanted to follow them, to confront them, but part of me was afraid. We were unraveling, and I didn't want to admit it. One night, there was a full moon, and I pretended to be asleep as he got out of bed, threw on his clothes, and went out. I watched from the window as he wandered past the house, and not a second later, she followed him again, but this time, she turned and I swear by all that's holy, she turned and smiled at me. What was I supposed to do? She knew I saw her, and she was all but laughing at me, knowing I was a coward who would do nothing to stop her. When he came back, we argued, and I told him what I'd seen." I knew this part of the story from the vision and I leaned against the wall as she took a seat.

"He denied it, of course, but I refused to believe his lies. He wasn't my Damien anymore, and I wasn't about to share him with his girlfriend. I packed the car up and the next day we left. I didn't care anymore, because a part of me died that night. Yes, I sent his letters back. I refuse to let him poison your minds against me, and I fought for custody. He didn't even bat an eyelash, so that shows how much he cared. He only wanted this place, his river, and his girl. I cut him off and never looked back. I know this must hurt you, but it's the truth." Her eyes spilled their tears, and I wanted to console her, but I knew how wrong she was. The question was, what to say to change her thinking.

Twenty-Eight

Breaking Apart Again

S he checked her watch and eyed me over her three-hundred-dollar glasses. "I've got a meeting to see to, but when I get back, I'm going to have Brett come over and board this place back up again until I can do something with it. You're leaving, now. You have no right to be here, Julien, and I suggest you return to school, so pack up your things and when I return, you'd best be absent or…" I leaned against the wall and shook my head.

"I know. Let's play make a deal. You love a good deal, right? Brett no longer lives next door, so I'll put the boards back up before I leave, but I can't leave yet. Someone's commissioned me to do a piece of artwork, and I need to be here to finish it. I can't work on it at school. My room-mate and I had a slight falling out and I'm gonna have to wait to get switched to a new room. He punched me, and I refuse to go back until I have a room to go back to. There's also the addition of a girl I met here, and I will not up and leave until I have time to say goodbye. I want another week, and then I'll leave. Swear on my… Father's potential grave. Can you live with that?" She watched my face, but except for the needing another room at school, it was the truth. I watched as she sighed, then she rolled her eyes.

"I need to do this, Mom. This is important to me, and we'll be all good when I'm done, if all goes well. One week… That's all I'm asking for." She nodded and sniffed, then wrinkled her nose.

"Fine, one week and then you're out of here. You had best not go back on your promise, Jules. It's bad enough I had to cut short my trip for this, so I'll find out if you're lying to me. One week!" I nodded and hid my inner grin as she strode to the door.

"No, this place is an eyesore. It still makes my skin crawl being here, and I'm surprised you don't feel the cold drafts. Something isn't right here, but no matter, it will be out of our hands soon enough." I nodded solemnly and walked her to the door, then forced myself to give her a hug goodbye.

"I'll call you when I'm done here, and then I'll head back to school, or maybe home. I can always go to school somewhere closer and get my stuff transferred. You'd like that, right?" I could see the look of concern cross her face and attempted to appease her. "Or maybe I could intern for a little at the firm and see if it's a good fit for me. I've got mixed feelings… So it would be a waste of money to send me to school for something I don't have a passion for, right?" She eyed me, but I doubt she heard what I said. Glancing down, I noticed the huge rock on her finger and I grabbed her hand.

"Um… Is there something I should know?" She blushed, which was something she never did, and shook her head.

"Oh… This," she said, as she twirled the ring on her fingers. "I was going to tell you, but being in this place always throws me for a loop. Carlos and I got married while we were in Greece. So, if you come home, you're going to have to find a place to live quickly, because I think it would be uncomfortable for you there. Carlos likes you, he does. It's just that we're newlyweds and, well, you know." I realized at that moment that I didn't care. She'd always did what suited her needs and to hell with the rest, I guess. Nodding, I gave a pat smile.

"Sure, Mom, you're right. I wouldn't want to intrude on your bliss. I'm happy for you and Carlos. But, I've got to get back to work. One week, I know." She beamed at the congratulatory tone and pivoted on her Jimmy Choo pumps and walked out onto the porch. Her eyes peered across the street and a grin reached her face.

"Yes, they're going to want to snatch this place up and the rest of the property that runs past it. Your father bought the patch of woods years ago, not wanting anyone to develop it and this land will go for a prime price, being on the river and all." I could see the dollar signs spinning in her head, like a cheap Vegas game where all the cherries pop up at once and the machine goes nuts. I held back, saying nothing, eager for her to vacate the premises. She turned to me as she headed towards her car.

"One week, Jules, and not a minute more!" She jumped in and revved the engine, then backed out, trying to avoid the puddles in the road. Her eyes moved to Brett's house and I could see that Em had come out onto the porch. Mom looked back at me and slid her glasses down her nose and eyed me, as if it finally dawned on her that the reason I was here was for the cute girl next door. She slid them up a second later and headed down the street, out of view. I glanced at Em as my spirits plummeted. One week wasn't long enough, nor would one month be. Em came walking across the yard and I plunked down into the rocker, my brain attempting to void itself of the poison called Simone. She stopped as she reached the steps.

"Are you okay, Jules? Who was that woman?" I motioned to the other chair and Em sat, her hands clenching in her lap.

"That, dear Em, from Wisconsin, was my mother. She demands I leave here and gave me a week to pack it all up and get out." I ran my hand through my hair and shook my head, my shoulders slumped, and I wanted to cry. Em stood, then kneeled at my feet.

"Can she do that? Make you leave here?" I shrugged and glanced at her, wanting so much for everything to be different, to not have to say goodbye so soon.

"She says when she gets my father declared dead, their will say's this reverts ownership to her, and apparently he bought the acreage that runs past this place, too. I know her, and I know she's all about the mighty buck. She told me she's going to sell it to the builders across the street and they can expand over here and have river access. My father would roll over in his grave if he could see what she's planning. I can't let her take this place, but I don't know how to stop her." Em patted my leg, then ran her fingers down my face, a

140

look of sadness filling her eyes.

"That would be a tragedy, Jules. I'll say a prayer that she comes to her senses and changes her mind. Besides, I think she'd have to wait seven years to declare him officially gone. If the books I've read are accurate, but I'll check it out, then let you know." I hoped what she said was true. She stood, then leaned over and kissed me on the cheek. "Don't let it bother you in the meantime. There's no point in getting stressed over something you can't change, so believe that it will all work out, okay?" I nodded and smiled, happy that I had someone in my corner. She turned with a wave, then walked home while I watched. My moods were swinging wildly, and for a minute, I wished my mother would drive her car off a bridge and get out of my life permanently. I leaned my head back, closed my eyes, and felt the tears come.

"Dad, if you're out there, tell me what to do? She's going to sell this place, and they will tear apart everything you've ever worked for. I can't let her do this, but I don't know how to stop her. Please, help me, Dad." It occurred to me that by asking, my heart knew he was no longer with me, and that hurt worse than anything. Not saying goodbye, and now, watching the destruction of his peaceful haven, felt like hot needles being jabbed into my brain. I sat for a few minutes, then walked in, intent on reading more letters or the journal.

On the table sat the jar Sara had left, and I grabbed that and the candle, then cloistered myself in my father's room. I felt him the most when I was in here, and I set the candle on the table, lit it, then grabbed the journals. I really needed to hear his words, and I dove in, eager to find out more about the life of the man I barely knew.

I've been spending time at the river, as my nights have turned into my days and vice versa. Knowing the time really doesn't matter anymore in the big scheme of things, I wander when my thoughts become unsettled, which is often. I suppose it would be easy to be angry, to be shouting to God, why me, but I know that a man's life gets pre-determined in some massive book in the sky somewhere and when it's my time, then that's it. To fight against the inevitable is a losing battle, so why try?

I know what is to come. Am I happy about it? No, but I can't change it. They've

141

finally come up with the diagnosis, and there's not much to do about it. These things work relatively fast, and to go to extreme measures for me, only to have the same result, is my definition of insanity. No, I will enjoy, to the best of my ability, each moment I take a breath, each song that I can lose myself in, and each laugh shared with friends. My only regret is that I don't have my children here. Those voices are the ones I hear when I close my eyes. Those faces are what I hold as the most precious of all things. But to regret is, again, a pointless endeavor, as I can't change things, so I'm learning to allow the world to keep moving, even realizing it will be without my physical presence. I'm letting it go and letting God handle it.

It's impossible to travel up North now, and to have a message delivered, perhaps this time to get through, would only cause them pain. What would I say? Time is running out and those moments are my hourglass sands, except I can't watch them drift away, only sense the emptiness of what was there and now falling faster than snow in a blizzard. I am refusing treatment, and instead, spend my days with Chino, walking to the river, or chatting with Brett, and lately, Sara. She is now writing this, as it causes headaches when I attempt the chore. I'm not saying it's a chore, it just is. Sara picked up some books on braille and has gotten pretty good at it, so she's teaching me. I told her don't bother grabbing War and Peace, as that's something I couldn't get through when I could see, let alone with my fingers doing the reading. It makes her happy to help, and I appreciate her willingness to do these things for me.

Sometimes I ask her to read to me, and she finds humorous books to fill the time, but lately I find I go shorter and shorter distances in listening, because the pain becomes too much. She is like my Annie to Helen Keller, and I'm grateful. She may or may not write this, but between the two of us, she's the most upbeat about the whole thing, but I'm sure when I'm not close by, she is hurting as much as me. It's funny, the things you can't see that you pick up on. My hearing and scent have increased, most likely to make up for my lack of sight, as has touch. I long to hold my kids once more, but in the meantime, I pet Chino endlessly, which he seems to enjoy. He is a lovable dog, but becomes distracted easily. Perhaps that's why he flunked school. Doesn't matter, though, because every day I have with him is a good day. My head is hurting, so I'll stop here. Be back soon.

I could almost feel him with me, as I read his words, and it made me ever more grateful that he had Sara to be his writing partner while he went through this. To imagine being at the mercy of your neighbors made me even more angry. We should have been here for him, to see him through whatever was happening. Part of me wondered if he would have gotten treatment had we been in his life. Would the attempt to keep living have been worth it if he had someone to live for? I felt sick to my stomach, knowing at some point, the writing would stop, that there would be an end, and I broke down again and cried.

Twenty-Nine

These Pictures of You

F our days later

I woke to a rhythmic knocking on the door and blinked the sleep from my eyes as I gazed around my father's room. The candle was out again, looking as if it had never burned, and I moved to the door. Nothing was surprising me any more these days. A man stood on the porch, his business suit screamed money, and I stepped back for a second, unsure who he was or what he wanted. His salesman smile wove its way across his face, and he pulled out a handkerchief and dabbed at the perspiration on his brow. Tucking it away, he slid a business card towards me. With his unusual looks, I expected the card to read Willy Wonka. He and Gene Wilder could be twins.

"You must be Julien? Your mother said you'd be here. I'm Sylvester Rausch and I'm with Steele Property Management and Shore Banks Realty. We're the builders across from you." *Man, my mother works fast.* I hesitated, then slammed the door in his face. The door rattled with the force and I leaned against it. He began knocking with more persistence, and I tucked in my anger as I ripped the door open again.

"I have no need for your services, Mr.... Rausch, you said?" My brains began firing on all their pistons and I held nothing back. "My father owns this house, and he is divorced from my mother. He has been missing for a year, and last I checked, it takes seven years for a person to be declared legally dead, so my mother has no claim on this house or his land. I suggest you tell her to wait the full seven years. This home isn't for sale, not now, and if I have my way, never!" I stepped back inside and slammed the door again, hoping he'd take my message back to mommy dearest. There was no further knocking, and I peered out the window as he hopped into his shiny silver Acura and drove away. As I stood there shaking my head, I watched my hands as they trembled. My brain was screaming for a beer. I felt the simmer of my emotions running through me like a freight train.

"I don't care, Sara, I need this." I yelled to the walls, not caring whether she could hear me, then I stalked out to my car and grabbed my beer from my trunk. "Piss warm or ice cold, it doesn't matter anymore!" I realized I was mumbling to myself, but I no longer cared. My mother was a tenacious badger on a free roadkill buffet with this house thing, and I was careening out of control. I threw two of the cases into the fridge and opened the third, then threw a few bottles in the freezer. As I stalked to the living room, I searched through the album collection, and not finding anything, grabbed my iPod and earbuds, two bottles of beer, and headed for my father's room.

My eyes glared at the images on the wall, and I ripped the wedding picture down, then threw it on the bed. I flipped the thing over, unlatched the hinges that closed it in, and removed the image. My hands were trembling, and I carefully tore my mother from the picture, then shredded it. The pieces fell like confetti to the floor. The next was an image of just her, and I repeated the process, laughing in between chugging my beer and annihilating every ounce of that woman from this house.

"You won't win, Mom. I will die before I allow you to tear this place down." I was shouting through my angry tears, but with no one to hear me, I didn't care. So, I chugged down another beer and peered around the room in search of anything else remotely connected to Simone.

"You are dead to me! I will not leave, and there's nothing you can do or say that will make me." A knocking on the door finally reach my ears during a song change-up, but I refused to answer it. Sara could pop in at will, and if it was my mother, well, heaven help her if she tried to make me leave. I ignored it and grabbed a few more beers from the refrigerator. Cranking my tunes louder to drown out whoever was at the door, I lost myself in the blaring music as my eyes fell on the journals and the jar that lay beside them. My fingers reached over and grabbed the small bottle, and I eyed the sparkles within.

"Sara, if you can make this stop, do it. I don't know what to do, and I need answers now. Please…" I twisted the top off the jar and leaned back against the pillows as an odd scent of something familiar filled the air. "Peace… Please, I need some peace, Sara." As I inhaled the rich scent, I closed my eyes and drifted once more into a hypnotic state of being, my vision now of Sara and my father.

* * *

"He's never going to understand, but there's always a bigger presence at work than what we see, don't you agree?" I watched as Sara nodded. Her pen drew symbols on the first page of the book and she listened as my father spoke.

"Yeah, I don't know, sometimes this hurts so bad I wish I were dead, but other times, I feel this sense of… Hmm… I guess you could call it peace. I had a dream last night and the girl Keira was there. I haven't seen her since forever, but suddenly, it felt like everything was falling into place, like it was going to be okay. She said something strange though, and I'm unsure what she meant, so I'll just say that it was nice to see a face so clearly in my mind again. Loneliness was always a foreign word to me, even with losing Simone and the kids, but being here, I always felt surrounded by light. This is a magical place, and I had forgotten that, but lately I'm getting reminders. I'd forgotten to believe in the magic. Pretty funny, huh? Here I'm wasting away into someone I'm kind of happy I can't see, yet my heart perks up when I remember that there's magic. Always believe in it, Sara. That's your words of advice for today. We should put that in the journal, huh? Don't forget to add that in somewhere." Sara stopped doodling and gave a light smile, and I watched as she eyed my father. He seemed almost skeletal to me, and it was a shock. She pushed a bowl of soup forward and gently slid a spoon into his hand, turning it upright.

"Eat something, Daddio, you've got to keep your strength up. You're not leaving today, not if I have my way. I'm not ready to let you go, yet, you hear me? We've got more writing to do. The life story of Damien must be told, right?" My father nodded and brought his hand up to clasp the bowl, then he tipped the spoon in before bringing it to his mouth. His hands shook, and he spilled a little down his chin. Sara grabbed the napkin and dabbed it, then gave a sad smile.

"You're going to wear more of it than you eat. Here, let me help." He relinquished the spoon, and I watched as this young girl carefully fed him. After several spoonfuls, he shook his head.

"I'm good, that's enough. I'm not that hungry. You can feed Chino the rest. He eats everything." I could see this large black dog laying at his feet and I sensed myself smiling, finally getting a look at the mystery dog. His tongue hung sideways from his mouth, but he jumped to his feet as Sara set the bowl down on the floor, where he sucked the entire thing up in one gulp. Sara giggled and retrieved the bowl, then walked it into the kitchen, where Chino followed close behind her.

"You stay with Daddio, Chino. Be a good boy." The dog looked at her and then turned its head and stared at the cupboard before turning his attention back to her. She chuckled again and shook her head.

"Daddio, can Chino have a Milk Bone? He's begging again." I could hear my father cough several times, then a light laugh rose from him.

"Yeah, I'm almost out, though, so just one. I've gotta have Brett pick me up more next time he heads to town. Remind me to ask him, okay?" Sara grabbed a biscuit, and I watched as Chino sat down on his haunches to wait.

"Look at you, you big beggar. Can you shake? Shake, Chino!" The dog wagged his tail but did little else. "Come on, you did it before. Now shake, Chino." The dog stood and shook his whole body, which caused Sara to burst into a fit of laughter. She handed the dog the treat, and he ate it in one gulp. Drool ran from the corners of his jowls and dripped to the floor.

147

Ruffling the fur on his head, she moved back out to the dining room where my father sat, staring at the wall in front of him, seeing nothing. She cleared her throat, and I realized she was alerting him to the fact that she'd come back in. He turned his head towards the noise and smiled.

"I feel like heading to the river? Does it look like it's going to rain?" Sara walked to the window and looked out while Chino lay back down on the floor beside my father.

"No, it looks pretty okay out. It's not supposed to rain until later, but you know how it is, but if you want to chance it, I'll come with." My father nodded, almost absentmindedly, and Sara closed the journal and eyed him.

"Do you want me to put this journal away until tomorrow? We can write some more then. You can tell all about your big river adventure. Maybe Roger will be down there and we can make up a story about the wild and elusive killer gator, Mr. Rogers and his Gator-hood..." Dad smiled and shook his head, and she carried the journal into the bedroom, where she must have tucked it away in the closet. I wondered why he felt it necessary to lock it away, unless he worried someone would come in and read up on the inner realm of his feelings. Chino stood and my father grabbed at the harness around the dog, then they walked to the door. With him standing upright, I couldn't believe how thin he was, and I felt my heart breaking. I knew I was reaching out with my hand as I saw the vision, wanting to hold him and tell him I could see him, that I was there. Sara strode in front of him and opened the door, and I watched as he allowed Chino to guide him into the yard and around the house. The dog took his job seriously, and walked at my father's pace, almost as if leaning against him to show him the way.

"It's kind of nice that it's cloudy. If the sun were out, it would be hotter than heck, don't you think? Ooh, wave, mom's pulling out and she waved to us." My father lifted his hand and stopped for a second, offering a wave, then the two continued down the path. His hand held the string that ran between the posts, and Sara chatted amicably about a book she was reading. My father would nod, and I wondered if he was listening or lost in thought. I'd never been around a blind person, but his facial features seemed stoic, as if void of expression. The words poker face came to mind, and I wished that

148

I could have been around, to talk to him, and to share easy banter like Sara had done. As they turned the curve, I could see the bench and the water. The current was running fairly fast, so I knew they had rain, or it would have been calm.

"Oh Roger, are you coming out to play today? Roger, are you home?" Sara's sing-song voice was loud and high pitched, and I realized she was pre-warning him so that he'd vacate the premises. I saw his log-like body move from the bank. Slipping into the water with a splash, he headed out and away from the two. Sara smiled at Dad and patted him on the arm.

"Okay, he's gone for a swim, so it's safe now." Chino eyed the form that moved and I felt my heart race. I hoped he didn't think it was a stick and go plowing into the water after it. My father took a seat on the bench, and Sara bent down to gather some stones.

"So, how many do you think I can skip today? I'm up to five, but I really think I can manage six. Want to bet me a quarter? You're not dead yet, so I know you're good for it. Besides, I know where you hide the change. What do you say, Daddio? Go for six?" My father chuckled and glanced down as he nudged Chino with his foot. I felt myself smile at Sara's easy way of dishing out gallows humor, and I could tell she was comfortable enough with him to joke around like that.

"Well, what do you think, Chino? Do you think this little slip of a girl can skip it six times? Now, you tell me if she cheats, because I'm blind and I think what she really wants is a quarter. She's probably robbing me blind when I'm not looking. Get it, robbing me BLIND?" He burst into laughter and Sara turned to him, a wide grin etched across her face.

"You're a funny guy, Daddio, just for that I ought to make it seven." My heart stopped as I watched Roger turn and come back towards shore. Its speed increased as it plowed its way through the current. An enormous wave pushed in ahead of him as he jettisoned through the water towards the thin legs that stood on the bank. Sara turned back as the alligator's face rose from the murky depths, her eyes wide as she registered he was almost upon her.

* * *

I woke up beaded in sweat, my breath coming fast and furious. My eyes darted around the room as my hands hung in the air, ready to grab her. The glass bottle lay on the floor where I must have knocked it, and the candle was out. I closed my eyes, blinking at the images that raced across my mind, and I swallowed, then took a breath, trying to calm down. My heart was exploding from my chest and I felt the tears burgeoning from my depths.

"Sara, I need you, now!" I screamed out as my body trembled. I heard only my wavering voice echo in the stillness, and I bolted from the room, intent on summoning her to tell me what I needed to know. She was nowhere to be found, and I don't know if that was good or bad. I needed to see her, to know she was safe. As I flung open the door, I gazed out to the front yard, where a fresh sign stood, embedded in the red dirt. Shore Banks Realty and a sale pending sign sat, all shiny and new. Sylvester's grinning face sat in the lower left corner and I wanted to smash it to pieces, but the man himself was long gone.

Thirty

The only Thing that's Real

My brain was pivoting in twenty different directions and I took a deep breath and held it, unsure what I should do next. A door slamming caught my attention, and I walked out onto the porch to see Frank. His cellphone was in his hand and he walked to the end of the driveway and gestured, waving wildly. A second later, a large truck came lumbering down the road. Its screeching beeps triggered as it backed into his driveway. Frank moved out of the way and glanced at me, a wide smile across his face. A man and woman jumped out of the cab and they lifted the large cargo door. I headed over, figuring I'd clear my mind and try to be sociable. Frank grinned as his head nodded. He met me half-way.

"Lookie, the canoe and gear made it. Oh, and I took your advice and will do the ballroom dancing thing at least once. Do you want to take a maiden voyage out on the river, just a little ways out, of course. We'll keep land close by at all times, just in case." I shivered, the vision I'd just lived through as fresh as a newborn in my mind. I shook my head.

"Can't do it today, Frank, but we will get to it. If you go out with Jasper or something, just be careful, okay?" Frank nodded and eyed the two who unloaded the gear. They set everything down and Jasper came rushing out of the house a minute later, giddy and grinning from ear to ear. Frank smiled

151

and nudged me.

"They'll unload his go-cart last. It's all he's been talking about. It's a little noisy, but if it bothers you, let him know. You know he's going to be racing up and down the street, churning up a lot of dirt, too." I smiled.

"That's okay, he's got to have some fun, right?" Frank nodded, and I eyed Jasper as he badgered the movers to go faster. You could sense the excitement, and for a second, it got my mind off of my own problems. Frank turned to me and sniffed. His eyebrows drew together in concern.

"Are you okay, Jules? Is there something troubling you?" He lay his hand on my arm, and where normally I'd yank it away, I crumbled, the weight of the day crashing down on me. Frank drew me away from Jasper and gave my arm a squeeze.

"You just give me a minute to talk to the movers and I'm coming right over. I can smell the alcohol on your breath and even I know it's a little early in the day for drinking. That, and you look like you're ready to come unglued, and I know what that's like. Heck, some days I feel like I coined the phrase. Wait for me, and I'll be right there." I stood there, my eyes peering up at the clouds overhead, attempting to stave off the tears that hung on the edge of my eyes. Frank spoke to the movers, then Jasper, then grabbed my arm and hustled me to my place. "Let's go inside, it's cooler." I nodded and led him up the steps and into the house. Frank eyed the place but made no judgments. His house looked modernized, whereas mine was rustic. He took a seat at the table and I sat across from him and lay my head in my hands.

"My mother showed up and as you can see from the sign outside, she's selling this place. My dad hasn't even been declared officially dead and she's sweeping in like a buzzard on road kill and selling his home. Tell me she can't do that." I shook my head as I sobbed, and my hand reached for a beer that wasn't even there. Frank offered a kind smile and leaned back.

"How long have you been drinking, Jules? I see you shake, and I know the signs. I have them myself, and I'm finally going to do something about it. Drinking killed my boy, and I'm no better, doing the same thing. I had a long talk with Em last night and she's concerned. Maybe it's something we can do together. It sounds like you need someone who understands, and maybe

I'm not that person, but I know I could use help." I dropped my hands into my lap and clenched the loose material of my pants.

"A few years now, it's gotten worse over the last year, dealing with my mother, school, and then my dad disappearing. It helps, that and painting. I started painting again and for the first time in eons, I didn't want, or maybe need, a drink to do it. There was a lightness. Wanting to create something perfect set me on a tangent. I've never felt that way before. Em wants a painting, and I'm making her one. I need to get my life in order, but I don't know where to start." I looked him in the eyes and could see genuine concern written in them. It made me feel like I could talk to him about anything, but now with Sara and what I was finding out, I wasn't sure if he would believe me or think that I'd gone off the deep end. I inhaled deep and took the chance.

"Frank, I've been talking to Em about spirits, you know, kind of like ghostly things." I waited, trying to gauge his reaction. He merely nodded and gave a soft smile.

"I believe, Jules. Some people do, and some don't, but I've always believed there was something more after we die, or at least I like to think there is. When business is unfinished, maybe there's a portal that can sweep the spirit in, even if giving solace. I felt Frankie Jr. around me after he passed, and I was angry, so I drank. I used him as an excuse, and I'm realizing now that I used his death and booze like a crutch. There's never any reason to bury yourself in a bottle. Life has so much to offer, and though it doesn't always feel that way, new doors open, you just have to remain aware enough that you answer the call when it happens. I moved over a thousand miles away to escape what was eating at me, but it follows you. There is no running, and I guess the easiest way is to stand up and face that fear." I nodded as he spoke and he leaned back as he tapped his fingers on the table.

"Rhythm, Jules, life has a rhythm, and for some it's fast, for others, kind of slow, but you have to follow your own beat. Don't let anyone set the tempo for you. Your path is yours alone to walk, but you can have friends and people to support you. But you need to be brave and carry on, even if in the storm and feeling alone. You've got me and Em, and I like to think I have you. You can't change what will happen. Good, bad, or otherwise, things will happen. It's how you handle it that makes all the difference." His words touched something in me and I reached out my hand and took his in mine.

"I need your help, and you, Frank, thank you." I felt almost lighter by saying those words and I exhaled. "When I came, it was to come to grips with my dad being gone, though he'd always been gone, to me. Now, I've unearthed his journals, which I'm slowly reading, and there is a spirit who keeps showing up and then I'm seeing these crazy, yet true, visions. Some days I think I'm going crazy, other days, it's like an unfolding. I'm afraid for the day when it comes full circle, and I'm unsure what will happen." Frank listened and smiled, his head nodding in understanding. "Did you ever read a fantastic book and you milk it, not wanting the story to end? Well, that's what this is like. When it ends, I'll know the truth. I'm not ready yet, and now with Mom popping up and selling my father's home, it's rushing me to get to the conclusion. How do I follow my rhythm when someone else keeps upping the pace?" Frank closed his eyes for a moment, then smiled.

"You keep on doing what you're doing. It will all unfold how it's supposed to. Your mother's a bump in the road, or more like a jack-knifed semi, but you'll get through it, and I'm here. What can I do to help?" I hesitated for a second, then explained what had been happening with Sara and the visions. I didn't mention the latest river one, though, as I was still processing it. Frank pondered things, and he took a deep breath.

"What was wrong with your father? You haven't mentioned the cause, but you knew something was amiss. Maybe you need to keep reading? Get to something concrete. Then you'll know where his head was at when he wrote it? And if he's gone, then what happened to his dog?" I recalled asking Sara the same thing. "If he were still alive, would you need an excuse to drink?" Now that one stung a bit, and I pondered it.

"I drink because I'm angry, and my father said violence is bad, and I think thoughts of it would be just as bad…" Frank shrugged and gave a soft smile.

"Anger is a reason, but it's like a coin. There's always a flip side. Kindness, forgiveness, you know, those things. When we got here, I thought a light would flick on and with our new life, everything would be hunky dory, right?

Wrong! I ran away, and I'm drinking more than ever. That is still running away. I need to learn to be okay with Frankie Jr. being gone. He was on his path. We only had him for a few years of it and I think there's a lesson to be learned in each loss we encounter." I listened intently as he spoke and felt myself relaxing with each bit of wisdom he offered.

"Think about what your father being gone has to teach you? Do you think it was to get angry? Ha, listen to me, I know what you're going through, Jules, because I'm going through it, too. Meeting you offered me hope that there's more to this world than dwelling on something you can't change. I don't want to live the rest of my life angry. Frankie Jr. wouldn't be happy with that, and my family doesn't deserve that. Last night I went to an AA meeting." I must have looked shocked, but I kept silent.

"I didn't talk, and they didn't expect me to, which I would have run right out the door had they forced it. I looked at the surrounding faces, men and women from all walks of life. You know what we all had in common? Escape and fear. We were escaping and making excuses for careening down our individual paths of destruction. I don't want to run anymore, and I hope when you finish your story here, that you'll move on and learn something amazing from it. You have a whole life ahead of you, and you need to be your own man and do what the big man intended." I nodded, listening to his words of wisdom. What he said next made me grin. "Em said your art is amazing, and I love my little girl and believe what she says. There is so much hope for your future, Jules, don't take it lightly, and believe in yourself."

I felt the tears stream from my eyes, and I nodded as he patted my hand. He was right, and Sara's words filtered through my thoughts. You can't be drunk and understand. To see things clearly, I had to let the crutch go and live these moments with a sober mind. I smiled at Frank as I wiped my eyes.

"Don't tell Em you saw me cry. How will she ever like a cry-baby?" Frank chuckled and looked at me kindly.

"I won't tell a soul, but it's okay to cry, Jules. Everybody hurts, and everybody cries. It's a fact of life, so don't sweat it, all right?" I nodded and stood, feeling stronger about the whole thing now that someone else knew what I was dealing with. It buoyed me, and I needed to continue reading more. Time was of the essence, and I couldn't hide in fear any longer. I smiled at him and nodded.

"Thanks, Frank. I appreciate your support more than you'll know, and you're right. I've got some more reading to do, and I can't cross the bridge until I get to it." Offering him a smile, he gathered me in his arms and gave me a hug. I hugged him back hard, wishing it were my father, but using him as a substitute in the meantime.

"I'll let you get to business, Jules. Don't forget, if you need to vent, or even cry, I'll be right next door. Just give me a holler, and I'll be there." I nodded, feeling lighter somehow as we walked to the door.

"Same here, Frank, if Wanda gets on your nerves, head on over. I'm sorry about Frankie Jr., and I feel he's proud of you for waking up and moving forward. I'm in your corner, too." Frank wiped a tear from his eye, patted me on the arm, then headed home. I closed the door and took a deep breath, ready to tackle some more of my father's last words.

Thirty-One

And I Thought I Heard you Speak

S ara remained missing in action, and I pulled the beer boxes from the fridge and set them on the counter. I opened every bottle and, with a sigh, dumped each one down the sink until they were empty. My mouth salivating as the aroma of barley and hops reached my nose. Shaking off the thirst for one, I set the cases out on the porch. Next garbage day, they'd be history. "It's now or never, so, reading time, Jules." My hands shook, but I moved to the bedroom and grabbed the next journal, then flipped through the pages. This one only had a few pages written in it and I grabbed the other two and found them to be empty, as if he'd run out of time. There wasn't much left to delve into, and my heart felt heavy. "Okay, Daddio, give me your best shot." I said a silent prayer for strength, and dove in.

Chino has been a godsend and I will be eternally thankful for the time I've spent with him. I can't return him after my ultimate day comes, and have asked Brett and his family to take him on. They were quite receptive to the idea, though Brett keeps asking me to keep the faith. "Miracles happen" has become his mantra for me, and I know they do, but I'm sure in my case, it will not happen. I'm getting to be okay with it.

I've now lost pretty much all of my sight and sleep most of my time. Sara swings by and writes for me. If she adds any embellishments, I think by now you'd know which are my words and which might be hers. She plays my albums for me, and she's alphabetized them by artist, which is something I've never done, and we are going through each one. It makes me happy to teach her new tunes, and she's quite the knowledgeable expert now on a lot, even teaching me some new things that she pulls up on her fancy iTouch. It's incredible the things they can do now, and she told me there's a speech to text thing, but at this stage, it would be pointless. I'm not buying a computer. I've set some money aside, and it will go to my kids when I'm gone. Jules must be almost eighteen, and Keira isn't of age yet, but I've had a new will drawn up and it pains me to say it, but I'm leaving the homestead to him. He loved it here, and I know he won't sell it. Heck, he may even hate me, but it's the last gift I can give him. They can split the money between them. It's not much, but it's something.

My tumor has grown larger and I have very little time left. Most days, I don't have the energy to get out of bed, and that's another thing I have to thank Sara for. If she weren't here, I'd have starved and slept like a dead Rip Van Winkle or something. She'd never heard of Rip, so she says she's going to go look him up. I loved fairy tales as a kid. My mother condoned it for a little while, then said I needed to be a man and grow up. I had Sara get a book from the library, Hans Christian Andersen fairy tales, and she read them to me. It feels nice to be a kid again and believe. Some can get dark, but it's kind of how life is. It can't always be a bowl of cherries... That was my mother's favorite book. Erma someone wrote it and I remember how she'd laugh and shake her head. I miss my mother's laugh, and I miss what could have been. I hope when and if they let me into the pearly gates, she will be there, an improved soul from what she'd been. Time will tell.

Some days I wonder if it will be my last, and I'm sorry my writings of late have become morose and melodramatic. Perhaps my "I don't care" will show through, because though dying, oh boy, now I've gone and said the 'd' word, I can only do what I can do, warts and all. I only pray that Simone isn't the one to find these journals, as I'm sure there would be one mighty bonfire as she celebrated. I can't fix us, and it's too late to try. But if I leave off with anything I'm adamant about, it's that I love my kids. Julien and Keira are my flesh and blood legacy, and with my last words, I will say as much, even if they're not around to hear it.

I'm getting tired and we're going to knock off for the night. See you next time. I sound like a soap opera now. (He's laughing at that)

I realized Sara must have added that in, and I thought it a pleasant touch, because I could see him dictating to her and giggling. He always had a good sense of humor and I was glad that even towards the end, he never lost that gift. My heart felt heavy, and I blinked my eyes as Sara materialized in the doorway.

"You're almost there, Jules. Keep reading and I'll be back to fill in the blanks." She disappeared as fast as she came as my mouth opened with a response.

"There are no more pages." I remembered the stacks of letters. I'd buzzed through most of them, but still had a few to go. Sorting through, there was one for Keira and the rest were for me. I grabbed the next one and settled back on the bed.

Dear Jules, heart of my heart,

Your world's already tossed around like a ball and I hate to do it more, but I've no choice. My doctors finally reached a consensus, and it seems I have a brain tumor. That's what all the headaches were about. It's called Glioblastoma and because I waited so long to get looked at, there's not much they can do. They talked about surgery, radiation, etc... But the prognosis isn't good. I weighed my options, and though it hurts, I see no solution to allow me to live a life without a lot of harmful side-effects, and I'll still most likely die, anyway. So, I've declined treatment. Now, I live out my days here, have Sara write my letters and in my journals, and though you may never even see these, it's my hope that someday you'll grow curious and come here and find them. I hide them away just in case... I'd hate for your mother to be the one to find them. Sara tucks everything in my hiding hole, and if you ever come and she see's you, she knows to show you where to find them. I made her promise and I trust that she'll do as I've asked.

What can I say? I've shed so many tears and words that I hope maybe they give you a little solace, knowing I wanted things to be different. Time is flying by, and I'm happy each day I wake, though the pain is unbearable sometimes. They've given me some medication to take the edge off, but I feel as if my head is going to explode and I have a hard time staying awake. Maybe our life could have been different, but I'm glad you're not here to see what's happening to me. Your mother never could have handled it, but I have a feeling that you're more like me and stronger than that. You will grow to be wise and fearless, Jules. I pray these find you while you're young and not gray like your old man, and this way, you can go next door and meet Chino, if he's still doddering around. He's a good boy, he is. I hope he brings Brett, Jill, Sara, and Lily as much joy as he's brought to my life. Although he's turned into a bed hog. I don't think guide dogs are supposed to sleep in the bed. Probably why he flunked superhero dog class. Regardless, I am blessed to have him. I just hope he isn't too sad when I leave, as he's gotten spoiled. Sara knows his routine though, so she'll keep him well fed with Milk Bones. Listen to me ramble, will ya? I should probably go, but I have found bursts of energy when I talk to you through these letters. I only wish you could read them, too, and feel the jolt they give me. It's like when you were a boy and we sat out at the river, just the two of us. Those memories get me through the days when I want to say enough is enough.

Hold tight to me in your heart, if you're able, and know that I loved you to the very depths of my soul. I'd cry if I could, but my eyes no longer shed tears. Know that when I'm gone, that I never forgot you, and that I never will. So, I guess I'll see you in the stars, my boy, and you may catch me drifting about on the Milky Way, not the candy bar, ha ha, but I'll see you again. I have faith.

Love you forever and always,

Dad

I swiped at the copious amounts of tears that were falling and moved to the next letter, which was the last one. I really wanted a beer, but I shook it off, and with trembling hands, pried open the seal on the last of his words.

Thirty-Two

To the Childhood I Lost

Hello Julien, this is Sara,

Your dad is doing pretty badly and has been delirious for the last day. The doctors came and gave him something, and he has lucid moments, but not enough to dictate a letter. He goes through the motions, and sometimes gets up and I can get him to eat something, but I feel it's going to be time for him to leave, and soon. I don't know if you remember me, but when you were here, you were always picking on me as I played with my dolls in the backyard. You called me Sara Beara, Care Bear, and other amusing things. You were always nice to me, and your dad doesn't know I'm writing this, but I wanted to tell you some things, in case you didn't believe him.

He loves you more than life itself. My father loves me, too, but to hear the way your dad speaks about you, well, it makes me almost jealous. He glows, and he gets a tormented look in his eyes. Unashamed, he calls out for you when he sleeps and gets cloudy-headed. That man is a wonderful soul, and I hope if you're able to forgive him, that it will make you happy to know how he felt. Love like that is scarce, and I won't tell you how to feel, but you should be honored. That's just my two cents about it, so take it as you will. He's the type of man who rarely, if ever, speaks unkindly about anyone, and I strive to be like him. Helping him has already encouraged me to learn braille, and I know when I grow up, I want to be

161

someone who works with the blind or maybe the terminally ill. I know, hard to believe for a teenager, and heaven knows I may change my mind in time, but my family is supportive. I hope that whatever you're doing makes your heart happy. Happy hearts are cool! Well, I just wanted you to know that we're doing what we can to keep him comfortable, and that he loves you so much.

Bye,

Sara (Care Bear... ha ha)

It was almost a letdown as I was longing for my father's words, but I understood she was trying to bridge the divide the only way she knew how. "Thank you Sara, for that, and for everything." She was still MIA and I set the papers aside. My fingers were twitching, and I knew I'd set them loose with some paint to take the edge off my mood. I gathered my supplies from Keira's room and decided that I would just paint right there. I pulled over the bookshelf to set my palette and paints on, and it surprised me to see there were no jars left. Shrugging, I chose not to worry about it and eyed the work in progress. "Music, get some music, Jules." I heard my father's voice in my mind and smiled, then slipped into the living room to choose. Eyeing the selection, it drew my eyes to Sgt. Pepper's Lonely Hearts Club Band. I set the needle down on Strawberry Fields Forever, not yet ready to tackle A Day in the Life. The music filled the room, and I headed back to paint.

My mind drifted off as I squeezed the colors, blending them together to create the desired shade, which remained undecided. Lost in thoughts about the words I read, I let my hands do what they needed to, swirling the paints into life. I smiled when I eyed the soft curves from the jasmine, and I embellished them with a highlight, coaching them to stand out and be noticed. Hours passed, and I yawned at one point. Content in this melancholic mood, my eyes watched as the scene sprung to life. A high, full moon in pale pinkish-blue took shape, and I wondered what time of year it was and what its name would have been. Two figures stood on the edge of what I now knew was rippling water, and taking a step back, I realized it was my father and I, though I wasn't a child, but a man. There were no features, just the silhouettes, as being witnessed by someone watching them. I wondered if it was Sara, putting this in my mind as my hands brushed stroke after stroke. The music kept repeating, but it had become background noise and I gave it no thought.

"I told you it would be beautiful. He would have loved it. Good job, Jules." I glanced over and noticed Sara leaning on the doorjamb, watching me as I went through the motions in a haze. Nodding, I continued, not ready to answer.

"You'll find the answers you're looking for. Turn every leaf and you'll see." I half-heard her, lost in thought, and I smiled as I added mysterious swirls around the two men. My hands felt like they were in a frenzy, and I couldn't stop.

"I've got to finish this, but it needs more." Sara shook her head.

"It'll feel complete when you want it to. That's how it works, right? Like I told you when you first got here, love shouldn't tear apart, it should heal. You won't forget him, especially knowing how he felt, but you've got to decide who and what you'll allow in your life. Trust in what your gut tells you, and though it may hurt, let the rest go. Your dad taught me that one, and he's right. But in the meantime, keep seeking and you'll find. I made a promise, and I've done pretty good at keeping it. There's more to the story, but you need to be ready. Are you?" I turned to look, and she disappeared, and honestly, I didn't know the answer.

I rinsed my brush off and eyed the color tubes, then began blending more shades. I added water to lessen the thickness, and though I'd never done it before, flicked some paint at the canvas. The effect made stars, and not caring if any landed on the moon or not, I filled that blueness with dots of light. My heart was racing, and I shook my head.

"This feels odd, but in a good way. Yep, I can deal with it. I hope you like it, Em, because I don't know if I'll ever paint another like it." It was a polar opposite of anything I'd ever created, and it shocked me in a good way. There was a lightness and depth to it my other paintings lacked, and I was pleased. My brain felt drained, and dunking the brush in the water, I knew I should stop while ahead. I closed the door and went back to the bedroom. A jar now sat in my reading spot and I glanced around, searching for Sara. I wasn't ready to see what happened at the river, and I went to the closet in search of the remaining paperwork housed there. I pulled out the file marked research, and pushed the thoughts of the jar away, then began peering through the pages. Most were articles on Glioblastoma and I didn't have the heart to read them to conclusion. There was a deed for the house and a will from some woman named Susan leaving the house to my father. Not wanting to waste time with legalese, I set it aside, too. There was a letter from my mother, and my hand shook as I pried that from the stack. I was eager to see what she had to say, and that one, I read. The date was from two years ago and I figured it must be good, because as far as I knew, she had had no dealings with him since the divorce.

Damien,

You've got to stop this. The kids want nothing to do with you and it pains me to say this, but you brought it on yourself. You had so many chances to come home and live a normal life, but for whatever reason, you chose a life of solitude in the sticks chasing non-existent ghosts. Whatever! I have moved on with my life, as have Jules and Keira, and they're better off without you. They don't speak your name or even think of you. Forget about them, as they may as well be dead to you, and I don't blame them. You may think of me as a harsh shrew, but I'm far from it. All these years, I protected them from your craziness and visions. There is no such thing as magic, just like there's no such thing as werewolves and witches that ride brooms. I hope your delusions aren't some kind of genetic defect, as now I'll have to spend the rest of my life peering over their proverbial shoulders, searching for a sign of your sick madness.

Back off, that's all I have to say. You're ten shades of nuts and I'm glad you live so far from here, because having you locked up in the loony-bin would be foremost in my mind.

I hope I've been clear, and if not, go see a shrink and tell them of the things you see and the phantoms you talk to... See how far that will get you. I'm done with you! Rot in hell.

S

The vehemence shocked me, and my heart broke, imagining my father reading these words. As something burst in me, I knew I'd never be able to forgive her for this nasty abuse my father suffered at her hands. After growing up the way he did, she may not have hit him, but this was just as bad. I felt my hands clench in the fit of rage and forced myself to sit and breathe as the need for a drink spiraled through me.

"Don't do it, Jules, be strong and believe in yourself. You've got this, just believe!" My father's words filtered through my mind and I wondered if maybe my mother's words held some truth. Did a mental illness run in the family, or was it even possible for that to happen? I wanted to rip her words to shreds, but chose instead to fold the letter back up and shove it in the envelope. A day of reckoning would happen with her, and I knew it was probably better to hang on to the evidence. Revenge wasn't on my plate, but a soft, flowing empathy moved through me for my father. Returning to his closet, I eyed the shoes and the cubbyhole, wondering if there was anything left. Not ready to let this chapter end, I brushed away the tears that fell and leaned back on my haunches. As I glanced up, I noticed a picture hung towards the back, set behind my father's shirts and his fall jacket he never needed after moving here. The blue tartan plaid wool coat was a gift from my mother.

"You should have burned this, Dad. It's obvious she didn't care." I moved the jacket aside, releasing a cloud of dust in the air, and I eyed the painting on the wall behind it. It was one I'd done as a boy, when he had bought me a set of cheap paints from the drugstore. I remember painting it, but had forgotten all about it. My work was juvenile. The image was of a swing set on the playground. A small boy sat on the swing and a man stood behind him in the position of readying to push the child. We were both smiling, and it looked more stick figure-like than anything, and I chuckled.

"I like to think I've improved some since then, heck, I know I have." He had it framed and matted, and I grasped the edges and pulled it off the hooks that suspended it. It shocked me to find another hidden compartment behind it, and my eyes widened in disbelief.

Thirty-Three

It's Time to Leave the Capsule

A knocking on the door brought me out of my stupor, and I set the picture down in the closet and closed it, then latched the bedroom door behind me. Em stood on the porch, her neon-yellow sundress as bright as the day. A tentative smile crossed her face, and she stepped towards me. Then she frowned as she reached out a finger and wiped at a tear I must have missed.

"Are you okay, Jules? I just got this really weird vibe that you needed me, and a cool mist moved through my room. I'm here for you. What's happened?" I opened the door wider and invited her in. She closed it behind her and as she turned, I wrapped my arms around her.

"I hate my mother. There, I said it, and I'm not sorry. I've been going through some more of my dad's stuff, and she wrote him a letter a couple of years ago. The hateful things she said. Heck, I have no words for how I'm feeling after that. She's the reason he didn't come, and she threatened him. I'll never forgive her for this." Em held me tight and I could feel the anger dissipate a little, and I knew I didn't want to release her and lose the feeling.

"How can someone hate another so much that they tear their kid's lives apart because of it? It's not fair." Em released me and I felt the tears falling again. She leaned in and kissed me softly, and I realized that this was what

I needed. I returned the kiss and crushed her to me, tasting the essence of peppermint on her tongue as I explored the soft sweetness of her mouth. This was heaven, and there was no place that I wanted to be than right there, holding her. She moved her mouth from mine and kissed my jaw, then worked her way down my neck until she reached the edge of my shirt. Leaning my head back, I closed my eyes and allowed her to piece me back together with her touch. Her hands lay on my chest, and I felt myself drifting into bliss as she moved them higher, then ran them through my hair. I shook my head, lost in the moment, yet very aware of this beautiful girl who cared. Stepping away a minute later, I looked at her and smiled.

"I have so many things I could say, Em, but it would pale compared to how you make me feel. I have enough respect for you to stop, but my head is in a place right now that I need to clear up. Don't get me wrong, I'd love to keep this up, but I need to be whole before I can take this farther." Em grinned and shook her head as her fingers stroked the stubble on my face.

"You do what you need to do, Jules. I'm not going anywhere, and I have no problem waiting for the day that you're ready. Besides, it'll be better for us then, I agree. Don't be mad if you have to cut your mother out of your life to heal. This is your life, and it's yours to do what you want with. She was the portal to get you here, and it took two, but you're grown now. If something doesn't sit well within your heart, it's okay to set it free. Blood makes you related, not family, remember? Set your boundaries and stick to them. Don't let anyone cross the line, or you'll hate yourself for it. She's lost your trust, and you need to do what's right for you." I knew what she said held merit, and it made me feel strong enough to carry through.

"I owe her a lot of money for school, though. If I leave, she's going to come after me for it." My head hung as I thought of my future, or lack thereof. "There's no way she's going to allow me to live here and start a new life. He says he has a will and left the place to me, but I haven't found it. Time's running out, and honestly, I really want a drink. That's a whole other issue, but I'm dealing with it as best as I can." I watched as the tears welled up in her eyes and she nodded.

"Frank told me about talking to you. I went to the AA meeting with him

167

and I have to thank you for that, too. Something he sees in you triggered his senses, and I'm going to be eternally thankful if he sticks with it. I love my father more than life itself. He's always stood by me and has done what he can to give me and Jasper a good life. It's kind of serendipitous with you coming here, and us picking the house next door. Magic is at play, Jules, and I feel it coursing through. If you could do anything in the world, what would you do?" I grabbed her hand and led her to the table. My legs were shaking, and I needed to sit. I motioned to the chair on the end and she sat, while I shifted my chair to be beside her.

"I want to paint, and to teach kids how to paint. Or own a gallery someday when I sell some paintings. I don't need to be famous and be the talk of the town. I only want a simple life where I can be here in nature and let inspiration take me where it will. But first, I want to find out what happened to my father. I don't think I'll ever be at peace until I know the truth." Em squeezed my hand, and I held it tight as I told her about the vision I'd had about Sara and my father at the river. By the time I finished, she was holding back tears, her mouth opened slightly in shock.

"It was over a year ago, right? If he was in the river, there wouldn't be much left of him. What does your friend Sara say?" I shook my head.

"She hasn't revealed it all yet, though she left me a jar. I'm terrified of knowing, of seeing it, if that's what she's going to show me." Em fidgeted in her chair and shook her head.

"What if I sit with you while you go through it? Would that help you any? I know it would scare me to death to see that, but if I'm here with you, maybe you'll sense me and know that you're not alone?" I thought about the words she said and could see that it might help, but would I be able to handle it without a drink? That was the million dollar question.

"I'm afraid that I'd want to get hammered and forget all about it. How can you 'unsee' something like that? It's traumatic, and I knew a guy who served over in Afghanistan. He's still having mental issues dealing with it. What if that happens to me? I can't talk to my mom about it. Heck, I'm never talking to her again if I can help it. I'm scared, Em." She thought about it and I saw a light smile cross her face.

"Would you allow me to tell Frank about what's going on? I've said nothing, just that you might need to be encouraged over the drinking thing. He may have more answers than I do, as he's kind of out of the loop of the whole thing. It may give him focus other than himself, too. He's always been there for me, and I know he'd be there for you." I thought about what she said and sighed. Having nothing to lose, I hoped I would find solace with company for this insanity. I nodded, and she grinned.

"I'm going to go home and take him for a walk. That way Wanda and Jasper don't overhear. That woman's got ears like jugs when she thinks something's up." I chuckled, imagining Wanda with huge ears, listening in like a neighborhood gossip, waiting for new tidbits of information to spread. "I'll be back in a little while, so hang tight in the meantime, okay? We will get through this together, I promise." I stood when she did, and walked her to the door, where she turned and held me tight, then planted another kiss on my lips. "We will be okay, Jules."

I watched her walk down the porch and closed the door. My hands were trembling, and I prayed for the first time in forever that I'd have some solace. If Frank would buoy me as I stepped through the next doors of this journey to finding truth, maybe I'd be okay. My feet carried me into the living room, and I tucked the Beatles album back into its sheath as I eyed the other albums. Moonlight Sonata was calling to me and I put that on the turntable and dropped the needle. I didn't notice the small green bottle sitting on the air conditioner unopened. I slid into the chair and leaning back, closed my eyes, allowing the melody to calm my nerves and mood, then I waited for Em to return. Another vision found me, and I relaxed as I let it play out.

* * *

"When are you coming home, Dad?" I sat beside him on the bench and watched as his shoulders slumped, and he turned and caught my eyes. He sat up straighter and gave me a tired grin.

"I'm not, Jules. This is my home now, and I know it hurts you, but it has to be this way." Large tears fell from my eyes and he wrapped his arms around me, but I was angry and pulled away, then jumped to my feet.

"You don't love me anymore. That's why you won't come home. Mom says that we won't come back here again. She say's that you don't love us." I was ten and my heart was breaking. His face looked pained at what I said, but I was afraid that she was right. I loved him, but he didn't love me. My father shook his head and stared up at the stars. A look of peace ran across his face, which confused me further. She was right.

"Look up at the stars with me for a moment." I wondered why he wanted me to stare at stupid stars when all I wanted was an answer. Even at ten, I felt a divide that split us and didn't know how to get us back to good. I began crying, but did as he asked.

"We are all stardust, Jules, every one of us. We can never be apart, and when you look at the stars, you realize how tiny we all are. Like little ants, we move here and there, going about our business. But we are specks in this world, and like the stars, we are infinite, just like love is infinite. I will never stop loving you. When people are in pain, they say things to make themselves feel better. You can't stop loving them just because they may be wrong, but you can distance yourself like the stars are way up there. We know they're there even when the sun is out and you can't see them, but they never leave us. Until the day I die, you are my stars, Jules, and I will be with you every time I see them. She can do and say a lot of things, but that's one thing she can't cancel out. You and me are a pair, my boy, and nothing will change that." I watched him as his head slowly nodded, and I could tell he was sad, but he had lost the fight. He opened his arms, and I fell into them, sobbing through the pain, holding on as if I'd never let go.

"Just don't you forget about me, okay? I will give her time to heal her heart, but I will see you again. You are my son, and I'll love you forever and ever. Love is magical and you can't banish the magic. It's not possible. But, it may go easier if you don't ask her about me, because she's like that old bee's nest we knocked out of the tree in the backyard. Remember how those things flew out, angry and bitter? Well, that's kind of how she's feeling right now, so don't stir the hornet's nest. After a while, it will calm down, and life will move on. We'll get together again like today, but better." I inhaled the scent

170

of his neck, woodsy and calming, and I believed what he said. He set me aside and nodded, then tousled my hair.

"Time to get heading out before the hornet buzzes. Believe, Jules, always believe." We began walking down the path towards the house and I reached out and took his hand. I knew enough as I sat there to cherish this moment. So, why I had blocked it from my mind? To touch him now, and feel his strong fingers wrapped around mine, stirred calmness and love through me I'd hidden away.

My tears fell as I shook my head and woke from the vision. "I'm ready now, Dad, and I will see you again."

Thirty-Four

Standing on the Edge

I never saw the jar until I woke from the vision, but I cradled it in my hands and thanked it for the gifts it had given me. For the first time, I could actually feel a part of my father enter my soul, and I think it's because I was willing and open to it. Strengthened by the memory reborn in me, I stood and gazed at the surrounding walls. I could imagine painting the room a different color and having my paintings hung around the room, a small area rug lay down over the wooden floors, and a brightness to what, in my mind, would be my home. "Where did you leave your will, Dad?" My heart raced and the space behind my childhood drawing flashed into my mind.

"Yes! That's got to be it…" I rushed into the bedroom and opened the closet door, and pushed aside his jacket. The material felt warm beneath my fingers and I pulled it off the hanger and crushed it to my face, inhaling the scent, which remained strong, even after all the time that had passed. "I love you, Dad, and I'll make you proud. I will follow my dream, because I know you'll be here, somewhere, supporting me. Help me, please, and I will see that she doesn't lay a hand on your home, my home." I bristled when I thought about my mother, but I would deal with her when the time came. First, I had to find the will. There was a deep hole in the wall and I saw nothing at first. I wondered if he hung it there just to keep mice from coming in from below the house, and for a second, my hopes plummeted.

"It's got to be here, I feel it. Believe, Jules, he told you to believe." I reached my hand into the wall and moved my fingers from side to side, praying there'd be no cobwebs or rodent nests in there. Moving closer to the back wall, I moved my arm deeper in and downward, then finally connected with a metal box. It must have been sitting on a shelf, but I could feel the handle. Grabbing it, I heard a knock on the door. "Must be Em and Frank." I hefted the box up, which was heavy, and eyed it. It resembled a metal fishing tackle box, but I knew my father wasn't into fishing. Eager to open it, I heard the knock again, and grumbled beneath my breath. "Coming," I yelled, and I set the box on his dresser and headed to see who was here.

Em and Frank stood on the porch, their faces etched with concern, and I smiled. "So, I guess you know what's happening now? Good, Em, I had another vision given to me and it was what I needed." She moved forward and gave me a hug as Frank smiled.

"Anything we can do to help, we'll do it. You're not alone, Jules, and I'm honored that you trusted in me enough to allow me to join you in this. I know you'd do the same if our roles were reversed. What can I do?" I released Em and ushered him in, then shut the door behind me.

"There's one jar Sara left for me, and the vision of the river was a doozy. I'm afraid this is the continuation of that. If Roger ate either of them, I'm going to freak out. I know they found Sara on the riverbank, but they didn't find my dad. I'm afraid of what I'm going to see." Frank eyed me, looking confused.

"Who's Roger?" I told him about my meet-up with Sara at the river, reminding him of why we had to be careful canoeing there. He nodded, a look of consternation on his face. "Okay, then. I'm as ready as you are." He looked nervous. "You ready, sport?" I exhaled and nodded.

"As ready as anyone could ever be. I've got to get this wrapped up. I found a box earlier but haven't checked it out yet. That project I can do alone, but I need to open the jar and see what she has for me. Let's go to the bedroom, because she said to open it there." Frank nodded, and he and Em followed me in. I glanced back and eyed them, and they looked as determined as I was, which gave me hope. Em doubled back and grabbed some chairs and I sat down on the bed and grasped the jar in my hand.

"I'm not sure if you'll be able to see it too, but they don't normally take a long time. At least they haven't. Hang tight and let's see what happens." They looked at each other and Frank took Em's hand, and she rested her other on my knee. I could feel her grip and I felt so thankful for the two of them for doing this. "Okay, let's get this party started." My hand trembled as I slowly twisted the cap off, then I lay back on the bed.

* * *

We were at the river again, and as I feared, it was the ending to the story of what happened that day. Sara stood on the bank as my father sat on the bench, Chino laying beside him. Roger meandered a few feet from shore and I watched as Chino jumped to his feet. A growl deep in his throat turned to a hysterical bark a second later. Sara was smiling, then concern crossed her face as she turned to see Roger moving in closer. She looked at Chino, her eyes filled with a sudden fear and she reached for the dog, as if hoping to save him. Roger moved in fast, and as his body rose onto the bank, his snout rammed Sara's legs. Her body tumbled backwards as her voice shrieked out, "Damien, get Chino. Gato…" Her words cut out as she landed half on Roger and half in the water. Roger pivoted around, searching for his prey. I watched helplessly as Sara emerged a few feet from shore, her legs kicking as she shouted. Her body went down once, but she came up a minute later, this time a few feet farther from shore. I watched as my father listened, and he patted Chino on his neck.

"You be a good boy and stay. I'll be back." Chino whimpered but did as asked. My father listened again as Sara's voice gasped for help. He dove into the water, moving towards her voice and I could feel my fists clenching, wishing to be in his place, needing to save Sara. He swam out towards her voice, and with no sign of Roger, I felt myself relax a little. Reaching out for her, his hand finally connected with hers and they began making their way towards shore. Sara hit land first, and my father pushed her from behind, as Chino ran to her, sniffing her and licking at her face. She lay there, exhausted, and I felt a small sense of relief. A second later, my stomach clenched in fear. Roger had surfaced again, then went under. I hated that alligator, and I watched, helplessly, as it pulled my father backwards, deeper into the water. I waited, expecting to see some sort of thrashing, like a Tarzan movie where he battled the fierce gators, but I saw nothing.

I could feel myself crying, and then felt a squeeze on my knee. Not ready to leave the vision, I continued to watch, praying for my father to surface again. Chino paced the bank and then returned to Sara's side. She wasn't moving. The dog lay down by her side, protecting her from Roger should he return. "Dad, where are you? Dad, I'm here, please…"

* * *

My shouting must have startled me from the vision, because I came to, shaking like a leaf with my face saturated in tears. Frank was crying and Em looked like she'd break in two if a wind hit her.

"Please tell me you didn't have to see that, too?" They both slowly nodded, and I realized that by touching me, they were privy to the entire scene.

"Gosh, Jules, I am so sorry. For you to be having to go through this, I don't think I'd be as strong as you. Ugh… Your father was a courageous man. To go in there without having sight and save Sara. She lived, right?"Frank asked, his voice, quiet. Sadly, I shook my head, and he looked at Em, then pulled her close to his side. "I'm forbidding you to go to the river, young lady. I would die if anything were to happen to you." Em began crying, and hugged him tight.

"I'm a big girl, dad, and I'll be okay. Don't worry." I watched the two of them and wished more than anything that I had my father here with me.

"So, I guess that answers the question of where my father went to. Em found out through an article that Sara died. She must have inhaled water when she first went under. Chino must have lived, too, because he alerted Sara's dad. That's how they found her. The sleep of death on the Peace River, and my dad missing and presumed dead. At least I know, not that it makes it any easier." Frank stood and reached out his hand and took mine in his.

"You are a stand-up guy, Jules. My heart is still having palpitations, and I know you're probably wishing you had a drink right about now, right?" I listened to his words, though I hadn't even given a drink a thought. Shaking my head, I looked at him, seeing the worry.

"No, I need to stop that. I've got a future ahead of me, and a young lady that I care a lot about, considering. How about you? Are you craving one?" Frank shook his head.

"Yeah, I kind of am, but I won't do it. I think I'm going to see if they have a meeting tonight, though. I may need to stop in and actually take part this time. Would you care to join me?" I nodded emphatically, not knowing what I'd be in for, but realizing it had to be easier than what I had just been through.

"I'd like that a lot, Frank. I'd be happy to go with you." Frank smiled, then gazed at Em.

"Well, I'm going to leave you two kids alone. Got some things I've got to work on at home, and Jules?" He said, as he turned to me, "Forget canoeing out back. I've lost interest in doing that until it gets cold and those things are sleeping." I wasn't sure when their sleeping time was, but I agreed wholeheartedly.

"Sure, I feel ya, and I'll stop by. Just let me know what time, okay?" Frank gave Em a quick kiss on the cheek and me a wave.

"Catch you kids later." He walked out and Em sat down on the bed beside me.

"Are you going to be all right? I can stay if you want me to, just say the word." I shook my head, then leaned over and kissed her.

"Man, I can't believe you guys held on to me through that. Part of me kind of expected it, but to see it, like I said, it's something I can't unsee now. I hope he went fast and didn't suffer." Em held me tight and sniffled.

"He was dying anyway, and maybe he was okay with doing this one last heroic act. When people get near the end, the idea of fading into nothingness and pain is daunting. Maybe to him this was his ultimate gesture of saving someone else. He was willing to die to help her, and that alone tells you what kind of man your father was. I'd be proud, and with what I've seen, being around you, you are a lot like him. You are an incredible guy, a talented artist, and I can just feel it, that you're going to be triumphant in anything you set your mind out to do." I had had no one say anything like that about me and I blushed.

"Um… Thanks, I guess, if you say so. I hope I can make him proud, but first I have to save this place. If his will is in that box, my mother can't touch this house. The will she has was from when they were married. That was ages ago, so a new will can void that one out. I just hope she doesn't battle me in court because I have no money to battle her with, plus I owe her. What if she comes after me for the college money and wants this house? I'd die before I let her sell it to developers." My hands were trembling. Every time I thought about her, it set me on edge, and the thought of a beer cropped into my mind. I shook it off and took a deep breath, then kissed Em. Releasing her a second later, I felt settled and smiled at her.

"You do something to me that no one else has ever managed. When I'm with you I feel this overwhelming sense of peace." Em blushed, and I stammered. "I mean, I don't know how you feel, but, I'm just saying." She grinned and touched my cheek, then ran her finger across my lips.

"I want to know more of you, Jules. We can take it slow, but I feel the same way as you. Frank doesn't have a problem with us hanging together, but I can't get too involved if you're going to be leaving me. I couldn't handle that, and I want to invest the time in us, if you're into that. What are you going to do now? That's why you came, right? To find out the truth? You've got that, so now what?" I leaned back and ran my hand through my hair, and turning, I eyed the box on the dresser.

"I'm going to think positively that his will is in that box, and I am going to claim this as home, and my mother can rot. How's that?" Em smiled and nodded.

"So, are you going to open it and see, or just sit there and bask in your positivity?" She giggled, and I joined her.

"You're right, let's look, okay?"

Thirty-Five

They will Vanish Away

I slid off the bed and moved to the dresser. My eyes took in the coat that had fallen from my hands and I stopped to pick it up and re-hang it. The coat still felt warm to my touch, and I set aside the feeling to hug it again, embarrassed that Em would see my need for closeness to a piece of my dad. Draping it over my arm, I held it towards her.

"This was my father's coat. I'm sure he had little cause to wear it here, but it still smells like him." Her fingers stroked the soft, worn wool and a smile rose as she pulled it close and inhaled.

"It smells like you, so you must smell like your dad." I shrugged, then on a whim, tried it on. Her eyes widened, and she glanced behind her at the pictures on the wall. There was one of him and he was holding me while in the coat. I must have been around seven, and my grin stretched from ear to ear. She pointed to it.

"He's wearing it in that one. Turn around and look at yourself, Jules." I swiveled around and checked myself out in the mirror over the dresser, then glanced back at the image.

"I look like him, don't I? I never noticed before, but I guess with the haircut and going the natural color route, it's turned me into my dad." Shock filled me, but it was a joyous thing. Em stood and came up behind me and wrapped her arms around my waist.

"You look like him, and I think you're very handsome. Do people still use that? Handsome? Well, regardless, I'm glad because it means a part of him will always be a part of you, so that should offer you some solace." I relished being in her embrace, and we stared at each other. I slid the coat off and took one last sniff before hanging it in the closet, then picked up the box and brought it over to the bed.

"Well, my dear Em, here goes nothing." I unlatched the two hinges and closed my eyes as I raised the lid. Hearing Em gasp, they flew open, and I expected to see a nest of spiders come tearing out of the thing and disperse themselves. Four stacks of cash, around four inches high each, took up most of the box and I grinned as I pulled each one out. Arranging them side by each on the bed, I pulled out a thick blue folded document at the bottom and eyed the law firm's name etched into the top, Hangerstone and Roy, Attorney's at Law. I looked at Em and giggled, then unfolded it. My eyes scanned the pages, and there, as plain as day, was the segment where he left this house, the property, and the other ten acres that lay beside the house to me. Tears fell from my eyes as I hugged her to me.

"This is it, Em, this is the will. He left it to me, and then some. The money is to be split with Keira, but according to this, it should be around eighty-five-thousand." Em held out her hand and I gave her the document. She perused it, then handed it back.

"It looks like he had this made out when he found out he was sick. They dated it a year and a half ago. He knew he was dying, but one of his last thoughts was obviously of you and your sister." Her eyes grew wide. "Hey, will that be enough money to pay your mom what you owe her?" I did the math in my head. A year and a half of school, minus the scholarships that I had, it would cover it and then some, and I began laughing.

"Yeah, baby, so as long as she doesn't contest it, which I don't think she can because of the divorce and now she's remarried, I will be free to live my life without her in it. Oh my gosh, I feel like it's Christmas." Em shook her head, then checked her watch.

"I hate to be a party pooper, but I've got to run. Are you going to be okay?"

I stood and pulled her up and hugged her tight.

"I'm as right as rain, Em, and I'm still going to catch a meeting with Frank if there is one." My thoughts drifted to Sara. "I wonder if I'll see her again, now that I've opened the last bottle. I hope so, because I'd really like to thank her and say goodbye." Em moved towards the door and I walked out onto the porch with her, and I kissed her one more time.

"If it is to be, you'll see her, and if not, know that she gave you a gift, too, no matter how harsh it was to see." I gave her one more kiss and released her.

"We'll talk soon and thank Frank again for me. I'm glad you were both here. It's good, I guess, to let people in, because it made my vision a little easier. Now I suppose I should call my mother and get her to call off the dogs with the house sale," I said as I pointed at the realty sign. Em nodded.

"Just speak your truth, Jules, and if she gets out of hand, know that you don't have to deal with her if you choose not to. Set your boundaries and do what you need to. Find your peace. It's the only way." I listened to her words and gave a smile.

"Yeah, I know, and thank you. Em, I couldn't have done this without you, nor would I have wanted to. I guess I'm trying to say that I'm grateful for having you beside me in my life." I felt a thrill as a blush rose to her face and she gave me a small wave, then turned to head home. Watching her dress move against her legs as the breeze blew, I took a deep breath. She made my heart feel better, and I realized I was falling for the beautiful Em. That wasn't a bad thing, but I still had some sorting of my own to do before I could focus on that. Walking into the house, I leaned against the door and let my thoughts drift. Music, I need music. Grabbing a Pink Floyd album, I set the needle down and sat in the chair as "One Slip" filled the room with its fast, driving beat.

"Tell me what to do next, Dad. I need your guidance, because I can foresee see this spiraling in so many directions, so help me see the right way I need to go." I sensed her before I saw her, and I opened my eyes. Sara stood in the doorway, a sad smile on her face.

"You were brave, Jules, and he would be so proud of you, or I'm sure he

180

is, but I can't put words in his mouth." She moved from foot to foot, as if uncomfortable. Something was weighing on her mind. "Are you ready for the end?" Realizing I could take that many ways, I chuckled nervously as she moved closer.

"I'm not dying, right? Sorry, just a little gallows humor to lighten the day, my bad." Sara giggled and shook her finger.

"Oh my, you are like him. Your dad had a wicked sense of humor, so now, not only do you look like him, but you're sounding like him, too. Good one, though, but no, there's the matter of closure, if you're not tired, that is." I thought I'd seen everything I needed to see, and I shook my head, confused.

"He drowned, or got eaten by Roger, right? There'd be nothing left, and I can't have anyone go diving to look because I'd have to tell them the story, and they'd wonder how the heck I knew what happened. They'd be locking me up and throwing away the key. I'm not swimming in that gator infested swamp! But I found the box in the closet, so there's that silver lining in this stormy cloud of chaos, right?" She sat down on the couch and eyed me.

"Good on you. I knew if I gave you long enough, you'd turn enough leaves and find it. That was his jacket for raking leaves. He told me that a long time ago, but he didn't use it much down here. So I'm glad that's one thing I don't have to tell you, but there is more." She eyed me, took a deep breath, and offered a sad tinged smile. "Are you ready, Julien?"

"Of course, I'm ready, though I don't know what else there is…" Her eyes looked down and for a minute, she looked upset.

"When I tell you, or show you, I have to leave. So I guess this is a goodbye of sorts. You may be happy to be rid of me, but I've done what they sent me to do, so there's no reason for me to remain here any longer. They'll give me another assignment, but you won't see me again." Oh, was I ready to say goodbye? The thought caused an ache to roll through me. I closed my eyes and wondered what my life would now be like without my little spirit to gift me with jars and visions. It made me sad, and I gazed at her and shook my head.

"I can't in my heart keep you here, that I know. So I guess the question is, are you ready? You've kind of become like my sister, though she isn't as much fun, that and she can't pop in and out of rooms at will. I wish my father could have saved you, and I'm sorry he couldn't." Sara shook her head.

"We all have our journeys to take, Jules. This was a part of mine, as your fathers was his. He isn't here because he's done what they've tasked him with. Look at the stars, because you know he's up there looking down on you proudly. Be the man he wanted you to be, choose kindness, but share your gift with the world. It's what we all were here for. Mine was to gift your father one last act of courage, and mine is to gift you closure. Let me know when you're ready, and we can go." My eyes went wide.

"Where are we going?" She grinned and then rolled her eyes.

"Well, to the river, of course. You've got to finish it, Jules." I jumped from the chair and shook my head.

"I am not going in that river. I told you that. Sorry, but I can't." She shrugged but walked towards the door.

"You're not going swimming, but you and Frank will take a ride down the river because you need to finish things. Don't worry, you will not get eaten or drown, I promise. That's now how it ends." I was almost afraid to ask her how it would, but giving her the benefit of the doubt, I followed her out of the house. We headed along the path to the Peace. The day was windy, and I prayed Roger was absent. Sara chuckled, and I realized she must be able to know what I thought. "Quit worrying, silly." We reached the bank a few minutes later, and I leaned down and grabbed a rock, then skipped it across the ripples. Managing six skips, I grinned like a kid.

"Not bad, huh? You were going to get six skips, right?" Sara nodded with a smile etched across her face, and she moved to stand closer to me. I glanced down at the spot and wondered if this was where my father got her to before she passed away. She nodded, and I wanted to hug her, but she shook her head.

"You can't, Jules, because I'm not really here, not like that, anyway. Look down river." I stepped away from her and gazed down stream where a multitude of clumps, mangroves, forced the water to move to the left and right.

"If you go to the left, you'll travel for about a half mile, and you'll come to another split like this. Go to the left again and you'll see an enormous tree that has an eagle's nest way up in the top of it. Pull up there, and get out of the boat, then look around. There's not much there, but there is some left. Bring him home, Jules. It's time to close the chapter." My mouth opened in shock and I blinked my eyes as I watched her form waver in front of me.

"Bring him home, Jules, and you'll find peace." She scattered in front of my eyes, turning to a thousand tiny sparks that took to the wind and blew away.

"Sara, wait, I have to say goodbye." I felt the tears fill my eyes, and I watched as the lights disappeared. "Goodbye, Sara…" I allowed the sob to come, and I stood there on the bank, unafraid of Roger, or of anything, except for the sudden overwhelming fear of goodbye. As my tears slowed, I glanced back out to the mangroves.

"Time to grab Frank and see if he wants to take a ride…" I headed back down the path, steeling myself for what needed to be done.

Thirty-Six

The only Truth I Know is You

❧

Frank answered when I knocked and he held up his finger for me to wait and he shut the door. A moment later, he slipped back out onto the porch and smiled. "There is a meeting tonight at seven if you want to come. It's not the same place as I went last time, more like a twenty-minute drive, but if you're game, I'll be there with you." Unsure how long this task would take, or how I may feel later, I shook my head.

"I need a huge favor from you. They brought something to my attention and I believe I may know where my father's remains are." Frank's eyes went wide, and he grabbed me by the arm and led me down into the yard.

"You can't be serious? Did you have another vision? How do you know?" I gave him a light smile and eyed the path to the river.

"My little ghostly girl dropped by after Em left and had me go to the riverbank. She gave me directions, though she said there wasn't much left, but I needed to close the chapter and bring him home. That, to me, means there's something there. Can we take a ride in your canoe and find out?" A flash of fear crossed his face, and I shook my head. "She said we wouldn't come to any harm, so I wouldn't worry about Roger or other gators. Sara has never lied to me yet. I trust her. So, can we?" Frank held up his finger and stalked back up the steps and into the house, then came out a second

184

later with a hat and work gloves. He motioned me to follow, and we went to his shed, where he grabbed a shovel and a plastic garbage bag. I eyed the shovel.

"She said nothing about having to dig him up," I asked, eyeing the pointed device in his hands. Frank chuckled nervously.

"Nope, this is in case we have a nasty gator. We can defend ourselves and bash that sucker right over the head." I could see the logic, and if it made him feel better, then I was all for it. We hefted up the canoe, and he ditched the shovel and bag inside, grabbed two life jackets, and we hauled it down to the riverbank. There was no sign of Roger, which made me feel good. "This is your quest, but I'm getting in first and you can push us off. I don't want to be sticking my feet in there." We set the canoe part way in and Frank climbed on board, while I pushed it out a ways and jumped in. My shoes got soaked, but I didn't care. My eyes peered around for rogue reptiles, but spotting none, I gradually relaxed. I pointed to the mangrove where we'd turn. Frank stayed mostly silent, and it was quiet here, except for the sound of the oars connecting with the water. We made the turn where Sara had asked, but I had no way to judge distance. The canoe moved effortlessly with the two of us paddling, and a short spell later, I saw another area where it forked off. Again, I took the path she requested. My eyes scanned the trees.
"We're looking for a tall tree with an eagle's nest way at the top. Let me know if you see it." The canoe drifted, and we both stared at trees, then the river curved, and as we moved around the bend, I could see it ahead. I pointed, "there, that's where we need to get out and look." Frank nodded, but said nothing. His eyes peered at the bank and I knew he was still fearing a gator attack, and I could understand his trepidation. I turned the canoe so that I could get out first and pull it to shore, alleviating Frank having to get wet feet. He grabbed the shovel as soon as his feet touched the sand and he stared at the surrounding brush.

"All right, I'm ready if one comes. I've got your back, Jules, so you look, okay?" I held back the chuckle that had formed in my mouth and nodded. We used the cable attached to the canoe to tie it to a tree, so that it wouldn't go wandering away without us. I didn't even know where we were, but getting lost would not be high on my priority list. Frank followed close behind as I scoured the shores, looking for remains. Not seeing anything, I moved farther into the brush, my eyes seeking any irregularities. Ten minutes later, I found my father. I stopped short and Frank bumped into me, and I felt it when he slipped his hand on my shoulder.

"I think I'm okay. She was right, there doesn't seem to be much left." I kneeled down and carefully cleared the debris that had fallen from the trees. His remains looked as if tucked beneath a dying blanket of palm fronds, leaves, and other refuse of nature. Frank gave me a moment to be alone, and I appreciated not having to speak. I knew what skeletons looked like from biology class in high school, and I assume that animals had spirited away pieces of him over the past year. Frank's feet shuffled through the brush a few minutes later as he returned with the plastic bag. I nodded. The weathered skull lay turned sideways, and I wondered if the water had swept him here in a flood, or if injured, he pulled himself here as his blood ran out of his body? It didn't matter that he had been dying. It still was like an icy knife to my heart. Frank patted my shoulder, then kneeled beside me.

"No one should have to do this alone. Here, let me help you." I watched as he plucked up a bone fragment and I held out my hand to stop him.

"Shouldn't we notify the police of what we've found?" Frank set the bone aside and nodded.

"I suppose you're right. It could be a crime scene investigation, but you're going to have to come up with a reason you're here and stuff. How good are you at creative embellishment?" I grinned and shook my head.

"Frank, we had to take a pee, and didn't want to go in the water because that's gross, right? Isn't that good enough? Then, I find this, and they can do an autopsy, identify the body, and with me here, they have a DNA sample." I tried my cell phone, but could get no reception. "Let's head back and make the call. They'll bring a bigger boat to get here. I can go with them to show where to find him. I suppose I can't say I think it's my Dad, 'cause that would look suspicious." Frank nodded and grabbed the bag. We headed towards home, and I could feel my heart beating like a racehorse on the last stretch. My father would finally come home, and I eyed the skies as the clouds began moving in.

"Looks like it's gonna rain. I sure hope Roger isn't guarding his territory when we get home." Frank's eyes bugged out and he snorted, then kicked the shovel.

"I'm ready for old Roger, Jules, have no fear. We're gonna get help, and get your daddy back to where he belongs. You holding up okay?" I nodded, eager to land and make the calls. "I'm gonna go on to the meeting. If you don't need me to go back with you. If they call the cops, I'm sure you'll travel with them," he said quietly as I eyed him and shrugged.

"Hey, I never asked, how are you holding up?" Frank sighed and shook his head.

"Not gonna lie. That vision thing was a little nerve-wracking, and losing someone is always hard, so I understand what you're going through. With Frankie Jr., I didn't have to be the one to find him, and he wasn't missing... I just wonder if I could have done or said something different, made him stay home that night, you know, that kind of thing. Would he still be here?" His shoulders hunched and I should have felt guilty for dragging him into my mess, but I was honestly happy to have him to talk to.

"You've helped keep me sane through this, both you and Em, and I'm grateful. With my dad, I couldn't change anything, though now I can. That makes me feel better, though not saying goodbye when I should have... That's on my mother. Time will tell what will happen between me and her, but I don't think it will go well. Regardless, I'm ready to tackle that, and I'll be happy when it's all over. Do you think they'll allow me to bury him in the cemetery out back? He didn't leave any last requests, but I think I'd like having him around. He loved this place, and I think he'd be at peace here." Frank nodded and smiled as we approached the river bank, which was void of Roger.

"Score one for us, sport. Looks like clear sailing ahead. No shovel needed." He giggled, but I could see the sweat beaded up on his forehead, even with the lack of sun. I smiled at him and felt a peace roll through me.

Frank headed home, and we left the canoe along the path in case I needed it again. He gave me a hard hug, and I watched as he walked away. We'd both been through a trial, but I knew we'd make it. Grabbing my cellphone, I dialed the police to report our find.

Thirty-Seven

Emptiness in Harmony

T he cop car arrived promptly, but it took another good hour for them to launch a boat downstream, pick me up, and carry us to our destination. I was nervous, as I always was around cops, but surprised myself by keeping my cool and not thirsting for my usual nerve calming beverage. I pointed towards the direction to head, told Officer Maldorado about the remains, but kept mum on the fact that I thought it to be my father. In Florida, things move at their own pace, and I didn't want to be seen as a crackpot by telling them that a ghost girl gave me a Google map mostly on how to find dear old missing dad. There are always people going missing around here and I trusted them to put one and one together to get two. It went faster this time, not having to paddle, and they pulled in close enough and we got out. I led the way to show them the body. Unsurprised, nothing had moved. Not that I had expected anything to get up and walk away. They took a gazillion pictures and did their stuff while I walked back to the boat to wait. The officers talked to each other between asking me questions about who I was and why I was at my father's house. Maldorado knew my father had gone missing, and treated me kinder, and I wondered if she suspected what I knew, that we had finally found him.

After they took a bunch of notes, they hauled me home, then resumed their combing of the area for debris, I assume. I pulled Frank's canoe further inland and walked to the house. My body felt charged, yet the ordeal spent my mind. Em sat on my front porch. She held out her arms, and I fell into them, basking in the comfort she gave. I released her a minute later and kissed her on the cheek.

"Frank went to the meeting, but he said to tell you he's sorry for your loss. I think he was a little rattled, but said he'd grab you for the next meeting if you're still game." I nodded, my thoughts back at my father's resting place, and she stopped as I walked in.

"I've got some things to do, but I don't want you to be alone if you need me." Her words lifted my spirits, and offering a light smile, I shook my head.

"Nah, I think I'm good. Besides, if I do any painting, I can't let you see your piece before it's done, right?" She giggled and grabbed my hand.

"So, you're working on it, then? How awesome is that?" I kissed her on the cheek, my hand shooing her away. She stepped off the porch, and I gave a small wave.

"Yeah, it's coming out better than I imagined. I'll catch you later, okay?" She all but skipped towards her house and I watched, loving each movement and step she made. Turning, she caught me staring and I could hear her giggle from where I stood.

"You are beautiful, Em, thank you…" I whispered as I closed the door behind me. I made a beeline for my parent's bedroom, tucked the box away back into the closet hiding spot, but not before re-reading the will.

"Now comes the hard part." I grabbed my phone and walked to the fridge, my body on autopilot, which stopped when I realized I had no beer. What I found was a pitcher of lemonade. Not having locked the door when Frank and I left, I knew Em had worked her magic and gave me a cool drink of something other than booze.

"Yes, incredible, and cute, too," I muttered as I poured a glass before moving into the living room. I flicked the Moonlight Sonata album on and turned the volume low, then dialed. She answered on the fourth ring, out of breath and laughing as if in the middle of a newlywed tryst with Carlos. The scene in my head of the two of them made me cringe, and, taking a deep breath, I waited for her to speak first.

"Jules, ah, I figured you'd be calling. Are you almost here?" I could hear her put her hand over the receiver and say something, then it became quiet. Figuring she must have shooed Carlos away from hearing our chat, I shook my head.

"Well, no, as a matter of fact, I'm still right here. I'm not coming home." I heard her breath blow out and I could picture her, red faced and fuming over my declaration.

"You were to be out of there by week's end. You're actually a day late. That's why I figured you were on your way. The will is in my lawyer's hands and they've begun processing things for transferring the property. I TOLD them you'd be vacated by then, so now you've gone and made me look like a liar. That pisses me off more than I can say, young man. Grab your things, take what you want, and GET OUT!" I held the phone away from my ear as her tirade escalated.

"Well, Mom, they dated your will back when you were married. Did you know he had a brain cancer and was dying? So, we never got to say goodbye, and why? Because you wrote him that horrible letter telling him we didn't give a crap. Now who's lying, mother? I've been reading all the letters he wrote us, that you had returned to sender, and I've found a new will dated over a year and a half ago, and guess what? This house is mine, not yours, so call off your Realtor. You have no claim on my home, and the proof is right here in my hands." I'm sure her body was shaking in anger, and she was likely ready to hurl something at a wall. That's how Simone rolled, but I didn't care. I kept my tone even and refrained from laughing over the call, which surprised me. Perhaps I'd gained a sense of peace knowing she had lost control over me and my future. I felt good, and I think she detected it in my voice.

"It doesn't matter, my dear Jules, because you owe me. I've paid for your schooling, and you're legally an adult. You should have been smarter and taken out loans, but you owe me, and I have documents to prove it. You don't have two nickels to rub together, so I guess you're going to have to sell the house, because I demand payment. I'm calling in the tab, so to speak, so no, Jules, the house will be sold and you can consider your debt to me paid off. And then, I believe an apology will be due." For that, I couldn't help but to laugh, which was as good as a slap in the face.

"So, I did the calculations, Mom, and here's what I've come up with. Fifteen thousand for the first year, right? Oh, and please, correct me if I'm wrong, and then one semester, which should be a quarter of that, I'm right, right? So, we're looking at under twenty-thousand dollars, give or take. Yeah, that sounds about right." I could sense her wheels turning and her fists clenching.

"Yeah, sure, that is right, but you don't have any money, and what little you have in your pissant bank account, which should be something like two-hundred fifty bucks, will not cut it. We're selling the house, Julien. I'm sorry, but say goodbye." I laughed loudly on the phone and shook my head as I took a sip of lemonade. As I smacked my lips, I allowed a long "ah…" to escape.

"Well, mommy dearest, you are right about the bank account, but there's one thing you haven't asked. What else did the will say? Did I hear you ask? I thought I did, but I could be wrong. Oh, yeah, he also left a sizable pile of cash, which I have to share with your mini-me, Keira, but that's okay. It still leaves enough to pay you off and to get your lying, cheating self out of my life once and for all. He left nothing for you, which I hadn't expected him to, but you know what the saddest thing is, besides the poor man dying alone, without his children? He still loved you, even to his dying day. Now that, Simone, you'll have to live with for the rest of your life, and I hope you choke on the misery that you've caused us all. Now, I'm gonna leave that there for you to digest. Call the realty office now and make them disappear, because I will hire a lawyer and get a cease and desist order if I need to. God knows I have the abundance of cash to do it. A certified check will go out to you tomorrow when I hit the bank, along with a letter signed by a notary that this pays you in full." There was dead silence on the other end, and I should have felt bad, but I felt lighter, somehow. I would be free of the one thing that had begun the unraveling of our family, and my boundary was now set in place. There was no need for me to see her, except to gather my artwork and belongings from home. For that, I prayed for no issues.

"How... How much money did he leave?" I hung up the phone and took another gulp of lemonade as I shook my head.

"Some things never change, and I'm not sorry to see you go, but bye-bye, Ma." I leaned back, closed my eyes, and allowed the soft piano music to carry me to a calm place. I wondered how the police were doing, but didn't want to call and seem too antsy. They had my contact information, now all I could do was wait. As I glanced around the room, I let out a heavy sigh. There would be no more Sara, so I could stop looking for her to pop in. It was a sobering thought, and an overwhelming sense of sadness filled me. Except for Em and Frank, I was adrift without a proverbial family. That would take getting used to, but a voice whispered in my head that I'd be all right.

Thirty-Eight

Seeking Grace in Every Step

~⊙⊙⊙~

Two weeks later

I pulled the door open on the small U-Haul trailer and eyed the contents, elated that nothing seemed to be damaged from the move. Em jumped out of the car and swung her head around the side of the door and grinned.

"How did we do?" I grinned as I spread my hands towards the paintings.

"We've done great. Now we just have to unload it all. How come packing seems so much easier than unpacking?" She shrugged, then an amused look crossed her face.

"You should demand a raise for doing all the bull work, don't you think?" I pulled her around the metal door and wrapped my arms around her.

"I think I deserve a kiss. With that pothole in Georgia, I was almost afraid to look and see if any paint cracked open. It seems to look okay, but we'll see." I released her and gave her the key to the house, then I grabbed a stack of my canvases and began hauling them in. My heart was soaring, and I was eager to have my cherished belongings in my own home. We'd lucked out getting my stuff. Simone, not expecting me, was away on a business trip. I don't know if Carlos let her know I was there, but we got in and out in a flash. I was thankful to Frank for allowing Em to travel with me. Knowing I'd be living here full time, he gave me his blessing to date his daughter, as long as I continued to attend meetings with him. How could I not say yes to that? Being with Em was a god-send, and we spent a lot of time talking about what I'd do in the future while we drove to and from New York.

* * *

"When I get back, I'm going to take some of the money and fix the place up. I know that painting the walls will be foremost to do, and the roof still seems solid. I'm going to see if I can gut any of the walls and make the place a little bigger. But I want to deconstruct Keira's room and maybe frame those posters and put them somewhere." Em nodded and grinned.

"Hey, I'm pretty good at painting, you know. Maybe I can help, if you want me to, that is." I grasped her hand and kissed it.

"You can help whenever and however you want, but thanks for helping me get my stuff. I'm not upset that you didn't get to meet the family, and I'm sure you most likely never will, so thank you for the boundary advice, too."

We'd found cheap motels with separate beds on the way, sidetracking here and there to do a little sight-seeing. There was no place I'd rather be than right there beside her, creating memories. As I drove, I wondered if my parents had started out this way. Realizing they didn't end this way, I let the past go and moved forward with my life instead of looking back. Not once did I want a drink, and that's another thing I was thankful for. Em was so easygoing, and we drove the miles passing time, finding out more about each other, and realizing we were very much alike in certain aspects. She'd read while I drove, or would find a radio station that would come in clear and sing along with old eighties and nineties tunes. I got to play my music here and there, but it was sparingly. After several eye rolls, I got the point and found something livelier. There had been no messages from the police yet, following up on the remains, which I found disappointing, but it would happen eventually.

"Do you think they'll be okay with me burying my dad on the property, or scattering his ashes, at least?" A solemn look crossed her face as she lay her hand on my arm.

"Are you okay with him being there? It's your house to do with what you want. But you're going to grow old someday and be at a point where you're going to have to decide where you want to be buried. Do you want to be buried there? Now, that's the big question." I hadn't thought about that. Another reason for having her around was she kept me sane and thinking about the bigger picture. As I kept my eyes on the road, I nodded.

"He loved that house, as did I as a child, and even more-so now. Yes, I can see myself there when I die, but that will be many years down the road. The funny thing is, I always loved hanging out in cemeteries and talking to the folks buried in the ground. They left me wondering how they died and why, and now, it seems a little more serious. When you're our age, you don't give death much thought, and why would you want to? You lost your brother, and I lost my dad, but we keep putting one foot in front of the other, living our lives. Life is short enough to worry about dying and I'll cross that bridge then. Right now, I want to dream, bring it to fruition, and be the best I can be."

Em squeezed my arm and yawned, then lay her head back on the seat and shut her eyes. It was all I could do to watch the road and not the beautiful girl beside me, but it thrilled me knowing she was there.

* * *

She waved her hand in front of my face. "Earth to Jules, come in, Jules... You're a million miles away. What are you thinking about?" I stood there in the driveway with a stack of paintings in my hand, woolgathering. A cool breeze blew past me and I shook it off and gave a smile.

"Oh, this and that, our trip, stuff like that." I realized then that I was finally home. My home. Em would now go next door and I'd go inside alone, and life would move forward from there. It grounded me, but I felt a twinge of fear, wondering if I could fulfill my own wants.

"You're looking weird, like something's bugging you. What's wrong?" I shook my head and smiled as she hugged me.

"We're back, and we have all of our tomorrows in front of us. You will learn what you need to and follow up on your future, and we will get through it together, one day at a time. Jules, it's going to be a beautiful life. I can see it, and I don't even need a spirit to tell me it's true, because I feel it here." She brought my hand up and rested it on her heart, and I grinned.

"Well, that's all good, sweet Em, from Wisconsin, but we need to get this unloaded before we can do much else. Looks like it's gonna rain, and you need to get home and tell your folks about our trip, and I have a masterpiece to complete that you commissioned me to do. Now that I have all my supplies, I know what needs to be done to it to finish it up. You don't want me to fail on my first real art job, do you?" I glanced at the sky and cringed. "Are you ready?" She nodded and grabbed some boxes while I continued stacking my art. I eyed up the pieces as I put one on top of the other. Some I barely recognized, and I knew I was no longer that same man living in darkness or who thrived on doom and gloom. I watched as she carried two boxes in and I shook my head as I followed her.

"Dang, how did I get so lucky?" I eyed the skies again, which bubbled darkly, and for a second, the sun found a crack in the graying darkness and the bright light of the sun shone through before disappearing again. The first raindrop found me, and I held my head up as I smiled.

"I'm gonna be okay, Dad. Thanks for shining your star light on me and seeing me through, just like you said you would." Tears rose to my eyes, melding in with the rain that began drizzling down, and I ran for the door with the last of my canvases stacked high in my arms. Em grabbed them from me as I hit the porch and I rushed back out to the trailer to shut the door. The boxes weren't going anywhere. I had a date with my future and suddenly, I couldn't wait to get started.

Thirty-Nine

Chasing Rainbows in the Setting Sun

One month to the day of the remains being found by Frank and me, the police department confirmed that the bones had indeed belonged to my father. It was like a punch in the gut all over again, but I knew I could finally close the chapter of that book in my life. I had him cremated, and Frank, Em, Jasper, and Wanda, held a small ceremony at the back property. Later, I would get a small stone to mark his place, but we buried the urn right beside his childhood spirit, Keira. I haven't spoken to my mother, nor do I intend to do so. My mood stays lighter that way, and the AA meetings with Frank are proving to be a good thing for when I get in a dark place. It doesn't happen often, but if I want things to progress with Emily, it's what I'm willing to do.

Last night, Em dropped by. I was deep into my next painting, and as I gazed at her, I could tell something was off. I'd never sensed her as being the edgy type, but knew she had the weight of something on her mind. Her smile never quite reached her face, and I felt my stomach plummet, expecting bad news. I ushered her in, and she wrapped her arms around me and held me tight. Not that holding her bugged me. I always loved the way she hugged me, but this was tighter than normal. She released me a moment later and swiped her hands through her hair, which lay in waves over her shoulders.

Em always had her hair in a ponytail, so something was up.

"How are you, Jules?" I eyed her and gave her a quick kiss.

"Well, Em, I'm doing all right. What's happened? You look like you've seen a ghost, and we both know that seeing them is more my thing, but shoot, what's on your beautiful mind?" I glanced back at the painting, unconcerned with her seeing my work in progress. She didn't even peek at the canvas, which, knowing her, meant something was off.

"Last night, I woke in the middle of the night and noticed you walking to the river. You walked to the river, right?" I smiled and nodded. There had been an amazing full moon, and it reminded me of my painting, so I headed to the river to find out if my painting did it justice. Afterward, I'd headed home to bed.

"Yeah, I stayed for fifteen minutes, or twenty, tops. Why? Does that bother you? Don't worry. I looked for Roger, but he wasn't hanging around. I was safe, and you know I won't take chances." She closed her eyes, and I sat down, unsure what she was so bugged about.

"No, I don't care that you went there, it's just that…" I eyed her, waiting for her to finish. She kept playing with the charms on her bracelet, and I reached over and took her hands in mine.

"Tell me what's wrong, Em. You can talk to me about anything. You've become my best friend, and we talk. That's what we do. So if something is upsetting you, tell me. I'm a big boy. I can take whatever you need to say." She shook her head and took a deep breath.

"No, I watched you heading along the path, but I caught something else, too, and I'm not sure what to make of that. You could see the girl, Sara, but you saw no one else, right?" I nodded, unsure where the line of questioning was going. A second later, the goosebumps rose on my arms as a cool draft blew through the room. The front door was closed, so I knew it didn't come from that. For a second, I wondered if Sara had returned and a wide smile crossed my face. Em shook her head.

"It's not Sara, or the other girl. It was a man, and he looked like you. He stood beside the house watching you walk the path to the river. I was going to come out and tag along, but it's like there were two of you. Do you think your father's spirit is here now?" I didn't know what to think, but realized it could be plausible. Heck, so many strange things had happened since I got here, but the idea of seeing my father again filled me with an overflowing wave of happiness. Glancing around, I grinned as tears rose in my eyes.

"Em, if it is him, I'm good with it. No, better yet, I'm super excited about that. What if it is, holy cow? This is good, Em, fantastic." She smiled, and I could tell she was calming down. "Everything will fall into place the way it's meant to, just like finding his words, and the will. I'm feeling so right with being here, and that's just icing on the proverbial cake. Wow. Thank you for telling me, and I only hope that at some point, he'll surface and show himself to me. There's so much left unsaid. I'd be grateful for that gift. I would." Em stood and wrapped her arms around me as I looked around the room. The coolness wafted through again, and I held her tight, blessed at the possibility of having some closure. Em left a short time later, and I settled down, gathering my peace so I could resume painting. My thoughts ran to Em, and I grinned. Every time I saw her, my feelings grew deeper.

I'm already sweating the day when I tell her I love her, and I almost said it out loud once, but caught myself in time. The look on her face told me she knew what I was holding back, but she gives me space I need and I think she feels the same way.

One week later

Em tracked down Brett and his family's address, and I'm on my way there, now. Brett seemed eager to meet me, and I think it comforted him to know they found dad's body. It's going to hurt like heck to hear the stories about my father from a man who probably knew him better than me. Part of me wants to tell him about Sara, and the role she played in allowing me to find Dad, the will, and the memories I'd forgotten. But first, I needed to meet Chino. Em came with me for moral support. My hands were shaking as we pulled into his driveway. They moved up near Orlando, so we had a two-hour drive to chat and calm my nerves. The house was a modest new-build, and I cringed, but understood how he had to leave the old river house behind.

Memories and losing loved one's can do that to a person.

I felt Em touch my arm as she pointed out the house. They all looked alike, and I decided not to fault Brett for his choice. There was a big fenced-in yard, so I knew Chino had plenty of room to play without worrying about the gators that most likely infested the large ponds dotted throughout the sub-division.

"We're there, this is the one." I pulled in and parked beside the large grayish Chevy Silverado. My hands trembled and Em turned me to face her, her fingers gently on my chin. She leaned over and kissed me, and I inhaled the subtle fragrance of her lemongrass, almond, and eucalyptus oil blend she often wore. That stuff was amazing and she knew I had a fondness for it. "Are you ready?" I shook my head and took a deep breath as the front door opened. A huge smiling black lab came rambling towards the car, barking up a storm, and I got out and told Em to wait, just in case he was one of those jumpy kinds of dogs. Chino came tearing around to where I stood, his tail wagging furiously. Brett waved at me and laughed.

"Don't worry, he's not the best behaved dog, but watch out, he may just lick you to death." I kneeled down and stared at the pup, his deep dark eyes soulful, gazed back at me. He licked me across the face, then leaned his whole body against me. I wrapped my arms around him and gave him a hug, feeling the tears well up and spill down my face. Chino wasn't in a hurry to get away, and I sat there on the ground and bawled like a baby into his fur as he, in his own way, consoled me. Brett kept back, giving me a minute, of which I was thankful. I stood a minute later and brushed my tears on my sleeve, then extended my hand to Brett. He took it and pulled me into a tight hug, tears present on his face, too.

"You look just like your dad, Julien. Chino likes people, but not once has he ever greeting anyone like he did just now with you. Maybe he thinks you're Damien?" The dog clung to me and I waved to Em that it was safe to get out. Chino never left my side, and that made me feel selfish, yet good. She walked over and patted the dog and I introduced her to Brett. His wife, Jill, emerged a minute later and waved us in. Em walked in first with Jill, while Brett and I followed, with Chino hugging tight to my side. At the front entrance way, Brett held up his arm and stopped me.

"I remember you from when you were a boy. You've grown into a man, and I know your dad would be so proud of you. He never stopped talking about you. Someday, maybe not today, but when you're ready, I'll be more than happy to take a drive to your house and tell you the stories. You know, kind of fill in the blanks for what you missed out on. I'd like nothing better than to tell you that your father was an amazing man. Even towards the end, he never gave up on seeing you again. My daughter Sara probably knew him best, though, but she passed, so I guess I'll have to tell you what I know." I gave a sad smile and shook my head.

"I'd love that, Brett, very much, I would."

Forty

Also by K.L. Laettner

T ales From The Thrift (The Thrift Chronicles Book 1)
  A Shot In Time (The Thrift Chronicles Book 2)
  The Corridors of Yesterday (The Thrift Chronicles Book 3)
Coming in 2022

Diary of A Middle-Aged Mermaid

The Sandcastle Society

A Sprinkle of Salt: Poetry of the Oceans Muse

The Magnificent Memory of Agnes McMuffinn (Humor/A not-so Cozy Mystery Book 1)

Agnes McMuffinn Gets Lost in Paradise (Humor/A not-so Cozy Mystery Book 2)

The Girl Who Captured The Stars

The Girl Who Captured Memories

Forty-One

The Girl Playlist

F earless- Pink Floyd
    Pictures of You- The Cure
    The Dangling Conversation- Simon and Garfunkel
One Slip- Pink Floyd
Hold On- Sarah McLachlan
Heroes- David Bowie
Moonlight Sonata- Beethoven
Rhapsody on a Theme of Paganini- Rachmaninoff
(Somewhere in Time soundtrack)
Clare de Lune- Debussy
Gabriel's Oboe- Ennio Morricone
Mother- Pink Floyd
Just Like Heaven- The Cure
Love Will Tear Us Apart- Joy Division
Elegia- New Order
Bring on The Dancing Horses- Echo and The Bunnymen
I Got You- Split Enz
How Soon Is Now- The Smiths
Cemetery Gates- The Smiths

It Makes No Difference- The Band

Alive and Kicking- Simple Minds

Don't You Forget About Me- Simple Minds

All The Things She Said- Simple Minds

Holding Back The Years- Simply Red

Stars- Simply Red

Yellow- Cold Play

Creep- Radiohead

I'm Not In Love- 10cc

Time Passages- Al Stewart

Disintegration- The Cure

Oh Very Young- Cat Stevens

Welcome (To The Pleasuredome)- Frankie Goes To Hollywood

Super Heroes- Rocky Horror Picture Show Movie Soundtrack

When Dove's Cry- Prince

Purple Rain- Prince

Strawberry Fields Forever - The Beatles

A Day In The Life- The Beatles

About the Author

K. L. Laettner originally hails from Hamburg, NY, a suburb close to Buffalo. She lives in Venice, Florida, with her husband, Jeffery, and their menagerie of fur babies. When not locked in her lair, writing, you'll find her perusing thrift stores, hanging poolside, or scouring the beach in search of shark's teeth. Her stories run the gamut from beach reads, women's fiction, magical realism, poetry, and a little paranormal thrown in for good measure. You can find her books on Amazon. Her poetry blog, Peace, Love, and Patchouli, on WordPress, has over 4200 followers.

You can connect with me on:

- https://www.amazon.com/K-L-Laettner
- https://twitter.com/klaettner
- https://www.facebook.com/PeaceLoveAndInfiniteZip
- https://zipsrid.wordpress.com
- https://www.instagram.com/k.l.laettner_author

Printed in Great Britain
by Amazon